Everything You Ever Wanted

Luiza Sauma was born in Rio de Janeiro and brought up in London. Her first novel, *Flesh and Bone and Water*, received widespread critical acclaim and she was listed by the *Daily Telegraph* as one of their 'ones to watch' for 2017. Luiza worked at the *Independent on Sunday* for several years before becoming a novelist. She has an MA in Creative and Life Writing from Goldsmiths, University of London, where she won the Pat Kavanagh Award.

Everything You Ever Wanted

LUIZA SAUMA

VIKING
an imprint of
PENGUIN BOOKS

VIKING

UK | USA | Canada | Ireland | Australia
India | New Zealand | South Africa

Viking is part of the Penguin Random House group of companies
whose addresses can be found at global.penguinrandomhouse.com.

First published 2019
001

Copyright © Luiza Sauma, 2019

The moral right of the author has been asserted

Set in 12.76/15.06pt Dante MT Std
Typeset by Jouve (UK), Milton Keynes
Printed and bound in Great Britain by Clays Ltd, Elcograf S.p.A.

A CIP catalogue record for this book is available from the British Library

HARDBACK ISBN: 978-0-241-36354-6
TRADE PAPERBACK ISBN: 978-0-241-36355-3

www.greenpenguin.co.uk

For Tim and Yara

EARTH
Eight Years Ago

0.

Another Sun

Iris first heard about *Life on Nyx* on a freezing winter's night. She was at a pub in London, drinking with her work friends. Winter, pub, London, work – she never imagined that these things would seem exotic one day, but they do. It was a Thursday. Her mind returns to that night over and over again. It's like rewatching an old film, hoping its ending will be different but it's always the same.

She had heard of Nyx, of course, but not the TV show – it had only just been announced. She knew that Nyx was a terrestrial planet, much smaller than Earth. She knew that its solar system could only be reached via an underwater wormhole in the Pacific Ocean. She knew it had no moons. She knew that Nyx was tidally locked, so that, unlike Earth, it didn't turn on its axis. On one side it was always day and on the other, night. Its light side was a pale pink desert and its dark side – who knows? Iris had seen photos online. In most of them, Nyx looked like a pink Sahara. In some pictures, in the distance, there was an indigo lake surrounded by forest. Everything was untouched, like Earth had once been. Iris had read that Nyx's atmosphere wasn't conducive to human life, but a few people were already living there, inside a sealed structure called 'the Hub'. They were there for good. There was no way back.

Not knowing about Nyx was limited to the old, the insane and the cut-off-from-humanity, though a British anthropologist, Maria Temple, once visited a remote tribe in the Amazon rainforest, and even they had heard of Nyx, through word of mouth. They didn't fully understand what a planet was, or a solar system, or the universe. A baby girl in the tribe was named after the planet. Dr Temple took a photo of baby Nyx with her phone. Two weeks later, after she uploaded it to Facebook, the photograph appeared in the *New York Times* and was shared by millions of people around the world. Iris had once seen it, briefly, while sitting on the bus to work, looking at her phone, but it didn't pique her interest, so her thumb continued scrolling.

The morning after the pub, she found the image again: a naked brown baby with tufts of black hair and a string of beads around her neck, adorably new and far away from civilization. And then she found what she was looking for. The *Life on Nyx* website was elegantly designed, with minimalist fonts and soothing, pastel colours. Iris worked on websites, so she couldn't help but admire it. The Nyx Inc logo was a discreet pale grey, almost hidden at the bottom of the page. The background was a photograph of some sand dunes, glowing pink in the sun. Another sun, not ours. A breeze whipped sand into the air. It wasn't a photo, she realized. It was a video. A button said 'Click for sound'. Iris clicked and heard the wind blowing on Nyx, this other planet, millions of light years away. *Sssss*, it went, both gentle and hypnotic. She was extremely hungover. Words appeared over the video, then disappeared and were replaced by other words:

a beautiful new planet

a meaningful new life

are you ready?

ENTER

Iris could taste bile at the back of her throat. She swallowed and took a few quick, shallow breaths. She was definitely going to puke – it was only a matter of time. But first, she clicked 'ENTER'.

4

There was a long, complicated application form. There were other videos. There was a list of funders, including several well-known billionaires. There was an architectural plan for the expanded Hub, where the *Life on Nyx* community would live: a central, circular building with eight long annexes – like rays of light emanating from a sun. There were computer-generated images of the Hub's interior. Everything looked clean and new, light-filled, immaculate. An indoor farm, abundant with fruit and vegetables, ready to be picked. A cafeteria with tables, chairs and a counter, and ceiling-to-floor windows overlooking the landscape. A large room where people were exercising together, while others sat on sofas, reading. The CGI people were identically dressed in elegant, loose grey clothes, their faces calm and content as they walked down corridors, worked, ate meals and socialized. They had similar, ageless faces, but a variety of skin-tones.

Iris clicked 'play' on another video. You can still find it online, deep in the archives of the *Life on Nyx* website, but it might not be up for much longer.

✳

A man in his fifties with longish silver hair sits in front of a control panel that's covered with hundreds of buttons, switches, knobs and monitors. Above the panel, through a large window, you can see Nyx's empty, pink landscape. The man's face is open, earnest and ruggedly handsome, like an ageing movie star. In his youth, he must have been spectacular. His skin glows and his eyes are blue. He leans into the camera and smiles.

'Hello there, I'm Norman Best,' he says, in an English accent with a transatlantic twang. 'I'm the director of the Hub, the future home of the *Life on Nyx* community. We're very busy at the moment, getting ready for our big launch. We can't wait to welcome you to our beautiful planet.' Big smile. Norman has great teeth.

The film cuts to a montage of Nyxian scenes: pink sand, indigo lake, CGI rooms. Electronic music pulses in the background. The film returns to Norman.

'We're looking for a hundred tenacious, committed, hardworking team players from all walks of life – and from as many countries as possible – to be part of our groundbreaking programme. There'll be room for all kinds of people – medical professionals, horticulturalists, cooks, teachers and makers – though there are some restrictions, which you can find in the terms and conditions at lifeonnyx.com.' Small smile. 'Above all, we're looking for dreamers: people with vision, people who don't want an ordinary life.'

Cut to images of packed train carriages in various cities across the world. People walking along streets, their heads down.

'We're looking for people who want to be part of a real, self-sufficient community, the kind that seems increasingly less viable on Earth. The kind of harmonious, close-knit society that humans lived in for thousands of years, before technology took over.'

The music takes a darker turn and becomes an ominous drone.

'I've been living on Nyx for four years now. From what I hear, life on Earth has become even more difficult than it already was. Here, there are no wars, no conflict, no climate change.'

The film cuts to a group of soldiers dressed in camouflage gear, holding guns, walking down a yellow, bombed-out street; then to a polar bear on an ice floe, surrounded by water.

'There'll be no internet. No cell phones. No more living your life through a screen.'

Images of people gazing blankly at various devices – on public transport, at their desks, at dinner tables.

'No TV, no shopping, no processed food – in fact, all of our meals will be delicious, healthy and entirely vegan. There'll be no celebrities. No more comparing yourself to people you've never met.'

Television sets, designer stores, a greasy pizza, a montage of social media platforms. Kim Kardashian and her sisters walking down a red carpet, smiling grimly.

'There'll be no salaries. No taxes. No distractions. Just friendship, community and genuinely interesting, useful work. It'll be a chance to learn new skills and enjoy your free time in a positive, enriching way. There'll be various activities, thousands of books available in our digital library and a great selection of music, chosen by our community.

'My team and I have loved every moment of our time on Nyx. Personally speaking, I haven't missed Earth at all. The planet is even more dazzling in real life than it is on screen. Truly, you've never seen anything like it. We're so excited about building our community.'

Cut back to the landscape, the dunes, the moonless blue sky. The calming *sssss* of the wind.

'Eventually we're hoping to bring many hundreds of people up here, to build a genuine alternative to life on Earth. But this is a once-in-a-lifetime opportunity to join the pioneers – the first Nyxians. It's a one-way ticket to an incredible new planet. A chance to make a difference, to make history and to live a better life.'

Norman appears. He smiles and raises an eyebrow.

'Are you ready?'

Fade to white.

✳

The sourness rose from Iris's throat to her mouth. She closed the laptop, kicked off the duvet, ran to the bathroom and vomited. Afterwards, crouched on the floor, breathing into the toilet, she realized she was still wearing the previous day's clothes. There were chunks of puke in her long dark hair.

Shit, she thought. I'm late for work.

✳

And what of Nyx, the baby girl named after that inferior pink planet? Maria Temple, the anthropologist, never returned to the

Amazon, because she couldn't find a good job in academia – not even with her Master's, her PhD, her various postdoctorates and her brief viral fame. Finally, she received a job offer from a market research company, where anthropological skills were better remunerated. Some years later, another anthropologist visited the settlement where Nyx was born, but found it empty, abandoned, half covered by the quick, green jungle. No one knows what became of baby Nyx.

NYX

Seven Years Ago

I.

Everything Was New

'Welcome, everyone; welcome to Nyx,' said Norman into a microphone, over the hubbub of people entering the cafeteria, greeting each other. The room smelled clean and man-made, like a new pair of shoes. Norman was standing on a podium, wearing the same loose grey outfit as the other Nyxians, but looking a bit unreal, as celebrities often do, with his handsome face, silver hair and smooth, tanned skin that seemed incongruous for someone who had lived inside the Hub, away from the sun, for several years. Maybe it was natural – good genes and charisma. He waved and smiled, showing his straight white teeth.

Iris had recognized him immediately. Most people would. He had been the face of the *Life on Nyx* recruitment programme, the star of its online content. He had been denounced by politicians, journalists and scientists all over the world. A prominent astrophysicist had described him as 'a modern-age pied piper, leading a hundred fantasists to their deaths'. Iris was star-struck.

'Please take a seat,' he said, 'if you can find one, but I imagine that most of you are happy to stand, after your long trip from Earth.'

The audience tittered in agreement. Some of them stretched their stiff necks and limbs. They had spent most of the journey lying down, strapped to their beds for an entire week. There were a hundred of them, not counting the old-timers who had been on Nyx for several years. The new arrivals kept glancing at the walls where large black cameras hung, transmitting to Earth.

'My name is Norman Best,' he said, 'and I'm the director of the Hub, your new home.'

Someone at the back whooped, then another, and then they all started clapping and shouting, a cheerful racket. Iris joined in. Her hair was still damp – she had just showered, with several other women, in Annex 2's shining white bathroom. For the past hour or so, since arriving on Nyx, she had been smiling so hard that her jaw ached, but it was a good, blissful pain. The noise of the crowd bounced cleanly off the new walls. Everything was new: their home, their clothes, their white trainers, their electronic wristbands, their lives. They were new and Earth was old, and they would never see it again – thank God.

There was a touch of impatience in Norman's frown, his pale eyes, his hands running through his hair, but he covered it with a smile as the clapping died down.

'Thank you, thank you. I'm glad you're excited! I am, too, and I can't wait to get to know each and every one of you. My team is here for you. If you ever need anything, anything at all, you can send us a direct message through your tablets – which will be issued to you later today.'

There were a few excited whispers. The tablets would have no internet access, of course – and therefore no news, no emails, no podcasts, no photos of exes on their wedding days, no videos of puppies running in the snow, no think-pieces about modern love – but still, they were something to look forward to.

'Soon you'll be able to access our incredible e-book library and all of the music chosen by you.'

At the training camp in California, everyone had chosen one piece of music to take to Nyx. Iris had picked Frank Ocean's 'Pink + White', a song she thought she might never tire of. Then again, it had only been in her life for a few years.

'On your tablet you'll soon receive more information about your various jobs and activities. If you'd like to run a class or a group, please do! We're here to learn from each other. You'll also be able to send messages to your fellow Nyxians, though this is quite a small place, so I don't think you'll be doing as much messaging as you did on Earth.'

Iris was standing at the back. She turned and smiled at her friends from Block G: Rav from Birmingham, Vitor from São Paulo and her roommate, Abby, from San Francisco. They smiled back. Abby's brown, freckled skin gleamed with joy. In California, the group had developed a giddy bond, like new best friends at summer camp. Iris didn't really know anyone else. They had been kept apart, so that viewers could watch them getting to know each other on Nyx. Everyone looked bright-eyed and attractive; they were from various countries, but most were American, and in their twenties and thirties, apart from a few of the old-timers, like Norman. There were no babies, no children, no old people, though that was bound to change. At some point they would age, they would procreate, they would spend the rest of their lives together.

'This is an opportunity,' said Norman, 'to leave all that behind: the emails, the messages, the notifications, the constant communication with people you hardly know. Instead, you're going to enjoy a closer connection with the people and the world around you.' He spread his arms. People looked around at each other, nodding and smiling hello. 'Make no mistake: you are part of a great experiment, one of the greatest the world – no, the *universe* – has ever seen.'

Iris's right hand went to her pocket. She was reaching, unconsciously, for her phone, but the pocket was empty, of course. She twisted the soft material with her fingers. Her phone was on Earth. It now belonged to a chambermaid in Los Angeles – someone she had never met. A panicky emptiness came over her, a distancing from reality. The kind she felt whenever she gave up smoking. After a few months, when the distraction of longing reduced itself to a faint hum, she would pronounce herself cured and ask someone for a cigarette. That couldn't happen now.

'This is history,' said Norman, 'happening right now.' He

pointed at the ground. 'This! This moment. The first human colony on another planet. Did you imagine you would see that in your lifetime? And that you would be a part of it?'

She would succeed. She was free. No more cigarettes. No more scrolling. She smiled. This was good. The emptiness was good – a sign that a deeper, heavier emptiness would soon dissipate, for ever.

'This is the culmination of a lifelong dream,' said Norman. 'Since I was a little boy, I've had my head in the stars. Most kids grow out of it, but I didn't. And neither did you!'

Applause. More whooping. Norman had tears in his eyes. So did Iris. Her cheeks were burning, her whole body burned, hot and bright like a sparkler. Earth was watching. Now they know, she thought. Now they know why I came here.

'Whatever happens,' said Norman, 'remember that you are all brave, formidable souls. You will be remembered. This is history in the making!'

The crowd responded with a hysterical roar. People were jostling, screaming, laughing, crying with happiness. Iris could feel their sweat seeping through their new clothes, into hers.

'Yes!' said Norman. 'Ha ha. Yes! Welcome home, dreamers. Welcome home! Thank you for making this boy's dream come true.'

Everyone cheered. Iris clapped and clapped until her hands stung. Norman bowed like an actor and laughed coyly, pointing at people and waving at them. At one point, he seemed to look straight at Iris. She felt an explosion of warmth in her belly. Through the windows, pink sand dunes shimmered under a hazy sun; even more exquisite than they looked on the website. In that region of Nyx, it was always the golden hour – her favourite time of day. This is real, she thought, this is happening. She continued clapping. Her hands ached, but she couldn't stop. Her face was wet with tears.

As Norman began to leave the podium, she joined in with the chanting:

'*Life on Nyx!*'

'Life on Nyx!'
'Life on Nyx!'

✳

Later, everyone from Block G joined a welcome tour led by a cheerful American woman called Amanda – one of the old-timers. They began in the cafeteria, where she gave them a speedy introduction.

'You might have already noticed that, from above, the Hub is designed to look like the sun – or even a flower.' She grinned. 'Everything radiates from the middle, from the heart.'

Most of the common areas were in the central, circular part of the building. Other than that, she told them, there were eight annexes: 1 to 5 contained Blocks A to Y, where most of the Nyx-ians lived; 6 to 8 contained the family quarters, the control quarters and the farm.

Next, she led them through the kitchen to an enormous store-room packed floor-to-ceiling with produce. They shivered in the walk-in freezer and peeked into a laundry stacked with industrial washing machines. The living room was still and pristine, with new sofas and tall potted plants. They flashed their wrist-bands at the entrance of each room, emitting a high, satisfying *beep*. After the tour, Amanda explained, access would be limited to certain areas.

'It's just a safety thing,' she said.

There was a workshop with hundreds of tools, waiting to be used. The medical consulting rooms were small, tidy and unin-habited; as were the family quarters, where couples and children would live together. Amanda led them past the control quarters, where the old-timers lived, but they didn't go inside. Instead, they went to the control room, where Norman was working with three members of his team. It was a semicircular space, with a vast view of the landscape. There were no cameras in there. As the group entered, he turned, stood up and smiled.

'Welcome!' he said. 'This is where the magic happens.'

He shook each of their hands, listening attentively as they introduced themselves. Iris's heart skittered when his blue eyes met hers. As Norman explained the various functions of the control panel, she gazed out of the window. Several metres away, two people in oxygen masks were taking measurements on the sand.

'Why don't you tell them what's going on out there?' said Amanda.

'Of course. As you know, we're eventually going to bring more people to Nyx. My colleagues out there are making preparations for our extension, Hub 2, which we're going to start building in a few months.'

'Awesome,' said Amanda, before turning to the group. 'OK, guys, I have one more thing to show you.'

As they walked into Annex 8, they were shrouded by a cloud of humidity. The air smelled green and ripe. The farm had the proportions and grandeur of a Victorian greenhouse – tall, lustrous plants and a domed ceiling; a thousand shades of green set off by the pink landscape, which could be seen through the glass walls.

'It's open to everyone on Sundays,' said Amanda. 'It feels so good to be around nature, don't you think? The rest of the time, it's a regular working farm. You'll all get the chance to work here. We want everyone to get involved with growing our food.'

Iris and Abby strolled arm in arm, like visitors at a genteel botanical garden, listening to the hiss of the water sprinklers and noticing the changes in climate – from hot and tropical in one section to dry and mildly warm, like a good day in England, in another. There were strawberries, courgettes, tomatoes, pineapples, avocados, salad leaves, plants that were more ornamental than edible – orchids, ferns, cacti – and many more that Iris didn't recognize. As they walked towards the exit, she reached out and let the plants stroke her fingers.

*

Afterwards, the group hung out in the living room. Iris sat close to Rav, leaning against his strong, solid body. He was a personal trainer with an easy demeanour, the youngest child of Indian immigrants. When they first met in California, Iris had felt a sharp, instinctive attraction to his form and scent, as if they were animals in the wild, but it had mostly worn off since then.

Everyone had a story and every story had the same ending – leaving Earth, coming to Nyx. Rav told them about his favourite aunt, who had died young and told him not to waste his life. Vitor, who was slight and clever, with a hint of steeliness, talked about being an A&E doctor in São Paulo, patching up kids with bullet wounds, and about his parents, who had no idea he was gay.

'Maybe they know now,' he said, 'if they're watching.'

A guy called Jonah bonded with Abby – both were Jews, from the San Francisco Bay Area. They spent a while figuring out if they had any friends in common, but they didn't. Hans from Berlin said he had spent a year nursing his mother, who had lung cancer. After she died, everything had felt pointless.

'That's why I'm here,' he said, beaming.

Elizabeth from Cincinnati, Ohio, told them she had dreamed of being a singer, but ended up working in HR. She wore her blonde hair in a long plait, like Iris's mother used to.

'God,' she said, 'I was so glad to leave.'

'That was one of the best days of my life,' said Iris, 'when I quit my job.'

'What was it?'

'I was a digital innovation architect.' She covered her face, laughing with delight at how far away she was from her old life.

'What does that even mean?' said Hans.

'Honestly, I don't know.'

'It doesn't mean anything,' said Elizabeth. 'None of it did.'

✳

Over the following weeks, the summer-camp feeling continued, fuelled not only by the novelty of new people and surroundings, but also by the distant knowledge that millions of people were watching them on TV, learning their names and memorizing their faces. They became accustomed to the cameras; to never seeing the sun rise or set; to the automatic blackout on the windows; to always dressing the same; to waking, sleeping and eating at regimented times. There was a comfort to this regularity. Friendship groups quickly formed based on where people lived and what jobs they had, much like they did on Earth, but unlike on Earth everyone made an effort to be inclusive and open.

At first, Iris made friends with the other social media producers, but they didn't work closely together, so drifted apart. Their duties were limited: taking a few pictures, writing some words and hitting 'send'. Most of the content was created on Earth, in an office, but Iris couldn't see any of it. She bonded more with Yuko and Stella from her cleaning team and, of course, with the other inhabitants of Block G.

In their spare time, the Nyxians slept well, ate wholesome meals and attended Rav's exercise classes, but mostly they talked till their mouths were dry – about their lives, their countries and their old jobs, which no longer defined them. On Earth, these conversations were edited into digestible chunks of content: a syndicated daily show, short clips, blogs, images, tweets and memes. There was a livestream, too, for the die-hard fans who wanted to watch them in real time.

No one on Nyx seemed unhappy; everyone was content. Iris hadn't felt so good in years. Sometimes she thought of home, but she didn't long for it. She hoped her family and friends were all right, she wondered whether they were watching, whether they had already recovered from her departure. A tsunami might have surged over London, sweeping the city into the sea, and she would never know.

It hadn't been long. They probably hadn't recovered.

It was autumn in London. The temperature would be cooling, the leaves reddening and falling from the trees. Iris's mother would be taking her long black coat out of mothballs. Her old colleagues would be tapping away at their desks, writing reports and presentations. The city probably hadn't been swept away. In all likelihood, everything was more or less the same – for now.

Fridays were her favourite. In the mornings, she cleaned with Stella and Yuko, who talked as much as they worked, and in the afternoons, she had a shift on the farm with Abby, Rav and Vitor. On Earth, Iris could barely keep a cactus alive. On Nyx, she learned to grow salad, tomatoes, potatoes, beetroot, squash – anything. Together, they sweated under the glass dome, enjoying the heat of the alien sun as they sowed, pruned, raked and picked, following the instructions of the head gardener, Sean – an American with several faded tattoos on his arms – until they were second nature. Afterwards, she would have a hot shower and lie in bed for a while, listening to something soothing and familiar from the Nyx playlist – the Frank Ocean song or Debussy's 'Clair de Lune'. Later, she would meet her friends in the cafeteria. They would eat the food they had grown together and then talk until the end of the day.

EARTH

Eight Years Ago

2.

Freedom

In London, January was the worst time of the year. The indolent fantasy of the Christmas period – long mornings in bed, long nights drunk, endless television – had given way to sober realization: oh, this is life. It was Iris's penultimate January on Earth. She worked at Freedom & Co, a creative agency with outposts in New York and Amsterdam. Halfway through the month, sober realization morphed into turgid acceptance. It was Thursday – *that* Thursday; the day she found out about *Life on Nyx*.

In the afternoon she held a probation appraisal with her colleague Eddie, who she managed, in the tiny meeting room that had recently been christened the 'IdeasBox'. (The boardroom was now the 'IdeasLab'.) Forty minutes before the meeting, Iris had swallowed a pink Propranolol, which she'd bought off the internet. She didn't like going to the doctor; she didn't want to be on the record as a crazy person. Pills smoothed over her anxiety and gave it a sheen, like make-up. Before she had discovered them, the adrenaline in her veins sometimes forced her to flee rooms, like an animal from an oncoming car. She wasn't comfortable with power, not even the small, insignificant kind. Alison, her boss, seemed like she had been comfortable with power since childhood. Would Iris ever catch up?

Most of her colleagues were around her age – somewhere in their twenties. Older people usually burned out, had children or nervous breakdowns, quit and retrained as something more meaningful, like pastry chefs or yoga teachers. The oldest person at Freedom & Co was Roger, the director, who rarely registered Iris's existence. He shone with wealth and confidence, from his thick grey hair to his Italian leather brogues. Iris didn't want to make pastries or teach yoga; she didn't know what she wanted. She often thought: What happens to people like me, when they're not young any more? The useless ones – where do they go?

It was an inconsequential meeting, but Iris thinks of it often. Memories are so strange. Some of them, even good ones, slip through her fingers like liquid, while others cling on for mysterious reasons. Snatches of dialogue from bad films, lyrics to songs she never liked. She remembers exactly how the IdeasBox looked that afternoon. The sun was coming down, casting a rosy shaft of light across Eddie's handsome, puckish face, his wavy blond hair and blue eyes. Otherwise the room was gloomy, with the indefinite temperature of offices – both air-conditioned and heated – so that Iris's arms prickled with goosebumps while her underarms leaked sweat. She hadn't been outside since 9.30 a.m., not even for a minute. It was now after 4 p.m. Her limbs felt heavy and underused. Both of their faces were shiny and red, but that shaft of light made everything OK. It made the meeting feel like it was already a memory – hazy yet precise. Despite the pill, Iris still felt a little nervous.

'Well, I'm pleased to say that you have passed your six-month probation,' she said, in a rehearsed but casual tone.

'Oh wow,' said Eddie, his shoulders relaxing. 'That's great. Thank you.'

'We're really happy with your work so far.'

He sighed with relief, which made Iris feel sad for him – and for herself, too – for being so dependent on insincere affirmations. Both of them were pretending they hadn't got wasted together countless times, that they hadn't been flirting since Iris arrived at Freedom & Co, a couple of weeks after he had started.

'You're a real, uh, team player. Everyone likes you. We all love your work.'

'That's good.'

'I was especially impressed with your content strategy for Pure Yogurt.'

Eddie smiled at her as though they were playing a game, which they were.

'You took the client's brief and went several steps further,' she said. 'They were really happy. It felt fresh and different.' She was reading from her notebook as though it were a script, but she tried to cover this up by smiling and waving her hands around. 'Alison and I particularly enjoyed the videos of people sharing their stories about the essence of purity. They were so . . . *poignant*. I almost had a tear in my eye. Honestly!' She laughed, cringing with self-loathing.

'Oh, good,' said Eddie.

'Meaningful content, the kind that really connects with people – it's the dream, basically, and it's so hard to pull off. The client was super-impressed.'

He laughed and she laughed, too.

'I'm glad you liked them.'

'There are a couple of other things to discuss, though.'

'Oh?' said Eddie, his smile falling.

'Nothing major, don't worry!' Iris grinned like a loon. She could feel her eyes popping out of her skull, her face hurting from all the effort. 'Rest assured, we're really pleased with your performance, but there are a couple of *things*. I mean, you know you've been a bit forgetful at times.'

'The Instagram thing?'

'Yes, there was that,' said Iris, disappointed yet empathic.

Eddie looked serious and apologetic. 'I don't know what got into me. I had so much work on that week.'

'There was also the Facebook thing. Then you went on holiday and there was no way of getting hold of you.' She didn't ask, 'Why didn't you check your emails?' but the question was implicit. Checking emails on holiday wasn't an official requirement, but a spiritual one.

'The client didn't notice that one, though,' said Eddie.

He didn't care – he was her polar opposite. At the very least, Iris cared about looking like she cared. She couldn't help but admire him.

'That's not really the point, Eddie. Alison and I spotted it before the client had the chance.'

'You're right, it was stupid.' He looked down at the table. 'I'm sorry. I just had so much on my plate. I've been feeling kind of, uh, burnt out.'

The golden-pink shaft of light was still shining across his face, over his eyes. Iris had an urge to take a photo of him because the light was so beautiful, but that would have been unprofessional. She would have to remember it instead.

Look,' she said, 'I know we're not saving lives here, but just keep a list or something. I can't keep covering for you. I want to make this work. Let's put those incidents behind us, OK?'

'OK.'

'But in future, if you're feeling like your workload is too much, just come to me.' Iris swept her arm in the air, like a wizard with a wand. 'I'm your line manager. I can help. We can find a way around these problems.'

'I really appreciate this, Iris. You're *such* a great manager.'

It was a pantomime. Iris knew it, Eddie knew it, and they both knew that the other one knew.

'No worries. Do you have any questions?'

'No,' said Eddie, which is what Iris had been hoping he would say.

'Let's get back to our desks, then, shall we?'

When they stood up, the shaft of light moved from Eddie's face onto a shelf of marketing awards. Iris pretended to need the loo so they wouldn't have to walk back to their desks together, making small talk. Her cheeks were sore from smiling and her head hurt from all the pretence – it was exhausting. She reached the door to the unisex toilets just as Alison walked out, neatly dressed in a blue trouser suit and white trainers, her blonde hair tucked into a bun. She smiled knowingly.

'How was the probation hearing?' she said, as if Eddie were a criminal.

Iris decided not to correct her. 'It was fine.'

'Shall we talk about it?'

'Yeah, if you want to.'

'Let's go in here,' said Alison, opening the door wider.

'In the toilets?'

'The disabled cubicle, not the main ones. There's nowhere else private on this floor.'

'We could go to the IdeasBox?'

'No, this is faster. We're already here. Just a mini-meet.'

A mini-meet was a five-minute meeting in which nobody sat down, for maximum efficiency. Iris didn't want to have one in the toilet, but generally she agreed to anything suggested by senior staff – it made life easier.

So she said, 'All right.'

Alison looked around to see if anyone was watching before they walked into the cubicle and locked the door. There were no disabled employees at Freedom & Co, so the toilet was mostly used for shitting as it was more private and spacious than the other cubicles. Hence it smelled like various shits by various people; a palimpsest of shit, faintly masked by a tropical-scented air freshener. They stood facing each other, smelling the shit of their colleagues.

'Smells a bit in here,' said Alison, wrinkling her nose. 'So disgusting – doing number twos at work.'

'You think so?' said Iris.

'There's a time and a place.'

'What if you really need to go?'

'You just hold it in!' Alison pursed her mouth and widened her eyes, as if she suspected Iris of being a flagrant work-shitter, which she was. Maybe it was the secret to Alison's success – abstaining from shitting. She was three years older than Iris and earned twice as much. She had a husband, a baby and a house. She was disliked by almost everyone at Freedom & Co, but she successfully performed an impression of competence for Roger, which was all that mattered.

Alison covered her nose with her hand. 'Anyway, how did it go with Eddie?'

'It went well. He was really apologetic about the things he messed up.'

She nodded energetically. 'What was his excuse?'

'He said he was feeling burnt out.'

'Ha! Come off it. Like he even does a fraction of what we do. I was working till one in the morning last night, *in bed*, and then I was in the office at seven.'

'Wow.' Iris pictured Alison typing furiously into a laptop as her husband tried to sleep. 'You must be tired.'

'I'm fine, I. Unlike Eddie, I can take it.' Alison had shortened Iris's name to 'I' in the last few weeks, a sure sign that she saw her as slightly superior to the other workers. 'I'm not expecting him to work as hard as *me*. But he's having a nervous breakdown? Please!'

'I don't think it's that bad. He made a couple of mistakes, but he's really sorry and wants to make a new start.'

Alison smiled indulgently. 'He's lucky to have you as his manager.' She touched Iris's arm. Her hand felt hard, like wood. 'You're really kind, I. Maybe *too* kind.'

'Uh, thanks.'

'Also, how are you getting on with the Project Salmon strategy?'

'Project Salmon?' Iris said it slowly, hoping to jog her own memory. There was Project Ground Zero, Project Elephant, Project Sapling. Which one was Salmon? 'I'm on it. It'll be with you next week.'

'Brilliant. Maybe by tomorrow morning, though?'

'Sure.'

It was now past 5 p.m., but Alison would definitely forget the new deadline.

'Excellent. I just want to read it over the weekend, to get

ahead of things.' Alison looked at her phone and sighed. 'Well, I have another meeting. I'll leave first, otherwise it might look a bit weird.'

'I was coming to the loo anyway, so I'll just stay.'

Alison frowned. 'This loo is for disabled people, I. It's not fair to use it.'

Before Iris could reply, Alison marched out of the toilet. Iris locked the door behind her and took a huge, serendipitous shit.

Back at her desk, in the white-walled, open-plan office, she checked her personal emails first. There was a message from a shoe shop. Subject line: 'We miss you.' No, you don't, she thought, and unsubscribed. There was also an email from Kiran, asking her to buy olive oil and toilet paper on the way home. She addressed Iris as 'Dearest' and signed off with 'Love you', as if they were a couple.

Several messages appeared on the screen in quick succession:

Jenny
Sup everyone? Drink tonight? Thursday's the new Friday?
Rich
yes, please
Eddie
I'm meeting someone, but I can come for one

Jenny, Rich and Eddie sat at the same bank of desks as Iris. Other colleagues could always tell that they were messaging each other because their breathing became punctuated with small, amused sighs.

Jenny
Meeting someone? A womaaaan?!
Eddie
Yes, my sister
Jenny
Boring

Iris had been included in the group chat since the Christmas party, which had started with lunch and ended with the four of them doing MDMA and singing karaoke till 4 a.m. It was nice being included, but Iris wondered if it was bad for her career to be so open and friendly with colleagues. Better to stay distant and unknowable, like Roger, or crazy and unlikeable, like Alison.

Jenny
Iris? Up for it?

Iris didn't answer for a minute – she didn't want to seem over-eager. She searched for emails in her inbox that mentioned 'Project Salmon', in case they included any clues. There were sixty-seven results. Fuck it, she thought.

Iris
Yeah, I think I can come.
Jenny
Yay!! 👽

Iris had no plans beyond buying olive oil and toilet paper, but it was always good to sound a bit unsure and unavailable.

Rich
eden?
Jenny
Too early in the year for Eden. Still skint from Christmas
Rich
yeah, you're right

Hierarchies shifted in the group chat. Though Jenny was the most junior of the four, and the newest employee, she called the shots. She was formidably confident, both glamorous and messy; her dyed red hair looked like it had been whipped up in a storm and she often stank of sweat, but sweetly.

Eddie
Pub?
Jenny
Yes!
Rich
great
Iris
Sounds good.

As Iris typed her response, she noticed that the program auto-matically capitalized the first letter of each sentence, which meant that Rich was manually changing his capitals to lower-case letters. It gave his messages a quiet, pared-back poetry. He was the oldest member of the group – thirty years old – and Freedom & Co's only black employee. Agency staff tended to be homogeneous and inter-changeable, a truth they contested on their website's zany 'team' page, on which everyone shared a fun fact – their favourite 'free-dom fighter'. Roger's was Che Guevara. Alison's was Gandhi. All the obvious ones were taken by the time Iris joined the company. After cruising Wikipedia for five minutes, she chose Spartacus.

Jenny
Let's leave one by one, so that people don't know we're going out. I can't deal with anyone else today
Rich
cool
Jenny
I'll go first
Iris
I have some more work to do – I'll see you in a bit.
Eddie
Ok
Rich
btw, did u guys see this? just launched today http://www. lifeonnyx.com

A few minutes passed.

Eddie
Pretty cool!
Rich
amazing huh, maybe i'll apply
Jenny
Ok I'm leaving now!

✳

Before she left the office, Iris skim-read dozens of emails about Project Salmon. Each message seemed more indecipherable than the last. She was so bored and tired that the words seemed to dance around the screen, blurring into a cloud of nonsense.

actionable insights　　　　　　　　dynamic, holistic social

cut up the data in new ways　　self-curated web experience

granular detail　　　　　　　multi-platform synergies

stats should tell a story

harness the brand opportunity

swim against the tide!

It was like being a detective, but instead of solving a murder, she was trying to work out what she did for a living. She opened a new Word document, wrote a title at the top, then underlined and bolded it:

<u>Project Salmon: Digital Strategy</u>

The others were at the pub. They thought Iris was a work-aholic, but it was all a ruse – she didn't know what she was doing. She added 'Project Salmon' to her to-do list. It wouldn't take long to whip up a little strategy in the morning, even if she didn't understand what it was for. As long as she used lots of buzzwords and phrases – the more obscure, the better – Alison was sure to be impressed.

She turned off her computer, stood up and took her coat off its hook. The office was still half full. As she walked out, she saw one of her colleagues, Mark, shaking his head at her, disapproving yet triumphant. He was one step closer to being the martyr of the day, the hardest worker, the purest of them all.

Outside, the winter air was cool and fresh against her damp, hot face. Iris felt like a bag of flour, heavy and dull. Bar a few meetings, she had sat at her desk for ten hours. A better person would have gone to the gym to make up for it, but she wasn't a better person. Alcohol worked faster than exercise.

'You're here!' shouted Jenny from a booth in the corner of the pub.

Iris composed her face into a thrilled grin. 'Yay!' she said.

Jenny stood and put her arm around her, as if they were BFFs who had been parted for several years. It made Iris feel both loved and uncomfortable. She wished she were more into hugging. She hadn't been raised that way. Her mother hadn't hugged her in years. Eddie and Rich glanced at her and nodded, but they were deep in conversation, their eyes bright and involved.

'Drink, anyone?' said Iris. Her skin seemed to be vibrating on the left side of her body, where Jenny was touching her.

'Just got a round,' said Jenny.

Finally, Iris was released and went to the bar. She returned with a pint of pale ale and two packets of salt and vinegar crisps.

'What are you talking about?' she said, as she ripped open one of the packets and laid it on the table. 'Help yourselves.'

Everyone took a few crisps.

'You know that link I sent you?' said Rich.

'I didn't get a chance to look at it.'

'It's this project to send people to live on Nyx – you know, the planet?'

Four years earlier, the Nyx landings had been a sensation – the greatest breakthrough in space travel since Neil Armstrong had walked on the moon. Sometimes the Nyxians, as they called themselves, appeared in the news – but not often. Their contact with Earth was sporadic, for technical reasons.

'Oh, yeah,' said Iris, 'I think I saw something on Twitter about that. Aren't there people already living there?'

'Yeah, but they're all scientists,' said Rich. 'They want to send a hundred people – normal people. Applications opened today.'

'*A multi-platform social experiment,*' said Jenny, doing air quotes. 'That's how they described it on the radio this morning.'

Iris sipped her beer. It tasted like hope and joy, like relief.

'The catch is that you can never come back to Earth,' said Rich.

She looked up, suddenly interested. 'Never?' The cold beer slipped down her throat too fast. She burped quietly into her fist.

'Yeah, like the original Nyxians. There's still no way back. You spend your whole life up there. It's something to do with the wormhole – it only goes one way.' He laughed. 'It's pretty wild.'

'Cray-cray,' said Jenny. 'Who the hell would sign up for that?'

'Did you see the pictures?' said Rich. 'That Hub place looks incredible.'

Jenny rolled her eyes. 'It looks like a cross between an Airbnb and a luxury spa.'

'Exactly!' Eddie laughed. 'The millennial dream.'

'They've already had 10,000 applications in one day,' said Rich, 'so obviously a lot of people want to go.'

'Ten thousand people out of seven billion,' said Jenny. 'That's nothing. Ten thousand suicidal lunatics – and that's a tiny percentage of all the lunatics on Earth.'

Everyone went silent. Jenny always went too far. She combed her fingers through her hair. Her red lipstick was smudged. Eddie opened the second packet of crisps.

'I'm not saying I would go,' said Rich. 'I mean, my mum would actually kill me. But it sounds pretty good – living in a commune, growing your own food, not just wasting your life looking at crap on a screen.'

'Hmm, I dunno.'

'Look at Earth, man. Look at Britain and the US, the Middle East. Look at Eddie over there, checking Twitter on his phone, even though we're all trying to have a conversation.'

Eddie looked up sheepishly. 'I'm just texting my sister –'

'There's no history up there. Everything starts at zero.'

'I'd rather, like, move to the countryside or something,' said Jenny.

'Yeah, of course you would.'

'The way Rich is describing it,' said Iris, 'it does sound kind of appealing. You wouldn't have to worry about your future, about making the right choices, having the right job. Everything would be taken care of. And it's a beautiful planet, from what I've seen.'

'You big weirdos,' said Jenny. 'Why would you want to leave Earth?'

'I'm not saying I'd go,' said Rich. 'I'm saying I *get it*.'

'Look at this,' said Jenny, gesturing at the room. The pub was packed with the after-work crowd: men in suits who worked in the City, men in casual clothes who worked in tech, a few women. A dozen people were crowded around the bar, waiting to be served. 'We're some of the luckiest people on Earth.'

'Why,' said Iris, 'because we're at the pub?'

'Exactly. We're free.'

Eddie glanced at Iris. 'Life's hard. Who doesn't feel like running away sometimes?'

'Our lives aren't hard,' said Jenny. 'Come on.'

Iris's eyes suddenly tingled with self-pity. She felt as if she were drowning in the stale pub air. She blinked until the feeling passed. It came, it went. Nobody noticed, nobody knew. It was ridiculously easy, hiding herself. Painful, but easy. Her greatest gift. Even she didn't know who she really was: the fun, capable colleague, or the revolting madwoman lurking under the surface. There was no singularity, no undeniable truth, no middle ground. She felt both sane and deranged, joyful and miserable, competent and crippled.

Jenny picked up Rich's packet of tobacco from the table and started rolling a cigarette.

'Yes, you may have one,' he said.

'I knew you'd say yes.' Jenny gave him a wink.

They went outside to smoke. Iris stayed inside with Eddie. The pub was getting rowdy. The air felt steamy and blurred. They had to lean into each other to be heard, but half the time they just pretended to hear. It was getting embarrassing saying over and over again: What? Sorry? What? Sorry? What?

But then Iris heard Eddie say, quite clearly, 'Thanks for earlier!'

'The probation?'

'Yeah.' His smile was ingratiating.

'No worries.'

Is that the only reason he's nice to me, she thought, because I'm his line manager? Probably. It would make sense. That was the only reason she was nice to Alison, after all. Perhaps Eddie sees me in the same way – his annoying, ridiculous boss.

'I know these things can be awkward,' he said. 'Especially when –'

She missed the rest of the sentence because of the noise. People were shouting, clinking glasses, doing shots.

'Sorry, what?'

Two men were standing near their table with their arms slung around each other, blazers off, ties askew, celebrating the near-end of another week. Soon the weekend would come and time would briefly belong to them – more or less, apart from the regular checking of emails. I'm projecting my feelings, thought Iris. They probably love their jobs. They're nothing like me.

'Especially when –'

Eddie's warm breath was in her ear. She thought she would like to kiss him. How unprofessional. But still, it would be easy, just to turn her head and feel his breath on her lips, instead.

'Sorry, I can't hear you,' she said.

'Don't worry.' He grimaced. 'Shall we go outside?'

That's all it took to make someone feel unhappy on Earth – not being heard in a noisy, dark room. No wonder people always pretended to hear each other. It was a lovely white lie, the idea that someone was always intently listening. Iris and Eddie left their coats in the booth so nobody would take their seats, and squeezed their way through the crowd. They would be cold, but losing their seats would be worse. Outside, Jenny and Rich were rolling more cigarettes. They were wearing their coats, which made Iris feel even colder. Eddie was shivering, too. Iris never bought tobacco these days, because she had officially given up. Eddie knew this, so he handed her his packet before she even asked.

'Jenny told me this weird story,' said Rich.

'Oh God!' said Jenny, covering her face. 'I've been biting my tongue ever since I joined Freedom. I'm so sorry.'

'What is it?' said Eddie.

'It's horrible. I don't want to put everyone on a downer.'

It was so unlike her to hold back. Iris was genuinely curious.

'Seriously, it's not even a story. It's just that I used to work with someone who had Rich's name.'

'You used to work with someone called Rich?' said Eddie. 'Cool story, bro.'

'No, no. His whole name. At my last agency, there was a guy called Richard Wolfson.'

'It's a Jewish name, isn't it, Wolfson?' said Iris, only just realizing it.

'Yeah, my great-grandfather was Jewish, I think. Someone way back.'

'What was so special about this other Richard Wolfson?' said Eddie.

'He killed himself,' said Jenny.

'Fuck.'

Iris wanted to know more. 'That's terrible. Was it recently?'

Jenny bit her red lips and nodded. Her eyes filled with tears. Iris put her arm around her, which felt strange and forced, but Jenny didn't flinch at all.

'That's why I left.' She exhaled a grey plume of smoke. 'That's why so many of us left. Only senior management stayed. No one else could take it. It changed the mood of the place. Everyone wanted to get the hell out.'

'How awful,' said Iris. She hadn't tried to kill herself since she was sixteen, but she thought about it almost every day. Whenever she heard about a suicide, she wanted to hear everything – their age, their level of success, their note, their method – but she had learned to hide this morbid obsession, because it creeped people out. 'Were you close to him?'

'No, not really. That was the strange thing. He wasn't close to anyone, so we all felt terrible, like we should have made more of an effort.'

'There's nothing you could have done. You barely knew him.'

'What an intense thing to go through at work,' said Eddie.

'Shall we go inside?' said Rich, covering his disturbance with boredom. 'Another round?'

Eddie left to meet his sister and the others stayed till closing time. The pub served proper food, but they didn't order any because the alcohol and conversation made their hunger small and quiet. Instead, they ate several packets of crisps in all sorts of flavours, till their mouths felt salty and sore. After closing time, Rich and Jenny went to get kebabs, but by then Iris was tired of their company. She went to another fast food place, bought a box of chips, covered them in salt, vinegar and ketchup, and ate them on the bus to Clapton. It's Friday tomorrow, she thought. Am I getting too old for this? Getting hammered on a Thursday night, eating chips on a bus. When she was younger, she assumed that she'd be happy and fulfilled by now – doing something meaningful, living in a lovely house with a kind, handsome man. Perhaps everyone dreamed of such things. But Jenny was right: she was lucky, even if it didn't feel that way.

She listened to pop music on her phone, the kind she enjoyed when she was trashed, with her head resting against the window; mouthing the lyrics to Sky Ferreira's 'I Blame Myself' as the

38

bus made its way down Hackney Road. There were lots of drunk people on the street – shouting, laughing, running, hugging, smoking. Did no one have work tomorrow or did none of them care? The bus shuddered, her head felt heavy, her stomach swirled. Shit, shit, shit. Someone sat next to her and she thought: I'm trapped now. I'm going to have to vomit on my lap. Twenty-seven years old, for fuck's sake. Nearly twenty-eight. Nearly thirty. Will I still be puking on the bus at thirty? She breathed deeply and then shallowly. It was hard to tell which was best for keeping the vomit inside.

As the bus reached Mare Street, Iris looked over at another double-decker on the other side of the road, going the opposite way. On the top deck there was a guy asleep at the front. Young hipsters in the middle, practically trembling with excitement. Iris could tell they were new in town. At the back there was a guy. Wait, no, wait. A wave of nausea glimmered through her body, making her head light, her legs numb. He was an Ortho-dox Jewish guy – black suit, black hat, grey beard – but there was something familiar about him. His blank expression, his wide cheeks.

'No, it can't be. Wait, wait,' she muttered to herself, pushing past the guy sitting next to her and running down the stairs to the lower level.

The bus stopped and Iris ran out, but the other bus was too far away, disappearing now, and she was alone, in the dark. She was drunk and confused. Her dad was dead and buried. Or had he been cremated? She didn't know. It wasn't him, they all look alike – same beards, same black clothes. It isn't racist to think so, right? She was almost Jewish. Technically she was a goy, thanks to her goy mother, but she had inherited her father's surname, Cohen. A lifetime of explaining, No, I'm actually *not*.

Iris entered the flat noisily and threw herself on her bed, feel-ing as if she were rolling down a hill. To quiet her mind, she scrolled through various apps on her phone. Twitter: bad news, people screaming at each other. Facebook: another girl from school had been impregnated by her lawyer husband. *Mazel tov!* Congratulations! She liked the post, even though she thought the girl was a desperado, with her nose job and butter-blonde hair, and her husband who would be obese and bald within two years – you could just tell. Under the post, Iris began to type, 'I hope your baby is born with your original nose,' but deleted it halfway through and switched to another app.

She found herself googling Richard Wolfson. Not Rich from work, but Jenny's ex-colleague – the one who killed himself. There were many Richard Wolfsons in the world. There was her colleague, looking smart and professional on his LinkedIn page. There was a wannabe writer. There was a casting director in Los Angeles, a psychiatrist, an oncologist and a plastic surgeon. But not the dead guy. She googled 'Richard Wolfson suicide' and found what she was looking for. A local news item. Thirty years old. Died by hanging. Suffered from depression. Office manager. Huh. She wanted more than this – much more. She wanted to know how it felt, whether it was worth it, whether Richard Wolfson would give five stars to suicide – thumbs up, highly recommend – or whether he regretted it at the last moment, whether the pain of hanging was greater than the one he suffered in life.

What am I doing, what am I doing?

Her heart was beating so quickly, she wondered if she might have a heart attack. *Boom-a-boom-a-boom-a-boom.* Whenever she became conscious of her heart as this dumb hunk of meat, it would beat terrifyingly fast, as if it were offended. I'll show *you*, said her heart. Breathing heavily, Iris scrabbled around on her bedside table for her sleeping pills. She popped one out, crunched it between her teeth – it tasted disgusting, metallic – and felt a surge of calm wash over her. She fell asleep with her clothes on, including her shoes.

That night, she dreamed she was at a meeting in the IdeasLab, the boardroom at Freedom & Co. Alison, Rich, Eddie and Jenny were there, and some other people, and everyone was talking passionately, gesticulating and laughing in unison, but she couldn't hear anything they were saying. It sounded like they were underwater – fuzzy and incoherent. Alison said something funny. Ha ha ha. Everyone laughed. They started to notice, one by one, that she was not engaging with the conversation.

'What do you think, I?' said Alison. It was the first thing that Iris understood.

Everyone turned to stare, none of them laughing any more.

'Yes, what do you think?' said Jenny, looking much more serious than she ever did in real life.

In her dream, Iris remembered one of the most memorable suicides she had ever heard of – that of a promising young gymnast called Ella Williams. On a Saturday night in early spring, Ella was at a party in west London – laughing and dancing, her friends said, but not drinking, because she was teetotal. At some point she disappeared. Everyone assumed she'd gone home, but she was on the roof, looking down at the street. It was now Sunday morning: ice-cold, the sky was lightening and the streets were almost empty, apart from an elderly dog walker, who saw Ella standing up there. (It's always a dog walker; they see all the bad things.) The walker stopped and looked up, wondering if she should shout something. Perhaps the girl was just enjoying the view. But then she saw Ella walk to the other side of the roof, take a run-up and leap off the building, somersaulting several times in the air – 'like an Olympic diver,' the woman told the police – before crashing to the ground. Iris thought of Ella often, of her sweet, childish face on the BBC website and the baroque manner of her death. How alive she must have felt as she flew through the air.

'What do you think?' said Rich, in Iris's dream.

'About what?'

Alison glared at her. 'I, this is really important. Have you not been listening?'

Iris stood up and stretched her legs, like Ella Williams had done, and looked at the window on the other side of the room. The clouds were pinking in the sunset. She took a run-up and leapt, crashing straight through the glass and into space, where she flew through the black sky, surrounded by stars that audibly twinkled.

Suddenly, she wasn't flying any more. She was lying on the sand in her underwear, on the planet Nyx. The sand was the sweetest shade of pink, like marshmallows. The alien sun warmed her skin, nourishing her. Everything looked the same, in every direction. Pink sand and blue sky, pink sand and blue sky, pink sand and blue sky. What a relief. Whichever direction she chose, it wouldn't make a difference.

When Iris woke, her mouth was dry and she was definitely going to puke, but she felt peaceful, for once. It was a great idea. The solution to everything. Softer than suicide, an almost-death. She didn't want to die. She just wanted to escape herself – her life, her work, Earth. Perhaps something of her would remain here, on this planet. All the bad parts. She would be famous.

She opened her laptop and searched: 'nyx'.

3.

Interview #1

The interview room was on the third floor of an office block in Canada Water that looked like it was waiting to be demolished. The lift wasn't working. As Iris walked up the stairs, she wondered whether it was an elaborate hoax, whether someone was going to jump out and attack her. But there was no one else around. Following the instructions from the email, she entered Room 303 without knocking. It was small and box-like, with black walls and a single light that hung over a leather office chair. Iris sat down and waited. It was early May, the Friday before the bank holiday.

'Welcome to the *Life on Nyx* recruitment programme,' said a disembodied voice – chirpy, female and American.

Iris jumped in surprise.

'Congratulations on having passed phase one of the programme.'

'Hello,' said Iris. 'Thanks.'

'Please state your full name.'

'Iris Sara Cohen.'

'Thank you. What are your parents' names?'

'My mother is called Eleanor White and my biological father was called Robert Cohen.'

'Why do you say "biological"?'

'He left when I was five and died a year later. He wasn't much of a father.'

'Why did he leave?'

Iris snorted. 'Why does anyone leave their children? Because they're awful.'

The voice didn't say anything.

'He had a religious awakening,' said Iris. 'That's why he left. He became an Orthodox Jew. I don't know what came over him. He was already Jewish, but he'd never been religious.'

'Did it upset you?'

'Wow, that's a really personal question.'

'We will be asking many personal questions. It's part of the recruitment process. I hope that's OK with you, Iris.'

It was the kind of bright, perky voice that waitresses used in American films, in suburban diners. Iris had never been to the US, so she didn't know if they really spoke like that.

'Sure, it's fine. What's your name?'

'My name is Tara. I'm not a human being. I've been programmed to interview *Life on Nyx* applicants. Please can you answer the question,' she said, still perky, but firm. 'Did it upset you when your father left?'

'I was five years old – I don't remember. My memory of that time is, like, a haze. I don't even remember his funeral.' She shrugged. 'I'm used to it. It's just this sad undercurrent in my life. We all have those, don't we? I mean, you probably don't. You're, what, some sort of AI?'

'Yes, that's what I am. How did he die?'

'He had a heart attack.' She swallowed. 'Oh, I also have a stepfather called Jack White.'

'Like the rock star?'

'Yeah. When I was a teenager I used to sing the guitar riff from "Seven Nation Army" to piss him off.'

'That's funny. What are their professions?'

'My mother used to be a schoolteacher. She doesn't do anything now. My stepfather works with property. I don't really know what he does.'

'And your father?'

'He was a lawyer.'

'What is your sexual orientation?'

'Heterosexual, more or less.'

'More or less?'

'I had a girlfriend when I was a teenager.'

'Do you have a boyfriend?'

'No.'

'Where did you grow up?'

'London. Tufnell Park and, before that, Temple Fortune.'

'Do you have any siblings?'

'I have a half-sister called Mona.'

'How old is she?'

'Uhhh . . .' Iris counted the years on her fingers, against her jeans. 'She's twelve. She'll be thirteen this year.'

'And you're twenty-eight – that's a big age gap. Do you have a good relationship?'

'Yes, I suppose so, though I worry about her sometimes.'

'What do you worry about?'

'She's so quiet and studious. I don't think she has many friends. She goes to the same school I went to. It's very pressurized. She isn't having much fun.'

'According to your application, you went to St Peter's Girls' School.'

'Yes, I went there for seven years.'

'It's currently the third-best-rated school in the UK. That's impressive.'

'My father left me some money so I could go to a good school.'

'Did you have fun as a teenager?'

'Yes. I got good grades, but I went to loads of parties. I acted in school plays. I got on with everyone. I still do. That's why I think I'd be good on Nyx.'

'Are you still in touch with your school friends?'

'A few of them.'

Iris realized that she had starting gently spinning herself on the chair, from foot to foot. She stopped and tried to concentrate on not doing it.

'Not many?' said Tara.

'I grew apart from some of them.'

They hadn't grown apart. They had stopped speaking to her after she did the *terrible thing*.

'Are you the kind of person who grows apart from people easily?'

'No, I was just a teenager. It's normal when you're young, don't you think?' Iris laughed, remembering that Tara had never been young.

'You studied English at the University of Bristol – correct?'

'Yes.'

'Did you enjoy it?'

'Yes. I had lots of friends. I got a first.'

'Who is your closest friend?'

'Kiran. We live together. We met at university.'

'What's her surname?'

'Virk. V-I-R-K.'

'What does Kiran do?'

'She's an account manager at an advertising agency.'

'Blanket Creative?'

'Yeah. Did you just look her up?'

'Yes. What did you dream of becoming when you were at school?'

'I . . . If I get accepted, will this interview be used on TV?'

'Did you not read the terms and conditions?'

'I did, but I can't remember. They were quite long.'

'It won't be used on TV. This interview is purely for the recruitment programme, but I would advise that you reread the terms and conditions. *Life on Nyx* is a very serious undertaking, Iris.'

'OK, Tara, I will.'

'Can you answer the question?'

'This is embarrassing, but I wanted to be an actress. People always told me I was good at it. I got all the best roles at school.'

'What happened?'

'I, uh, I don't know. I lost interest. I don't think I was good enough.' Iris's hands were clammy. She could faintly smell her own armpits. Hopefully the AI couldn't smell them, too.

'Are you a leader or a follower?'

'I think I'm a follower, actually. I'm good at following orders. That's why I think I'd be good for this programme.'

'You're a digital innovation architect at Freedom & Co – correct?'

'Yes.'

'That sounds exciting. What does it involve?'

'I work on digital strategies for brands. Web development, content, social media, that kind of thing.'

'How long have you been there?'

'Almost a year. I worked at two other agencies, previously.'

'Do you enjoy it?'

'Yeah.'

'If you enjoy your job, why are you signing up for *Life on Nyx*?'

'Oh, sorry, I don't really enjoy my job. I don't know why I said that. It just came out. You're supposed to enjoy your job, aren't you?'

'Please answer the questions honestly,' said Tara, with a small, human strain in her voice. 'How do you really feel about your job?'

'I feel like it doesn't contribute anything positive to the world. I just help companies to sell things.'

'Why don't you find something you enjoy more?'

'I can't think of anything else to do and I can't quit, because I need the money. But yeah, I would like to do something else. Something with a higher purpose.' Iris laughed at herself, nervously.

'Would *Life on Nyx* be a higher purpose?'

'Of course. Living on another planet – wow. It would be an incredible honour to take part.'

'Where does your boss think you are now?'

'At a doctor's appointment.'

'Do you find it easy to lie?'

'It's only a white lie. You didn't offer any weekend appointments, so this was my only chance. I imagine that most of your candidates would have had to lie to their bosses.'

'How would you feel about being filmed every day for the rest of your life?'

'I'm sure I'd forget about it, after a while. I liked being on stage. Maybe it'll be a bit like that.'

'But you'll never be able to walk off stage.'

'Never?'

'Not really, though we've decided not to film participants in their bedrooms and bathrooms.'

'I think it would be OK.'

'You would be very famous. How would you feel about that?'

'I would feel fine. I mean, I'd be too far away to even notice my fame. It's not like I'd be photographed while buying a pint of milk.'

'You would never be able to buy a pint of milk again – or anything else. You would never return to Earth. You would never see or speak to your family and friends again.'

'Hmm. I don't know how to answer this without sounding like a monster. It would be difficult, but I think I would cope.'

'It's going to be extremely challenging – emotionally, mentally and physically. Is this really something you want to do with your life?'

'Yes. Can I ask a question, though?'

'Of course.'

'Why won't they be able to contact Earth? I mean, it must be possible, since the show will be streamed on the internet – right?'

'Again, this is explained in the terms and conditions.'

'I know, but –'

'Cast members will not be able to contact friends and family on Earth due to technical and financial limitations.'

'Right.'

Tara went on, reading from the terms, word for word: 'The only contact cast members will have with Earth is for regular psychological evaluations, which will be carried out by Earth-based mental health professionals.'

Only the terms and conditions referred to the Nyxians in this way – as 'cast members'.

'Above all,' she continued, 'after consulting several specialists, Nyx Inc has come to the conclusion that this is the best way to maintain cast members' emotional and mental well-being, which is our primary concern.'

It didn't make sense to Iris, but she said, 'OK.'

'Thank you, Iris. We've now come to the end of our first interview.'

'Thanks. Did I pass?'

'We're interviewing thousands of people around the world, so it will take a while to assess the results. We'll send you an email to let you know whether you've progressed to the next round.'

'I just want to say that I really want this.'

'Thank you. Goodbye, Iris. I hope you have a great weekend.'

'You too. I mean, thanks. Bye.'

4.

Cygnets

Later that day, Iris was standing at the head of the IdeasLab, giving a presentation about hashtags, holding a clicker in her sweaty right hand. The long bank holiday weekend was within reach. She remembers that day perfectly, from beginning to end: toast for breakfast, the interview in the black box, the presentation, cocktails at East of Eden.

'So, in conclusion,' she said, 'hashtags are, of course, an integral part of any social media strategy – a fun, simple way to increase engagement, spark debate and tell the story of your brand to potential customers, beyond your core community. But remember: always think before you tag. Any questions?'

Fifteen faces looked back at her, expectantly. It was almost over, but first they had to go through the song and dance of pretending they had questions. Most people didn't give a shit about anything on Friday afternoons, which took the pressure off, but still, the attention was unbearable. As a child, Iris had loved attention. Plays, assemblies, music: she involved herself in everything. It was hard to pinpoint when everything changed, when she became this other person, this wreck. A scarecrow made of hay and rags, passing as human.

'No questions at all?' said Alison, narrowing her eyes.

Iris felt a single drop of sweat fall from her armpit, trailing down the right side of her body to her waist, under her silk blouse. She sniffed the air. Yeah, she thought, I definitely smell bad. Shouldn't have worn silk – it would stain. Eddie looked at Jenny, Jenny looked at Rich. They cocked their heads, hoping someone else would ask a question. Finally, Eddie raised his hand, offering himself up for sacrifice.

'Really interesting presentation, Iris. Some great insights there.'

'Thanks, Eddie.' She smiled modestly.

Eddie was slumped low in his chair, leaning backwards. He ran a hand through his messy blond hair. His T-shirt was old and bluish grey, threadbare under the arms. There was no dress code at work, but he took it too far. He barely tried to hide how little he cared.

Another drop of sweat fell from the same armpit, underneath Iris's blouse.

'But don't you think it's important to sometimes *not* use hashtags,' he said, 'just so that brands appear a bit more human and approachable?'

Iris nodded. Eddie had no interest in this question. He was just helping her out. She opened her mouth, not knowing what she was going to say, but hoping that if she randomly strung a few of Alison's favourite words together – learnings, stakeholders, narrative, synergy, analytics, strategy, conversion – then she'd be OK.

But Alison got there first. 'Wait a sec,' she said, her voice quick and shaky with anger. 'Did you listen to anything that Iris just said?'

Eddie sat up straight. 'Yes, of course.'

'Good, well, she already said – half an hour ago – that it's important to maintain a balance between marketing, curation and humanization.'

He shrugged, but he wasn't nervous – he wasn't scared of her.

'Sorry, Alison. I must've missed that.' He hung his head like a schoolboy, and smiled.

'Any other questions?' said Alison, taking over. 'Well, I'll take that as a sign of how thorough Iris's presentation was. It was really excellent, I. So many valuable learnings for us to take away and ponder.'

They filed back to their desks and immediately logged on to their group chat.

Eddie
Drinks tonight?
Jenny
Fuck yes
Iris
I definitely need one.
Rich
i need 20
Jenny
Let's go crazy

They were mute, but typing furiously, desperate for the end of the day to come.

Eddie
Eden?
Rich
yeah
Jenny
Yes! Let's leave one by one. Iris?
Iris
Yeah, I'm up for it.
Jenny
OK. Go team. I'll go first. See you upstairs. By the pool xx

✳

It was one of the first beautiful evenings of the year, with a soft, golden sky that, coupled with alcohol, made Iris forget her unhappiness, momentarily. She was sitting by the blue swimming pool on the roof of East of Eden with Eddie, Rich and Jenny. It wasn't warm, but it wasn't cold. Spring was her favourite season because it hinted at the summer, yet to come. The sun was fairly high, just creeping to the other side of the world, casting tall shadows and a hazy light as they drank delicious iced cocktails made with esoteric ingredients. They were laughing.

'Look at that,' said Jenny, pointing at the city, which glowed silver, blue and brown beneath them.

They all nodded and smiled. Jenny and Rich put on their sunglasses. All of them agreed, inwardly, that they were very lucky at that exact point in time. Everything was fine, more than fine. Everything was sparkling, ecstatic. Their veins were delivering alcohol to their fingers, legs and brains, making them feel warm and wonderful in the stiff spring air. They were talking shit about Alison, that awful bitch, and peering over their shoulders to check that no one from Freedom & Co was behind them, listening.

A young woman with blonde bobbed hair, wearing a retro, high-waisted white bikini, walked out of the changing rooms and stood at the deep end of the pool, preparing to dive. There was no one else swimming – it was still too cold. Her nails were painted red. She looked like a Golden Age film star. Everything goes around in cycles. It would be a relief, thought Iris, to be immune from that. The girl dived elegantly into the pool, barely making a splash. Iris zoned out of the conversation, as she often did, and watched the swimmer glide through the water. She's much prettier than me, thought Iris, and younger, too. But one day we'll both be old and ugly.

'You OK?' said Eddie, nudging her shoulder with his.

'Oh, yes.'

'Want another drink?'

'Yes, please. Same again.'

Iris slurped the end of the cocktail and crunched the ice between her teeth, enjoying the brief snap of pain. She watched as the swimmer pulled herself out of the water unselfconsciously, even though she was surrounded by fully clothed people, and stood up straight, squeezing the water out of her hair. She was close enough for Iris to see the goosebumps on her arms and legs. She was magnificent, really. No older than twenty-five. Probably some sort of model or actress. Someone who didn't think of death twenty times a day.

The moment passed; the sky darkened. What a terrible waste, to feel even mild sadness on the first Friday in May, sitting next to a swimming pool in one of Earth's great cities, with a long weekend ahead of you. Iris had been so consumed by work and the *Life on Nyx* interview, which no one else knew about, that she had forgotten to make plans. The others were talking about parties, dinners, family get-togethers, trips to the countryside: a sure sign that the conversation had dried up, that they hadn't drunk enough alcohol. On Earth that's what you asked people when you didn't know what else to say: 'What are you doing this weekend?'

'How about you, Iris?' said Rich.

'Not much – just chilling out.'

'I *wish* that was my weekend,' said Jenny. 'I'm going to be so knackered by the end of it.'

She was just being kind. Jenny never stood still. Eddie came back with the drinks. It was coming, it was coming: the Smog, the gaping blackness. The weekend would be finished. Iris had lived with the ever-present threat of the Smog for sixteen years. She had her guards, her night watch; she was familiar with the signs. Kiran was going away with Ben, her married boyfriend, so Iris would be alone. She was almost relieved. She could revel in it, swim in it, lie in bed all day, allow it to sit on her chest, laughing at her. Nothing would stop her from succumbing. Wait – she had lunch with her family the next day. How could she get out of it?

Someone dive-bombed into the swimming pool, splashing them with water.

Jenny shouted, 'For fuck's sake!'

They stayed by the pool until 9 p.m., when the rooftop closed for the night, then they moved inside and drank several more overpriced drinks. Someone produced a wrap of coke, so they took their turns at creeping to the bathroom. Jenny insisted that she and Iris should go together. The bathroom walls were elegantly scrawled with lines from *East of Eden*, the John Steinbeck novel. Something about beauty and truth, something about freedom, about good and evil. She had never read the book. As Jenny bent over the toilet lid, Iris caught a whiff of her greasy hair, but it wasn't so bad – earthy and rich, the kind of smell you'd enjoy on someone you love. As she squatted down, Iris tried not to think about how many particles of shit she was snorting, how many people had handled the banknote before she stuck it up her nose. As she inhaled, all of this was forgotten. Her blood seemed to vibrate; every cell in her body was singing a show tune. The Smog was filed away to the back of her brain for another time, probably the next day, but there wasn't going to be a next day – there was just the bar, the drinks, her friends, the city, a never-ending night. At 2 a.m. they took a taxi to Iris's flat, where they drank Kiran's gin and tonic, and when that was finished they drank some dessert wine that Jenny found in the back of a cupboard.

They moved from the kitchen to Iris's bedroom. Eddie and Iris sat on the bed, leaning on each other, and Rich and Jenny lay on the floor on piles of cushions. At 5 a.m., silence bounced around the room. Everyone looked rubbery and old. Rich ordered an Uber. Jenny went to the loo and didn't come back. Eddie and Iris were alone, on her bed. He put his arm around her, smiling his Peter Pan smile. Neverland – was that somewhere near Nyx? Iris's mind felt fluffy and soft. Her mouth tasted like shit, literally. This wasn't how she had wanted it to happen, her mind jangling with chemicals. She was his boss. It wasn't right. Who cares? Alison would care.

Eddie kissed her shitty-tasting mouth. The kiss sent disappointingly weak sparks through her body, not because she didn't like him, but because she was wasted. She couldn't keep her head up. They slid down to the fuzzy carpet and lay face to face, lips to lips, barely moving.

'We're fucked,' he said into her mouth.

Iris woke up in bed, under the duvet, wearing only her knickers. Her clothes were in a pile on the floor. Her mouth was dry, her nostrils crusty and her head heavy, as if filled with gravel. She picked at the crusts and flicked them away, before remembering that she wasn't alone. Eddie was asleep on his back, still on the floor, covered with a sarong Iris had bought on holiday a long time ago. She couldn't remember which country it was from. It was red and yellow, printed with folkish drawings of the sun. How would it feel to look up and see another sun? She drank some water from an old plastic bottle. It tasted like dust.

'Oh God,' said Eddie, now awake, putting his hands over his face. He opened one blue eye, then the other and then shut them.

Iris laughed. 'Good morning,' she said. She raked her fingers through her long hair, which felt dirty and warm at the roots.

Eddie stretched his arms over his head, showing the worn-away, stained armpits of his T-shirt. 'I feel like shiiiit!'

'Same.'

He kicked the sarong off and stood up. He wasn't wearing his jeans. His legs were sharply muscled, covered in blond hair – a runner's legs. Iris moved under the duvet towards the wall and felt his warm body slide next to hers. He put his hand around her waist and leaned in for a kiss.

'I've wanted to do that ever since you walked into the building,' he said.

'Really?'

'Of course. Couldn't you tell?'

'No.'

Eddie's stubble scratched against her skin. He breathed into her ear. Her body felt hot all over. Blood was rushing between her legs. What would his face look like when he came? Eddie pulled Iris towards him. This is joy, she thought, like a bird-watcher glimpsing a rare, lovely specimen. Remember this for later, when the Smog descends. Remember the joy.

That afternoon, Iris went to meet her family at a pizza place near Parliament Hill. She had an insatiable hangover. As she walked into the restaurant, her stomach growled. She found them at the back. Her mother looked too smart for the restaurant. Not just her shiny, highlighted bob and pearl earrings, but also her general haughty demeanour. She sat up straight, like a dancer, and enunciated every word. Mona, by contrast, was hunched down, looking at the table, wearing a baggy black hoodie and wire-rimmed glasses, her curly auburn hair half pulled back. There was a bowl of green olives on the table.

'Sorry I'm late,' said Iris, sitting down. 'Where's Jack?'

'Oh, he couldn't come,' said her mother.

'What's he doing today?' Iris took an olive from the bowl.

'Just working at home. He had an emergency.'

Her stepfather was permanently attached to a gadget, replying to emails, huffing or tutting at something, head down. Iris hadn't seen him in a few months, but she tried not to take it personally.

'Oh well. How's it going?'

'Fine,' said Mona, glancing up.

'I'm very well,' said Eleanor, 'and you?'

'Yeah, I'm OK. Are you looking forward to the summer holidays, Mona?'

'It's miles away,' said Mona, frowning. 'It's only May.'

'Oh yeah, I don't know why I asked that.' Focus, Iris, focus. A thought passed through her head: if only a sinkhole would open right here, right now, and swallow us up. Uh-oh, thinking of sinkholes was a giveaway. She looked up at her sister. There was a touch of unreality to the scene, a distance between Iris and her family. Am I actually here, am I alive? She blinked and said, 'Any plans for the summer, though?'

'We're going to the south of Italy for two weeks,' said Eleanor. 'We're renting a house.'

Iris felt a tug in her heart. She didn't want to go, but she wanted to be invited.

Eleanor seemed to notice this. 'Do you want to come?'

'Yeah, maybe.'

'Are you planning to go anywhere?'

'No, just working.'

'How is it at, uh, the office?'

Eleanor could never bring herself to say 'Freedom & Co'. Iris knew it was a stupid name, but most agencies had wholesome, feel-good, incongruous names. It was her life, what could she do? Her mother had wanted her to do something proper, like medicine or law.

'It's fine,' said Iris.

'What have you been working on lately?'

'Mum, you're not interested in my work. You don't need to pretend.'

'I *am* interested!'

'OK, at the moment I'm working on a campaign for a new organic beauty brand called The Farm.'

'Are the products any good?'

'I don't know. I haven't used them yet. I haven't had time.'

Eleanor raised her eyebrows. 'Hmm.'

Mona was silent, her eyes studying the menu intently, as if she were reading a newspaper.

'How's school?' said Iris.

Her sister set the menu down. 'It's all right.'

'She won an award recently,' said Eleanor, 'for maths. Didn't you, darling?'

'Mum, *please*.'

'That's great. Congratulations. What are you up to this weekend?'

'Nothing. Sitting here with you.' Mona kept her eyes on the table. She ate an olive.

Iris more or less remembered what it was like, being twelve, but at the same time it was like recalling the memories of another person. She had been doing well – making friends, studying hard – but underneath it all there was a low hum of white noise. She had started to feel like a rotting peach, no longer fresh and sweet. Her school reports described her as energetic, a leader, a doer, but inside, the Baby Smog was nourishing itself like a tapeworm. Mona was different. She didn't hide it. Awkwardness radiated from her face. Iris wanted to shake it out of her. She wanted to tell her: *Learn to hide it or the world will break you.*

'I'm going to the loo,' said Mona, standing up.

Eleanor watched her walk away until she was out of earshot. 'Stop foisting your ideas on her,' she whispered.

'What ideas? I was just asking what she's up to. She doesn't seem to have any friends.'

'She's one of the top girls in her year.'

Iris laughed – she couldn't help it.

'Don't be so envious.'

'She's having a bad time,' said Iris, 'and you're not helping her.'

'Mona isn't like you.'

'Not like me? What do you mean? I was good at school. Maybe not as good as Mona, but where did it get me?'

'How is that my fault?'

'I'm not saying it is.'

'She's coming back, Iris. Please.'

Mona slumped back on the chair and pulled her sleeves over her hands, poking her thumbs through the holes. A waiter came over and they ordered their food. Eleanor chose a salad. Her eyelids flickered slightly when her daughters each ordered a pizza.

By the time the food arrived, Iris's hunger had melted, along with the rest of her. The comedown was now a crescendo, gross and humid like fungus. There was sweat all over her body: on her back, trickling from her armpits, shining on her forehead, oozing from her pores. She struggled to talk and think. She managed to eat half of the pizza, somehow, and drank two Diet

Cokes, but her mouth still felt like a desert, full of sand. She didn't order a third Coke because her mother was looking at her with concern. She breathed deeply, which made the sickness more profound. Her heart fluttered like a panicked bird. Will I die like this, she thought, eating a pepperoni pizza while my mother and sister talk about the school fete? Neither of them noticed her crisis, or they pretended not to. Iris went to the toilet and threw up, which made her feel better.

'What are you doing now,' she said to Mona, when their mother went to the loo. 'Fancy going for a swim in the pond?'

'Bit cold, isn't it?' said Mona. 'I don't have my swimming stuff.'

'We can go in our underwear.'

'I don't know.'

'Just come and watch, then. We can have a little walk.'

Outside, the sisters waved their mother goodbye and walked up Parliament Hill, past the chatting dog owners. Iris was happy that Mona had agreed to come – she had assumed she would say no and scurry home with their mother. Iris sometimes worried that Mona didn't like her very much, that she saw her as damaged goods – the disappointing first child, poor fatherless Iris – but then she remembered that twelve-year-olds don't think like that. She wanted to be closer to Mona, like a real big sister – someone Mona could turn to, especially now, on the eve of her adolescence, the most ludicrous years of anyone's life. They were accustomed to a fond, mutual distance. Iris hadn't been around when Mona was growing up. She had been at university, at work, on the other side of London, off her face, uninterested in children.

They took the long way to the Ladies' Pond, up the green hill. The air cooled the sweat on Iris's skin. She wondered if she smelled like puke. Beside her, Mona seemed so clean and new – never been drunk, never taken cocaine, never stayed up all night. But they were sisters all the same, across those fifteen years, across the two fathers who separated them.

They reached the woods. Under the trees, it was much cooler – the dregs of winter, refusing to leave. For once, Iris was grateful for those dregs. The colder the water, the better it would feel.

'Are you really going to swim?' said Mona.

'Yeah.'

'You don't even have a towel.'

'I'll be OK.'

Beyond the gates, five or six women were swimming in the pond, surrounded by trees. There was no sign of the city there – that was what Iris liked best. Usually she only went on hot summer days, when the water and grassy areas were always busy, humming with female voices, but there were women who went all year round, who cracked the ice and leapt in on freezing winter days. They were a different species, tougher than Iris.

The sisters stood by the lifeguards, watching the sun glimmer on the murky pond. The trees weren't quite as full and green as they would be in a couple of months. Iris stripped down to her black underwear, leaving her clothes in a pile, out of the way. Her skin puckered in the air.

'You're mad,' said Mona. 'It's so cold.'

'Do you think I should jump in or use the ladder?'

'Jumping is easier.'

One of the lifeguards glanced at them, unimpressed by Iris's cowardice.

'OK, I'll jump.' Iris stepped towards the concrete edge of the pond and looked down.

'Do it!' said Mona.

Iris leapt into the air. The cold water took her in, closed over her head and held her. For a second, she floated under the surface, feeling like every atom in her body had been shaken awake, but it was so cold and the urge to breathe was too much. She stuck her head out and took a lungful of air. It was pure and sweet, like country air.

'How is it?' said Mona.

'Not that bad. Come in!'

'No way.'

'You're missing out.'

Iris turned and swam quickly, to keep warm. Her arms moved through the water like scissors through silk, while her feet were tickled by tendrils of underwater plants. All the bad feelings had gone. She breaststroked her way to the end of the pond, where the swimming area was roped off. Beyond that, a family of swans – a large white mother and her fluffy grey babies – were rooting around at the water's edge. The mother sized up Iris with her beady eyes. What are they called, thought Iris, the baby swans? Mona would know. When she turned back, she saw that her sister had stripped off her clothes, too. In her pants and vest, without her glasses, Mona looked so young. She *was* young. Her legs were skinny, her hips narrow and her chest almost flat. She was twisting her waist-length hair into a topknot. My lovely little sister, thought Iris. Or perhaps she just thinks this in retrospect. It's hard to tell.

'Jump in!' she shouted. The lifeguard shot her another look. 'Sorry,' she muttered, too quiet to be heard.

Mona walked down the ladder, dipped a toe in and cackled. There was something about cold water that teased out joy or even wrung it out, where there had been none before. There was a splash and her sister disappeared into the pond, then reappeared, gasping for air and giggling. Iris swam to her.

'Ahhh, it's freezing,' said Mona. Her teeth chattered and her pale cheeks blushed in the cold.

'You'll get used to it.'

'I'm glad I came in, though.'

'Me, too!'

When they reached the end of the pond, where the swans were resting, Iris said, 'What are they called, the bab–'

'Cygnets!' said Mona, before Iris had finished.

'I knew you would know. I always forget.'

Mona smiled with pride. 'Ask me the capital of any country,' she said, as they swam. 'I've been memorizing them.'

'OK – Sweden.'

'Stockholm.'

'Australia.'

'Canberra. Give me a hard one.'

'Uh, Fiji?'

'Suva!' said Mona, grinning.

'Wow,' said Iris, 'I'll take your word for it.'

'Another one!'

'The Bahamas?'

'Oh, I don't know that one,' said Mona, but she didn't seem to mind. She was like a different person, now that their mother had gone.

The two sisters swam back and forth a couple of times, delaying the inevitable: getting out of the water, the cold bite of the air, wet underwear under their clothes, shivering and laughing all the way home.

5.

Destiny

By bank holiday Monday, Iris felt clean and renewed. She hadn't left the flat since Saturday, or spoken to anyone other than a takeaway delivery man, to whom she said hello, thank you and bye. She had wrapped herself in blankets, watched an amazing amount of TV and masturbated twice. Eddie had texted her from his family home in Kent, where he was staying for the weekend:

> Hello! Are you feeling as shit as I am?

It pushed back the bad feelings, knowing that she existed in someone's mind, that she hadn't disappeared. The Smog didn't fully descend that weekend. False alarm.

Late in the afternoon, she heard a key in the door and felt relieved, her loneliness and boredom dissolving like sugar in tea. Kiran was back from her weekend away with Ben, her awful married boyfriend.

'Heyyy,' came her voice, as she knocked on Iris's door.

Iris was lying in bed, scrolling through the internet on her laptop. 'Come in!'

Kiran walked into the bedroom looking smart and polished – her hair and knee-high boots were both glossy and black, in contrast to Iris's faded T-shirt, tracksuit bottoms and damp hair. Iris stood and they hugged.

'How's it going?' Kiran sat on the edge of the bed, her coat still on, and sighed. She was holding a small brown parcel.

'All right, and you?'

'I'm fine.' Kiran held out the parcel. 'Oh, I found this down-stairs – it's for you.'

Iris snatched it and put it on her bedside table. It was her latest delivery of pills.

Kiran laughed. 'What's inside it?'

'Just make-up,' said Iris, too quickly. 'How was the trip?'

'Yeah, it was good. It was good and bad.'

'Why bad?' Iris knew why. She was asking out of politeness.

Ben was married with three children – that was the bad. Kiran was obsessed with him and he made her feel alive – that was the good. Feeling alive is always good. But Ben's wife and children were always there, hovering in the corners of her happiness. There were six people in the relationship. Kiran had only met one of them.

'You know, the stuff with Ben's wife. It's not easy.'

Kiran had been involved with Ben for a decade, on and off. They met when she was eighteen and he was thirty, at a pub in Soho, but he ended it soon afterwards, when Kiran went to university – where she and Iris became friends. In that first year, she spoke about Ben non-stop, as though he were the Messiah, sent to Earth to save her. He got back in touch a few years later, when he was an unhappily married father of two. When Iris finally met him, she was seriously disappointed – Ben was just a fat, sweaty City boy with a red face. He called Kiran 'my Indian princess'. His only redeeming feature was that he paid for all their drinks. That's when she realized: love is bizarre and can't be trusted.

'What's new?' said Iris, already bored with the conversation they'd had so many times.

'Ben wants to leave her, but she's really depressed. I get where he's coming from. He says that she might kill herself if he leaves. So yeah, I don't want that to happen. I'd rather wait a little bit longer.'

'Why does he think she'll kill herself?'

'I mean, he's, like, her *life*. She doesn't work, she just looks after the kids. Apparently she's Prozacked up to the eyeballs. I get why he's worried. He's thinking of the children.'

'What are you going to do?'

'I'll wait a bit longer, but I'm not going to wait for ever. Till Christmas, maybe.'

'Last year you said you were going to wait till Christmas.'

'Yeah, but, you know. We love each other.' Kiran held her chin up and shook her head. 'It's not easy, but we'll get there in the end.'

Iris didn't know what else to say. She didn't approve of the relationship. Not just for moral reasons, but because Kiran was obviously being duped by Ben and, more generally, by TV shows, films and songs into thinking that love was worth the sacrifice, the humiliation. She was a true romantic. She believed in destiny, as if a higher power had brought her and Ben together. 'Of all the pubs in Soho,' she often said, 'we were both in *that one* at the same time. Isn't that funny?' Iris didn't think it was funny – there were dickheads in every pub in Soho – but she never said this, because she loved Kiran.

By contrast, every time Iris started a new relationship her feelings got smaller and smaller, like a well-used bar of soap. She hadn't always been like this. When she met her ex-girlfriend, Edie, the summer after sixth form, she still believed in love. Back then, Iris had few friends left, because of the *terrible thing* she had done. She and Edie worked at the same cafe. Edie didn't need the job – her parents were rich – but she was clever, gener-ous and kind; no, *magnetic*. She made a crack in Iris's loneliness. It lasted two months and Iris ended it, but still, she thought of Edie all the time. She dreamed about her at least twice a month. The recurring special guest star of her unconscious. Edie was the first, the model for the others. The original bar of soap.

'Well, you know what I think,' said Iris, 'and there's no point in going over it again.' Though she knew, of course, that they would go over it, again and again.

'Yeah, you're probably right.'

'Really? Which part?'

'That I'm deluded, maybe.'

'You do realize he'll never leave his wife?'

Kiran shrugged. 'Maybe he will and maybe he won't.' She didn't want to think about it. The fantasy felt so much better. 'Look, I know what you think, but when I'm with him, everything seems better. I can talk to him about anything. I can be myself.'

'Are you not yourself now, with me?'

'Yeah, but . . .' Kiran sighed and took her coat off. She didn't look depressed, just thoughtful. 'Anyway, how are you?'

'I hooked up with Eddie. You know, my colleague?'

Kiran jumped and clapped her hands together. 'Really?! How was it?'

'It was good. We were really fucked, though.'

'I'll make some tea and you can tell me everything.'

Kiran got up and went to the kitchen. Iris settled back on the pillows, comforted by the sound of her friend clicking on the kettle, opening and closing cupboards. She was doing it all super-fast because she wanted to hear about Eddie. Maybe *we're* soulmates, thought Iris. Kiran and me, rather than Kiran and Ben. She wouldn't see it that way, though. Sex always wins. Everything swirls around it. A hole into which everything disappears.

6.

Thank You, Smog

For several weeks, the Smog stayed at bay. The absence in Iris was filled by Eddie. Despite her cynicism about love, she wasn't entirely immune to its effects. When she heard his name – even when it was Alison saying, 'Eddie, what learnings do you hope to glean from your social media listening project?' – it sounded so clean and beautiful: *Eddie!*

Eddie and Edie. Edie and Eddie.

She thought about him all the time, even when they were sitting next to each other, which they did for several hours a day. There were two Eddies: the human made of meat and bone, and the one in her mind, who made her insides glow with warmth and longing. Somewhere, in between their desks, the two Eddies would meet. She tried to remind herself that he was just a person. Probably a terrible person, like Iris, but his newness made him special. Even a two-hour brainstorm about web analytics was bearable, because Iris and Eddie could spend it avoiding each other's eyes and thinking about the myriad ways in which they wanted to fuck each other. Thinking about fucking was often better than doing it. During one particular meeting, she conjured up a blaze in her belly that spread to her genitals and the tips of her fingers. Afterwards they had sex in the disabled toilets, which was OK – despite the smell, despite the fact that she didn't come.

✳

One day Iris woke up feeling like there was a great weight bearing down on her body. She found it hard to open her eyes. The

Smog's long, smoky tentacles were reaching around her in an unwelcome, suffocating hug. She managed to get up, but it clung stickily to her skin, hair and eyeballs. When she looked in the bathroom mirror, her face was grey and flat, like a pavement. She seemed to reek of cabbages and mould. Showering didn't help. She walked down the street, bought a coffee, caught the bus and sat on the top deck. Her head was still damp from the shower. She rested it against the glass, leaving a wet mark. She tried to ignore the tentacles worming their way into her body, making her blood run thick. Focus on reality, she told herself. Be *mindful*. She'd recently read an article that said mindfulness could help. Here was reality: the coffee tasted sweet and earthy, the air conditioning on the bus made her skin bristle. It was a warm day in early summer, but there was a tinge of sadness in the air. In a couple of months, summer would end, like everything.

She had been with Eddie for two months. Inevitably, that would end, too. When would he reveal himself? When would she? There was a flutter inside her, like an animal trapped in a cage. Stay inside, she thought. She looked out of the bus window and saw a little girl in a private-school uniform – maroon blazer and kilt, knee-high socks, a straw hat – walking down the street with her father. He looked kind of Jewish and lawyer-y. Something about his blue suit, his jowls, his thinning hair, his wire-rimmed spectacles; a melancholy, thousand-year-old heft. A Jewish lawyer father – she had once had one of those.

The girl on the street was six or seven, skinny legs skipping, smiling brightly, while her father looked tense and distant. There was a strangeness in Iris's limbs, like they didn't belong to her. Maybe she was becoming one of those lunatics obsessed with cutting off their legs – she loved reading about those people because they made her feel so sane. It was comforting to know that there was a limit to her madness. She wasn't like that homeless guy in front of Shoreditch Town Hall with terrified eyes, shouting at the sky. She didn't see things, she didn't hear things, she had a job. She seemed like a normal person. All this pretending, performing, it was her life's work – so much harder than anything she did at Freedom & Co.

That morning, she had her annual performance review in the IdeasBox. The first ten minutes were fine. Alison praised Iris's passion for digital innovation, her relationships with clients, her talent for project management. Iris was pleased to have passed for someone who was interested in those things.

'The thing is, though,' said Alison, in the eleventh minute, 'and I've heard this from several people round the office . . .' She gave a small, curt smile, as if she were sorry she had to share such dreadful news. 'Everyone thinks you're fab, you're such a great asset, but we just feel that you lack leadership skills. Do you know what I mean?'

'Uh, sure.'

The Smog was taking a break. It was reliably good at disappearing at crucial moments, so that Iris wouldn't embarrass herself. Thank you, Smog.

'Good, so this isn't coming as a surprise. That's what I like about you – you're self-aware.'

You don't know the half of it, cuntface, thought Iris.

'I'm only bringing it up because you have such potential. I mean, where do you see yourself in five years?'

On another planet, thought Iris. Failing that, I'll get plastic surgery and a brain transplant and live under a new identity in the Sahara Desert.

Instead, she said: 'Working in such a technologically driven field, it's hard to say where I'll be in five years' time. The perfect job for me in five years probably doesn't even exist right now.'

Alison smiled and nodded, like a proud mother. 'Exactly! We're on the same page. You know, I see a lot of myself in you.'

Iris widened her eyes and said, 'Wow, thank you,' as if she'd been told this by Nelson Mandela.

'In a few years, you could be sitting where I am, but it will take a lot of work. You're just not –' Alison made fists with her hands and slammed them on the table. *Bang!* 'You know what I mean?'

'Yeah, yeah.' Iris made fists with her hands, too, but she didn't slam the table.

'You need to lead more, from the front. You should be like . . . like a commander leading an army into battle. And the battle is to get people clicking, engaging, interacting with content –'

'And buying stuff?'

'Yes, but you need to think more holistically than that. It's not just about conversion. It's about telling stories.'

What would the Dalai Lama do? thought Iris. That kind-looking man in red and yellow robes. Iris didn't know very much about him, but he would probably tell her to give up this job, all her possessions, and become a monk. Maybe that was the answer.

'You performed so well on Project Salmon,' said Alison.

'Thanks.' Iris still didn't know what this was, exactly.

'But what about Project Salmon Egg?'

She didn't know what that was, either.

'Yes, Salmon Egg is a really interesting one.'

'It is, isn't it? And I feel like that's the perfect project for you to sink your teeth into. It could be your baby, something that you *own*.'

Was Alison passing the project over because she didn't understand it herself? Iris studied her boss's face. Her blonde hair was neatly pinned back, but her eyes were dark and wild.

'I'd be happy to play a bigger role in Project Salmon Egg,' said Iris.

'Great. So you know what I mean, about being a leader.'

'You know, I'm sorry, but I'm not entirely sure.'

'Look, I –' Alison winced in frustration. 'I know it's hard to receive negative feedback, but the important thing is to concentrate on the future, on your personal and professional development. That's what we really care about, here – you.'

Iris held back a hysterical, incredulous laugh, but couldn't hide a hysterical, incredulous grin.

71

'Perhaps it's a confidence thing,' said Alison. 'I know what it's like, we're both women here.'

'It's true, we are.'

'You should walk into meetings and be like –' *Bang!* 'You know?'

'Like this?' Iris hit her fists against the table. *Bang!*

'I don't mean literally. I mean like in the way you talk, the way you move, the way you present your ideas.'

'Like, my personality.'

'Exactly! You've got it.'

'OK.' Iris was bored now. They were just passing the time, playing their roles, like bad actors saying their lines too quickly, without conviction, because they wanted to walk off stage and go home. It didn't matter how she performed. It didn't matter if she didn't change. All that mattered was staying in character and knowing your place. Nod, smile, promise to try harder, be grateful for the opportunity – always grateful.

'Great!' said Alison. 'I'd really love to send you on a leadership-building course. I know of *such* a good one. I did it myself. How would you feel about that?'

I don't want to be a leader, Iris wanted to say. *Is that allowed?*

'That sounds like a great opportunity,' she said in a level voice. 'Thanks, Alison, that would be fantastic.'

Their smiles had become gurns.

'Back to work, then!' Alison picked up her iPad.

They both stood up. Iris was at least four inches taller than her. She could see right over the crown of her head, striped with bleach. If this had been the Stone Age, Iris could have wrestled her to the ground and throttled her to death, since she was the bigger, stronger human. But things had changed since the Stone Age. Alison was superior in the only way that mattered: she believed in herself. They left the room and went in different directions. As Iris walked towards her desk, she could hear Alison running down the corridor to her next meeting, with the uneven gait of a cow. And then: *bam!* Iris turned to see her lying face down on the floor, spreadeagled, with her loafers hanging off her feet.

'Oh my God,' said Iris, quelling the laugh in her voice. 'Are you all right?' The last word caught in her throat. She forced the sides of her mouth down.

'Yes, yes, of course.' Alison stood up, her face pink with embarrassment, and walked briskly away.

Once she was out of earshot, Iris let the laughter spring out. Her face crumpled like a piece of paper. It was one of those laughs that are more like a cry, something primitive and desperate. She was sobbing, sobbing with happiness, at the image of Alison lying on the floor. Tears streamed down her face onto her chest, under her shirt. Back at her desk, she held a hand up at Eddie, tried to speak, but couldn't. Finally she put her head down and gave in to it.

'Are you . . . OK?' said Eddie.

Again, she tried to speak, but only managed: 'I can't.'

'It was that good?'

'No, no, it wasn't good.'

Her face trembled with hysteria. She felt like she was having a stroke. She wanted to see it again and again, like one of those online videos that automatically replays, for ever.

'I'm so happy, I could just die.'

Once the moment had passed, Iris spent several hours staring at her computer. She fulfilled her tasks, ticked them off her list and replied to emails, but every few minutes she lost focus. The shoe shop emailed her again: 'We miss you.' No, you don't, she thought, and unsubscribed again.

In the afternoon, the staff gathered in the office kitchen to sing 'Happy Birthday' to a guy from accounts who wore a woolly hat every day, even in summer, to cover his bald patch. Iris ate three types of cake, made small talk with various people and then walked back to her desk, feeling sick. She stared out of the window at the clear blue sky, listening to the deranged squawk of seagulls – so very far from the sea – and the sonorous hum of building work, and people walking down the street. She looked up at the ceiling and thought, for maybe the hundredth time that week: I could definitely hang myself off that light. What would they think when they found me?

I should be busy, I should be moving forward, I should be working on my leadership skills, making plans to take over the world. But what she really wanted to do was to stand up and scream, 'I don't give a fuck!' What a fine release it would be. Perhaps her colleagues would join her, they would all scream it together, 'We don't give a fuck!' or they would sing it, like the chorus in an opera, and then they would tear around the office like the animals they were, unplugging computers with their teeth and pushing them out of the window, pawing at each other, fucking on their swivel chairs. She pictured Alison standing on her desk, screaming with her arms aloft.

To be so lucky and so miserable, it was insufferable. I should be put down like a dog, she thought. I need to leave London. I need to leave the country, the planet, the solar system.

After work, Iris's colleagues asked her to come for a drink and she pretended to have a headache. Jenny tried to convince her to come by grabbing her arms and pulling her along the corridor, as if the night would be ruined if she didn't comply. Strength in numbers: another person around the table to bitch about Alison, to reassure them that they were loved.

Iris went home, feeling guilty. Kiran was out. She lay in bed with her computer on her lap, scrolling through clothes on various websites, imagining how they could improve her. She bookmarked a few items, didn't buy anything, had a shower, made herself come and felt ashamed afterwards, as if someone were watching and judging her. She went back to the laptop wearing a bathrobe, with wet hair. The doorbell rang at 10.30 p.m. It was Eddie, smiling in a carefree, drunk way, with shining eyes. One of the first things he did was reach into her robe. She slapped him away. They went to the bedroom and she let him touch her, but then she told him to stop, so they just lay under the duvet, smoking a spliff he had brought.

'Are you all right?' he said, stroking her hair.

Iris blew a long, thin cloud of smoke into the air. Eddie was disappointed because he had wanted to fuck. Iris was disappointed by his disappointment.

'You know, I had my performance review today,' she said.

'Is that why you're in a weird mood?'

'I'm in a weird mood because I don't want to have sex right now? Do I have to be up for it all the time?'

'Well, I am,' he said, smirking.

'But does that mean I should always comply?'

'No, no.' He exhaled and sighed at the same time. 'Forget about it.'

The room smelled dirty and sweet, of weed and unwashed sheets. How long had it smelled this way? Far too long.

'You know, Iris,' he said, 'if you ever want to talk to me about anything, you can.'

She glanced at him and briefly laughed, before looking back at the ceiling. 'What do you mean?' She could see him watching her, at the corner of her vision.

'I don't want to be presumptuous, but like, you don't have to keep anything from me. You can talk to me.'

'About what?'

'About how you feel – you know, generally.'

Iris's throat contracted. A cold tremor passed through her body. Did he know? Did Eddie know that she was rotten under the skin? Could he see the Smog, hovering over the bed like an evil spirit? Could he hear it laughing at Iris, at her feeble attempt to pass for human? How could he know, when even Kiran, Mona and their mother didn't know?

Iris deflected the question. 'Alison told me I need to improve my leadership skills. She's sending me on a course.'

'You never know, you might find it useful.'

'You think so?'

'Well, if you don't find it useful, it's not the end of the world.' Eddie made it sound so easy and logical.

'But the whole idea of it, of going on some shonky course, as if my personality is deficient –'

He dropped the spliff into a glass of water. 'That's what work is like. You have to play the game. That's just how it is.' Eddie didn't have a Smog. He was Smog-free.

'I spend most of my life at work. I don't want it to be a game. I want it to be . . .' Iris was going to say 'fulfilling', but it was too embarrassing to admit. She let the sentence trail off. They were now both lying flat, looking at the ceiling. She traced the familiar crack that ran across the mottled white paint from a corner of the room.

'I'm tired,' she said.

'I'll go.'

'No, stay – it's late.'

Soon Iris would get under the covers and turn the lights off, and the Smog would take its usual place on top of her, pinning her to the mattress, making her smaller and more insignificant, less able to breathe. Eddie went to the bathroom to brush his teeth and Iris checked her phone, because that's what you did on Earth when people left you alone in a room – you checked your phone and guarded yourself against loneliness. There was an email from Nyx Inc.

Dear Iris Cohen,

Thank you for attending the first round of interviews for *Life on Nyx*. We are delighted to invite you to a second-round interview. Please –

She stopped reading and flagged it for later, smiling so hard that when Eddie walked back in, he said, 'What's so funny?'

'Just something stupid on Twitter.'

The Smog held up its fat, smoky hands, and retreated unhappily into the wall.

Sometime in the night, Iris woke with Eddie pressed up against her back, warm and constricting. She fought the urge to push him away.

'Iris, are you awake?' he said.

She didn't reply, but she opened her eyes. The sun was rising. At the edges of the blinds, the sky was going blue.

Eddie whispered, 'I really care about you. You know that, don't you?' He paused, wallowing in his declaration. 'I know you're awake.'

Iris squeezed her eyes shut. It was frightening, hearing those words from him, sensing the weight of their emptiness, but soon this feeling passed and she fell asleep.

7.

Terrible Thing

On the night Iris tried to kill herself, she stood at her bedroom window, enveloped by the curtains, looking for the full moon. According to the internet, it was supposed to be there, but she couldn't find it. The sky was dark grey and murky, not quite black. No stars. Is this a sign? she thought. She was sixteen, so everything was a sign. I need to disappear, she thought, like the moon.

Over the past few years, the Baby Smog had been gaining strength, learning to walk and talk, gathering evidence against her. She had stopped acting. She had stopped playing music. She had started loathing herself. Smogs grow quicker than humans.

✳

Some weeks before, on a Saturday, Iris had been getting ready for a party when her mother called her downstairs. Eleanor had got home an hour earlier, after seeing her old friend Antonia, who lived nearby. When Iris walked into the kitchen, her mother was clearing away some leftovers. Mona was sitting in a high chair, holding a plastic spoon and babbling to herself. She was eight months old.

'What is it, Mum? I need to leave soon.'

Everything was newer, back then – the house, the kitchen, Iris, Mona and even their mother, with her long grey-blonde plait hanging down her back as she moved between the kitchen table and the sink. She'd worn her hair that way for years, but soon she would chop it off and dye it.

Eleanor turned, tugged the plait over her shoulder and said, 'Sit down, Iris, I need to tell you something.' Her eyes were full of dread. She always looked serious, but usually in a more vacant sort of way.

Both of them sat down at the kitchen table. Eleanor put her cleaning cloth to the side.

'I don't want to ruin your evening by telling you this. I keep putting it off. It never feels like the right moment. But Antonia thinks I should tell you – and she's right, I suppose. Jack thinks so, too.'

'God, what is it?'

Her mother sighed. 'I've wanted to tell you this for years. It's about your father.'

'Robert.'

'Yes.' She twiddled her fingers. They were shaking. 'I never told you how he died. And I really should.'

Mona squealed and laughed. Her mouth was shiny with saliva.

'He had a heart attack,' said Iris.

'No, I'm afraid that wasn't the truth. You were six years old. I couldn't tell you what happened. You were too little.'

All at once, Iris understood. Her organs felt as if they were made of lead. Of course, it had been a lie. Of course, Robert was like Iris. He was her father. She was made of him.

'How did he do it?' she said.

Her mother widened her eyes, surprised by Iris's guess. 'Your father wasn't well for a number of years. He found it hard to cope.'

'How did he die?' said Iris.

Suddenly, Eleanor seemed to regret the conversation. She shook her head and closed her eyes. 'Maybe we should do this another time.'

'No, Mum, you have to tell me now. Did he take an overdose?'

'No, but –'

Their voices were rising in pitch. Mona had stopped squealing. She watched them silently, as if she were following the conversation.

'Did he jump off a bridge?'

'*Iris –*'

'Did he hang himself?'

'No.'

Mona banged her chewed spoon on the table of the high chair. Eleanor touched her nose and averted her eyes. She reached for the cloth and began to wipe the table frantically. Weren't these all signs of lying? thought Iris. She'd read that somewhere online. How to spot a liar – the top ten signs. Her mother looked up and pursed her lips. Her skin was so pale and thin. She was developing soft jowls under her chin.

'That's it, isn't it?' said Iris.

'Maybe you shouldn't go out tonight. We could . . . just stay in, watch a film, get a pizza – anything you like.'

'No, I want to go out.'

Her mother nodded. 'Well, if you think it's best, I can't stop you. Maybe it's a good idea to see your friends – to take your mind off it.'

But Iris wanted Eleanor to stop her. She wanted her to hold her, stroke her hair and sing 'Silent Night' to her, like she had once done, even though it was April, even though it would feel strange. She wanted to talk more; to hear her mother explain. The strangeness would eventually dissolve.

'Yeah,' said Iris. 'I'm fine. I mean, it's been years, so . . .'

Eleanor smiled a little. 'I'm relieved. I'm glad I told you.' Her hand moved tentatively across the table, but didn't quite reach Iris.

As she walked upstairs, Iris felt like her blood was turning to ice. She rubbed her hands together to make the feeling go away. In her bedroom mirror, she looked exactly the same. She finished doing her make-up: gold eyeshadow, black mascara, lip balm and a cheap, sugary perfume.

'It's fine, I'm fine, everyone's fine, we're all fine,' she whispered, lightly patting her face in the mirror. 'Aren't we? Yes, we are.'

She smiled at her reflection and almost believed it.

At the party, in someone's bedroom, Iris allowed a boy to put his hand under her skirt. Not just any boy – it was James, her friend Beth's boyfriend. Beth wasn't at the party. She and Iris had once been best friends, but as they grew up, they struggled to maintain a mutual appreciation. Beth had become one of those girls who regularly shot tiny, barbed insults with such elegance and subtlety that you couldn't even accuse her of being mean – but everyone was terrified of her.

James had been fawning over Iris all night, constantly topping up her glass of vodka and Coke, which she drained every few minutes, until the news about Robert Cohen ebbed away, temporarily. As two of James's fingers jabbed inside her, Iris tried not to wince. She sighed breathily, like girls did in films, but mostly she just felt a juddering fear in her heart, cutting through the vodka, making her almost sober. She had never thought herself capable of such a *terrible thing*, but there she was. James pushed her head down to his lap and she gave him a blow job – her very first. He came quickly: a salty, vile cream that she instinctively swallowed. He wasn't even handsome. She wasn't sure why she'd done it. Afterwards, they were both embarrassed.

A few days later Iris received a message from an unknown number – a close-up photo of her face, sucking James's cock. She hadn't noticed him taking it. Her eyes were closed, almost blissful, concentrating on the task at hand. There was a strange beauty to it. The photo spread. Everyone saw it. There were more messages, from both known and unknown numbers.

COHEN YOU FUCKING SLUT

Suck my dick!

You love it you slag :)

In the corridor at school, Beth shouted, 'Skank!' at her, surrounded by their friends, laughing. They looked so happy. It was
a real bonding experience. Iris ran away and cried in a toilet
cubicle, biting her hand to keep herself from making any noise.

'Hmmm, delicious,' said the Smog, licking up her tears, one
by one.

And so it continued, for several weeks. The messages. The
Smog. The late-night calls to her mobile phone – sometimes
silent, sometimes giggling girls, but mostly boys whose voices
she didn't recognize.

'Suck any dicks today? Ha ha ha.'

'Cohen loves cock, Cohen loves cock, Cohen loves cock.' Sung
like a football chant, by a crowd.

'Ugly fucking dyke.'

'Are you going to kill yourself?'

Her number was being passed around. They all knew she was
rotten, even the people she'd never met. She lay in bed, clutching her phone, waiting for her punishment, rereading messages
in the dark, barely sleeping. By night, everyone was obsessed
with her. By day, at school, she was a ghost, acknowledged by
teachers alone.

✳

It was a Wednesday night. Everyone was asleep – her mother,
Jack and baby Mona. Iris crept to the bathroom and searched
through the cupboards. Eleanor liked to stock up on things. Iris

popped pills on the counter, dozens of them, and swallowed them with a glass of tap water, almost choking as they went down. She didn't bother with a note. She went back to her bed, lay down and waited for the Smog to take her away.

'Robert fuckface Cohen,' she whispered. 'I'm coming for you.'

Two hours later, she woke up vomiting down her front. It hadn't worked. She puked some more, into the toilet, changed her pyjamas and went back to sleep. In the morning her face was red and raw from all the puking.

'Must be a stomach bug,' said her mother. 'Just stay in bed – I'll call the school.'

Eleanor hadn't mentioned Robert Cohen since her revelation and she would never bring him up again – not with her voice, anyway. Sometimes she would look at Iris, especially when they were alone, and a gloom would cloud her blue eyes, which Iris interpreted as 'I'm sorry your father killed himself' though it could have meant something else entirely.

'Yes,' said Iris. 'There's a bug going round at school.'

And she told no one. Not until she met Edie, two years later – and even then, Edie was the only one.

It was for the best. Her mother wouldn't be able to handle it. Jack would have her sectioned. Everyone at school would know. She would never live it down. Crazy Cohen. Being a slag was bad enough.

In the afternoon, she crept into Mona's bedroom and watched her sleeping in the half-darkness. The curtains were drawn. There was a violet tinge to Mona's closed eyelids. Her face was plump and unblemished, delicate and new. She was wearing a rainbow-striped Babygro and pink socks. Her breathing was loud and sticky. It's amazing, thought Iris, her instinct to breathe, to live, to carry on, when she's so small and unformed. I must have been like that, once.

'I'm an idiot, Mona,' she whispered. 'I'm so sorry.'

The baby breathed faster, flickering her eyelashes. Could she hear her? No, she was just dreaming.

'My father didn't love me. I don't blame him.' Iris wanted to cry, but she was too tired. There was nothing left. Everything had been puked up. 'But I won't do it again. Never. I promise.'

She bent over and kissed the baby on her head. Mona smelled like sweet milk, like heaven.

8.

Interview #2

Iris was back in the black room, sitting on the swivel chair.

'Welcome to your second interview, Iris,' said Tara.

'Thanks for inviting me.'

'Out of over 500,000 applicants, only 10,000 people around the world have made it this far in the recruitment process. Congratulations!'

'Wow, that's great. How do you choose people?'

'We're looking for a balance of different personality types and skills.'

'OK.'

'Are you still interested in joining *Life on Nyx*?'

'Of course. I'm here.'

'Some people come to the interviews out of curiosity. Several people have attended in order to write articles about us.'

'Oh yeah, I saw that piece in the *Guardian*. But I'm not a journalist. I'm more of a content strategist.'

'Those sorts of skills will come in really handy on Nyx.'

'Great.'

'OK, first question: who in your life are you closest to?'

'It's hard to say. I suppose most people would say their family, but we're not that close. Maybe my friend Kiran. We've lived together for years. I know her better than I know my sister.'

'How do you mean?'

'I didn't really grow up with my sister. I'm a lot older than her.'

'Can you expand? Here's what you said about her in your first interview.'

Iris's recorded voice echoed around the room: 'I worry about her sometimes . . . She's so quiet and studious. I don't think she has many friends.'

'It's weird to hear my voice,' said Iris. 'I don't know, I can't explain it. It just seems like there's no joy in her life. No, that's too dramatic. She's really lucky in so many other ways and things will probably change for her. I'm closest to Kiran, but I don't know if that will be for ever. Friends seem to come and go. Mona is the person I love the most.'

'How would you feel about leaving Kiran and Mona behind for ever?'

'It would be hard . . . gut-wrenching. Kiran would be OK in the end – she has lots of other friends. I would be more worried about Mona.' She paused. 'Look, I'm not a psychopath. It would be the most difficult thing I have ever done in my life. I'm not sure that's the answer you're looking for, but I still want to go.'

'We're not looking for particular answers and we're definitely not looking for psychopaths. That wouldn't work – we're trying to build a community. If you love Kiran and Mona so much, why do you want to live on Nyx?'

'Loving two human beings isn't enough to keep me here.'

'Are you unhappy?'

'No, I'm fine. I'm happy.'

'Then why?'

'I want to do something different with my life, something special. I want to be – this is terrible, but maybe I'd like to be remembered, in some way.'

'Why is that terrible?'

'It's not the most noble aim, is it? My work feels inconsequential. I want to do more. I want to make a difference in the world, even if it means leaving the world behind.'

'Have you ever been in love?'

'Yes, with my ex-girlfriend, when I was a teenager. She's the only girl I ever went out with. Maybe it wasn't love, but I was obsessed with her.'

'What was her name?'

'Edie.'

It was shameful, really, how much Edie still lived in Iris's mind, like a pesky lodger who refused to move out. Iris dreamed about her so frequently that she sometimes forgot she hadn't seen her in ten years. Didn't I see her at that apocalyptic music festival, roasting marshmallows over a fire? Didn't we swim in the North Sea together? And when we got back to the shore, didn't she tell me she loved me? They were just dreams. Dozens of them. Hundreds.

'What was her surname?'

'Dalton.'

'Edie Dalton?'

'Edith Dalton.'

'Any middle names?'

'I don't remember. Are you going to track her down or something? We haven't spoken in years. I don't even know where she is. I mean, she might be in London, but I don't know.'

She had looked her up, of course – countless times – but Edie didn't have much of an online presence. Iris had tried to ignore the rumours: that Edie was a mess, a drug addict, that she'd been sectioned – they couldn't all be true. Instead, she focused on her memories, which grew more vivid and brilliant with each passing year: hours spent staring into each other's eyes, lying on Hampstead Heath, snogging; the silky feel of Edie's short golden hair; the sick ecstasy she inspired in her, for all of two months; the surprise that a girl could make her feel that way. Iris's memories and dreams entwined to create an eternal Edie Dalton, forever eighteen years old, a beacon of love and hope. In a way, Iris was thankful that Edie wasn't on the internet, thankful she hadn't seen her in a decade. It would have ruined her fantasy.

'If you reach the next level of the recruitment process,' said Tara, 'we might get in contact with a few key people from your life. This may or may not include Edith Dalton.'

'OK. I don't think she would be of any use to you, though.'

'How many people have you had sex with?'

'Fourteen.'

'Was Edith the first?'

'No.'

'Have you had one-night stands?'

'Yes. Not many.'

'How did you feel about them?'

'Not the best sex I've had in my life.'

'How often do you drink alcohol?'

'Quite frequently.'

'You know there'll be no alcohol on Nyx.'

'That's fine. I'm not an alcoholic.'

'But you might miss it – don't you think? You might find your-self missing all kinds of small, seemingly insignificant things.'

'How do you know?'

'There are people already living there.'

'Yeah, I know.'

'They're a specialist team of engineers and scientists. They're building a home for the *Life on Nyx* community.'

'Do they miss Earth?'

'They miss it very much.'

'Do they regret going there?'

'None of them has come out and said that, no.'

'Well, there you go.'

'Do you not enjoy your life on Earth, Iris?'

'Didn't you already ask me that?'

Tara didn't reply. Iris noticed that her arms were crossed. She uncrossed them and rested them at her sides. When she was a child, her mother always said, 'Don't cross your arms – it makes you look severe.' But now she didn't know what to do with them.

'This feels like a trick question,' said Iris. 'If I say I hate my life on Earth, you'll think I'm too miserable to go to Nyx. If I say I love it here, you'll think I don't want to go.'

'It isn't a trick question. Those are two extreme points of view. There's a spectrum between love and hate.'

'I don't hate my life on Earth. It is what it is. I think I would find it more interesting to live on Nyx. More fulfilling.'

'OK. I have some questions about your health.'

Iris's heart fluttered once, like a plastic bag in a quick wind. Her palms were sweating. She rubbed them together and placed them on her jeans.

'How is your health, generally?'

'It's fine.'

'Have you ever had any health problems?'

'Beyond the usual colds and flus, and a broken leg, no, nothing.'

'Do you take any regular medication?'

'No.'

'As you might recall from the terms and conditions, unfortunately we're not able to recruit people who rely on medication – we don't have the capacity for that.'

'Sure.' Iris had read a think-piece, a few weeks earlier, about how *Life on Nyx* was discriminating against trans people, the disabled, the mentally or chronically ill. 'What if people get ill when they're up there?'

'There'll be medical care available, but we're trying to minimize the need for it.'

'OK. But what happens when the medicine runs out?'

'As you might have seen on the website, this is only the first phase of *Life on Nyx*. Over the next decade we're hoping to send many more people, along with supplies. Eventually the planet will become completely self-sufficient, with fully equipped labs and hospitals – just like Earth.'

'OK.'

'How's your eyesight?'

'It's perfect, I think.'

'Have you ever received treatment for a mental health issue, including anxiety and depression?'

'No.' Did I say it too quickly? she thought. Her heart did a little dance, a pirouette, but she ignored it.

'Have you ever experienced suicidal ideation?'

'What's that?' she said, knowing full well.

'Have you ever thought of committing suicide?'

'No!' she said, pretending to be horrified.

'Have you ever taken any illegal drugs?'

'Never.' The pores on her forehead opened with the force of her lie.

'If you pass the recruitment process, we will administer a drugs test.'

'That's fine.' She would just give them up, until then.

'Do you give permission for us to check your medical records?'

'Yes.'

'Great – there's a form outside. Please sign it on your way out. If your records do not meet our requirements, we will request that you undertake our own medical examination.' Tara sounded so formal, all of a sudden. 'We'll be in touch if you progress to the next level.'

'Thanks, Tara.'

'Enjoy your day. Goodbye.'

There was a crackle, and then silence. Iris left the black room. By comparison, the corridor was too bright. She leaned on a wall and waited for her eyes to adjust.

9.

I Want to Win

Iris swallowed a pink pill forty minutes before her course at the London School of Leadership in Camden. It was a Friday morning in late September. The workshop room looked like it had been hastily refurbished: a shiny lino floor, green plastic furniture, a tiled office ceiling and framed Andy Warhol prints of Marilyn Monroe, Elvis Presley and a cow. A dozen chairs were arranged in a horseshoe in front of two whiteboards. Most of them were taken by men and women in their twenties and thirties, apart from one guy in a suit, in his fifties. Too late for you, dude, thought Iris. Too late for me, too.

'Hi,' she said, as she sat down next to him. 'I'm Iris.'

He jumped slightly. 'Oh, hi there.' His hair was the same shade of grey as his suit, which hung limply around his body. 'I'm John.'

They shook hands, both of them clammy. Iris tried to hide her hand as she wiped it on her jeans.

'What do you do, Iris?'

She took a deep breath, as she always did before sharing her job title. 'I'm a digital innovation architect at a creative agency.' She smiled and rolled her eyes a little to show that she knew it was an absurd title, that it didn't define her.

'Well, that sounds very impressive.'

She laughed. 'It's all right.'

'What does it mean? If you don't mind my asking. I'm just an old fogey.'

'It's just a fancy way of saying I work on digital strategies for brands.' John nodded again, still unsure what this meant. 'How about you?'

'I'm an IT manager at a mental health charity.'

'What brings you here?'

'Well, we recently hired a new member of staff in the IT department, and our chief executive decided I might need some training. I've never really managed anyone, you see.'

'I'm new to it, too.'

'Yes, but I'm a bit longer in the tooth. How many people do you manage, Iris?'

She always loved it when new people remembered her name. It showed that they cared. Or that they wanted something from her, but that was not the case with John.

'Just one person, right now,' she said, thinking, And I'm fucking him! 'My manager wants me to improve my leadership skills.'

'Right.'

A man strode in wearing a grey long-sleeved T-shirt and black jeans. He was stocky and brutishly handsome, with slick dark hair, an orange tan and intense eyes, which he used to scan the participants, nodding slightly at each person, as if thinking, Yes, I can fix you and you and you.

All the students stopped talking. He clapped his hands twice to grab their attention, though it had already been grabbed.

'OK, OK, guys,' he said. 'Welcome to the Fast-Track Leadership Workshop, where leaders are made, not born.' He was English, but had a strange, flat intonation that suggested he wished he were American or even Australian. 'My name is Adam Sickler-Jones and I'm going to help you find your inner leader today. Does that sound good?'

Everyone murmured – a low-spirited, multi-layered hum of despair.

'Wow, is that all you got? Here I am, telling you that I'm going to transform your lives in the next few hours, and all you can say is, *Uhhh okaaay*. This isn't going to be like other training courses. Mark my words. And if you're not happy with the outcome, I will personally give you the money back from my own wallet.

Now, I'm going to ask the question again, but this time I want more energy. Ready? Does. That. Sound. Good?'

'YES!' said everyone, because they had been trained from an early age to obey people who demand more energy – at rock concerts, at work, at home, in bed.

'That's more like it!' Adam Sickler-Jones clapped his meaty hands together. Thick black hair sprouted from the neck of his T-shirt. He pushed his sleeves up to reveal furry arms. He was some sort of gorilla-man. Iris wondered if he had a hairy back, too. Thinking about it made her feel kind of turned on, even though she'd never had a thing for hairy men. It was a bio-logical trick: his high testosterone making her crazy. An image flashed through her mind of Adam Sickler-Jones pummelling himself into her body.

'Hello?' he said to her. 'Are you listening?'

'Sorry,' said Iris.

'Pay attention. You only get one chance to learn this. Now, can each of you introduce yourselves, tell us a bit about your job and why you're here – starting with you.' Adam pointed at Iris. He looked super-serious, like a film star pretending to be an angry schoolteacher in a bad film.

'Hi, I'm Iris. I work as a digital innovation architect at a cre-ative agency, managing digital projects for various clients, delivering strategies on social media, content, marketing and development. I'm here because I'd like to build my confidence as a leader.'

Adam nodded, but his eyes were blank, as though he'd been thinking of something else. Fucking a woman from behind, thought Iris. Pumping weights at the gym. Doing high-fives in the air with his ripped male friends.

'I'm John, and I manage IT at a mental health charity. Our department has expanded and I don't have much experience of managing people, so I'm here to learn a few tips.'

'I'm Amy,' said a woman with red hair and lipstick, wearing a burgundy skirt suit. Everything about her clothes and demeanour screamed, *I'm confident!* 'I'm a marketing manager at a bank. I've been managing people for years, but I thought I should freshen up my skills with some new learnings.'

On they went.

'I'm Ruth.'

'I'm Steve.'

'I'm Madeline.'

'I'm Holly.'

Other names. Other job titles. Other lives.

'I'm Tom,' said a good-looking man in his thirties with dark hair. 'I'm the director of marketing at a film distribution company. I don't know why I'm here. My boss thought I should come.'

Iris was impressed.

'Now, Tom,' said Adam, 'that's not really the attitude I'm looking for today.'

'Isn't it? Why's that?'

'Aren't you keen to learn something new and find your inner confidence?'

'My inner confidence?' Tom looked around the room. 'Where's it hiding?'

'Obviously you already think you're the big man, I can see that. But what I see, my friend, is something entirely different. I see someone who is afraid of personal growth. But please, if you don't want to be here, feel free to leave the class.'

Most of them didn't want to be there, but they couldn't leave without a good excuse for their bosses, like: 'The workshop leader said something racist, so I walked out in disgust.' Better still: 'I received a text from my mother informing me that my uncle had died, so I had to fly to Australia, immediately.'

'No, no, I'll stay,' said Tom.

'OK,' said Adam. 'Let's do this.'

First, he ran through a role-playing exercise in which he and Tom pretended to be colleagues. Adam was trying to convince Tom that they should fire their copywriters and replace them with minimum-wage interns.

'Tom, we're going to save so much money!' Adam trilled.

'But that's ridiculous. We have so many experienced writers – why would we give the job to a bunch of kids? It'll be stressful for them and for us.'

'But writing is just putting a bunch of words together! Anyone can write!'

Tom broke the fourth wall. 'What is your job title supposed to be?'

'What do you mean, Tom? You know I'm the vice-president of digital marketing and communications.'

'It's just that I can't imagine why someone in your position with your level of expertise would ever say such a thing.'

'And *cut*.' Adam clapped his hands. 'You have to stay in the moment for this to work, for the learnings to get in here.' He pointed at Tom's head. 'Good job, overall, but don't be afraid to stand your ground. Don't just explain why the person is wrong; be firm and tell them that you're not going to kowtow to their demands. Have confidence in yourself.'

'But what if they have confidence in themselves, too? At some point, someone has to give in.'

'But do *you* want to win?'

'Win at what?'

'At life, motherfucker, at *life*!'

'What the –?'

'Just answer the question.'

'Jesus. Yeah, I suppose so.'

'*I suppose so?*'

Amy raised her right hand, jittery with excitement. Iris noticed that her nails were painted red, too. It must be her favourite colour.

'I want to win,' she said.

'What do you want to win at?'

'Life!'

'What do *you* want to win at?' Adam said, looking at Tom.

'Life,' he said, giving in.

'And you?' said Adam to Iris.

'Um, life,' she said, though she was fairly certain that she didn't want to win. How does one win, anyway? What are the telltale signs of winning? Wealth, fame, popularity, high status, regular sex with an attractive person – but Iris knew that people could be unhappy even with all of those things.

'Everyone repeat after me,' said Adam. 'I want to win! I want to win!'

'I want to win, I want to win,' they said, in varying tones of boredom and enthusiasm.

'This is your new mantra, people. Mantras have been absolutely crucial to my progression as a business leader and self-improvement activist. Believe it or not, I was once like you: a middle manager stuck in a boring job, coasting through life, choosing the easy route, rather than asserting myself. I knew, deep down, that I was capable of more, if only I pushed myself harder. One day I woke up and thought: What the hell am I doing? I was a loser. I looked in the mirror and said, "I want to win." That's how it began. Just that simple mantra can do so much for your self-esteem.'

He paused and an embarrassing silence washed over the group. Iris looked at the other participants. Unease rippled through her body, from her head to her toes. She looked around the room, at the windows speckled with city dirt, at the floor, at her fellow future leaders, from the sincere ones, who were taking copious notes, to the uninterested, who were slumped in their chairs, rolling their eyes. The only sign of hope was the water cooler in the corner – the simple promise of cold, fresh water. Apart from that, it was so undignified. Better to be a strong, silent gorilla, striding through the jungle with a baby clinging to its back.

Her mind had gone for a walk. It felt calming and peaceful to let it go where it wanted. She was like a reed being blown about by the wind. Somewhere in the distance, Adam was talking – for hours, it seemed – about his journey to leadership, which mostly seemed to consist of screaming 'I want to win!' at the mirror and quitting his job. There was more role play, though Iris wasn't called on to perform, thank God. She was just a reed by the sea, listening to the crash of the ocean, the rustle of the pines, the cries of seagulls. But then Adam did a double clap and said it was time for lunch. They moved their green plastic chairs to the green plastic tables by the window and were presented with a selection of sandwiches, snacks and drinks.

'What's your job like?' said Tom.

It was like coming to after blacking out. She looked up at him. They were eating sandwiches at a table, each with an open packet of crisps and a box of apple juice. A meal for children. There were two other people at the table, eating but not talking. People look so vulnerable when they're eating, thought Iris. Like cows in a field, nibbling on grass, waiting to be taken away and slaughtered.

'It's OK,' she said.

'Just OK?'

'It's, you know, just a job. Jobs are only ever OK, unless you're an astronaut or a movie star or an artist who can shit on the floor and sell it for a million pounds.'

He pulled back in surprise, and then crunched a crisp between his teeth. 'Wow, I like my job.'

'What do you like about it?'

'I like films. I like my colleagues.'

'Fair enough. Films are important. I help companies to sell shampoo and yogurt.'

'Why don't you leave?'

'I need the money. I don't know what else to do.'

'Something you're passionate about?'

'Passionate?' said Iris, as if hearing the word for the first time. It had become diluted through overuse – so many job applications, so many presentations. 'Passion' was a homeopathic remedy, a placebo.

'What do you love?' said Tom. 'There must be something.'

Drinking outdoors on a sunny day, thinks Iris. Jumping into ponds. Coming.

'Just ignore me,' she said. 'I'm having an existential crisis.'

'How old are you?'

'Twenty-eight.'

'Ah, you're having your Saturn Return,' said Tom, smiling.

'My what?'

'It's an astrological thing.' His face flushed and he laughed. He was extremely cute. 'No, I don't believe in astrology – I'm not crazy! – but that's what they call it. When Saturn returns to where it was when you were born, you're supposed to experience some kind of crisis or change. It happens every twenty-nine years.'

Iris sipped her apple juice. 'I'll blame it on Saturn, then.'

They both laughed and Iris thought: Is he better-looking than Eddie?

'You'll feel better after you hit thirty.'

Yes, he is.

'I hope so,' said Iris.

'Or you'll care less about your own unhappiness.' Tom raised his carton of apple juice. 'Cheers.'

After the workshop, Iris wondered whether Tom might ask for her number, but he didn't. They said goodbye on the street and he walked off in another direction, looking at his phone. The sky was a pale, queasy grey. She walked away from the building, whispering, 'I want to win, I want to win, I want to win,' so quietly that she could barely hear it herself, but she hoped it would be enough to scare the Smog away. She became so focused on the mantra that she ended up walking in the wrong direction, finding herself at the entrance to Regent's Park.

That's what I need, she thought: fresh air, trees, grass.

The park was busy with dog walkers, mums and babies, tourists admiring the flowers, and several attractive young people, enjoying the beginning of the weekend, walking hand in hand, drinking beer, smoking, laughing and talking. How do they do it? thought Iris. How did they get so good at performing their lives? She didn't feel human, or like a gorilla. She felt like a mad, stupid monkey wearing human skin, barely passing.

The weather was mild, but there was an autumnal stiffness in the air. As she walked, the sun began to glow soft and peachy through the clouds, casting a pink light across the sky. It was glorious. Even in her gloomy state, Iris could see that. Earth was magnificent, it was undeniable. But the planet had been doing just fine before we came along, performing its wild loveliness – sunsets, sunrises, rivers, mountains, jungles, beaches – for dinosaurs and Neanderthals. In the pictures Iris had seen, Nyx was not nearly as interesting as Earth. Miles of bland pink sand. Not enough oxygen. She would stay indoors for the rest of her life, would never feel the sun on her skin again.

Among the various groups of people in the park, she spotted someone she vaguely knew – a girl from one of her university seminars. Anne, Annie, Anna, Hannah? She had wavy dark hair, green eyes and was absurdly beautiful, like a Disney princess. Sometimes, in seminars, Iris had found herself staring at her in awe. How did it feel, to be so attractive that you made people feel demented? But now she couldn't remember her name. The girl was a bit older and heavier now, but still gorgeous. She had her arms around a man, both of them laughing. What does she do, these days? Even if it was unimpressive, she would always be impressive because she had that face. Iris looked at her phone, so the girl wouldn't be able to catch her eye. She liked her face, but didn't want to talk to her. This was the problem with London: everyone was there. Even if Iris moved to another city, another country, she could still run into people she knew. She wouldn't know anyone if she left Earth.

She scrolled through Twitter. Someone had blown themselves up in another country. Dozens of people had been killed. My life is full of embarrassing comforts, she thought. Look at this city. Look at my charmed life. Then she checked her emails.

The shoe shop had emailed her again, even though she had unsubscribed twice: 'We miss you.'

On the Tube from Great Portland Street, she listened to music and stared at the adverts for hair loss remedies and vitamins. A middle-aged couple got on: a chic, blonde woman with her craggy husband. There was something curious and pleading about the woman's damp, pale eyes, as she looked around the carriage. A tear ran down her cheek to her painted red mouth. Soon she was silently weeping, while her husband looked ahead, ignoring her. Jesus, thought Iris. The couple got off. The train ran alongside another train; both of them going the same way, sharing the tunnel for two seconds. Iris always loved it when that happened. She could see people on the other train, sitting, standing, being carried along. And wait, no – that man again, the Orthodox Jew she'd seen on the bus, who reminded her of her father, reading the *Evening Standard*. He was gone now. The train had passed. Don't be silly, thought Iris, closing her eyes. He was just some guy.

10.

Robert Who?

On Sunday she went to her parents' house to celebrate Jack White's birthday. She hadn't seen her family in a while. Eleanor wasn't one of those mothers who test their children's patience with constant phone calls. Instead, she tested Iris's love by rarely getting in touch. It seemed impossible that Iris had grown inside her, that they had once shared a body.

The previous night, Iris had gone to a party with Eddie. They had drunk a thousand beers and now she felt like sour blood was running through her veins.

Mona opened the door. The house smelled like roast chicken and potatoes. (What Iris would give now, to eat a single crisp roast potato.) Mona was wearing a blue hoodie, with her thumbs poking out through holes in the sleeves, her curly hair pinned back. Iris leaned in for a hug.

'How's it going?' said Iris. 'School OK?'

'Yeah.'

What else do you say to a thirteen-year-old? They walked to the living room, where the table was set for four.

'Where are they?'

'Upstairs.'

'So you're OK?'

'You already asked that.'

'We should go swimming sometime. It's still quite warm.'

Mona seemed to brighten up. 'Yeah, OK.'

'Next weekend?'

Eleanor walked into the room, followed by Jack. In contrast to Eleanor's glossy hair and pearls, Jack was portly and casually dressed, with untamed, curly hair. Iris greeted them with a nod and a smile, rather than bodily contact. As she did, she recalled a memory from her childhood – how she would curl up in her father's lap and he would put his arms around her. How he kissed her on the forehead before turning the lights off. She had forgotten about that.

'I've brought you a present,' said Iris, giving Jack a wrapped package.

'Ah, thank you. How kind.' He unwrapped it and nodded when he saw the label of the whisky. 'It's a good one.'

'My . . . my boyfriend recommended it.'

'You have a boyfriend?' He raised his eyebrows, impressed.

'Yes, he's called Eddie. I met him at work.'

Eleanor nodded and smiled. 'That's good. Shall we eat?'

They didn't ask anything else about Eddie: what he did at Freedom & Co, how old he was, how long they had been dating, where he was from. Instead, they ate lunch over a conversation that skated over the surface of things, never breaking through. The weather's nice, the news is bad, this food is good. Moments of silence were punctuated by knives and forks clanking on plates – but lightly, as though even these inanimate objects were too embarrassed to pierce the turgid atmosphere. Iris and Mona cleared the table and brought in a chocolate cake that Mona had made, but they didn't sing 'Happy Birthday', because Eleanor thought it was only acceptable for children. 'So silly,' she would say, when people started singing in restaurants. The cake was decent but dry, a tad over-baked.

After the table was cleared, Jack retreated to his man cave on the top floor and Eleanor stayed in the kitchen, cleaning up. Iris followed Mona to her bedroom, which had once been hers, and sat on her single bed – the same one she had lain on while waiting to die, twelve years earlier. But the rest of Iris's room had more or less disappeared – the heavy curtains had been replaced by blinds, the pale green walls had been painted white, the posters of New Rave bands had been recycled. Instead of bands,

Mona had posters of Jupiter, Saturn, the Milky Way and a basket of yellow Labrador puppies.

'Can I tell you something?' said Mona.

'Of course.'

'I started my period.' She covered her face and laughed.

'Oh my God! When?'

'Two weeks ago.'

'Congratulations!' Iris reached over and hugged her, and Mona hugged back.

'It doesn't feel like an achievement or anything.'

'It's a big deal.'

Mona shook her head. 'I kind of wish I'd never had it, that I could stay the same.'

'Stay thirteen years old? Really?'

'No, more like . . . eight. I liked being eight. Everything was easy. I remember at my eighth birthday party, playing musical chairs and thinking, I've always been a child and I always will be.'

'Was I there?'

'I don't think so . . . Mum is insane, isn't she?'

'You only just realized?'

Mona laughed. 'Was she weird to you, when you started your period?'

'She was all right, but she seemed embarrassed.'

'Exactly. What's wrong with her? All my friends' mums were really nice to them.'

Iris was happy to hear that phrase – 'all my friends'. Mona was smiling, pleased with it herself. Things were changing for her. Maybe Iris didn't have to worry any more.

Before she left, Iris went to the basement, where her mother was ironing Jack's shirts. Eleanor hadn't had a job in years, but she was always occupied. She rarely sat down, read a book or watched television. Iris wanted to say something.

She dug the nail of her index finger into her thumb, to distract herself with pain, and said, 'I know it's silly, but I thought I saw Robert the other day. On the Tube.'

'Robert who?' said her mother, hanging a white shirt on a rail.

'Robert Cohen.'

'Your *father*?' Eleanor widened her eyes and took a step back from the ironing board. She lifted a shaking hand and smoothed back her bobbed hair. Her eyes were suddenly coated with tears – just a little. 'Well, that's impossible.'

'Yeah, I know. It was an Orthodox Jewish guy. He just looked a bit like him. Actually, he looked a lot like him.' She paused. 'Why do we never talk about him?'

Eleanor took a deep breath. Her eyes were dark and focused. She took another shirt from the plastic basket, shook it out and laid it on the board. She looked upset or even angry, but at whom? Iris, Robert, the world? Iris wanted to ask, but she couldn't.

'Right,' said Iris. 'Never mind. I'll go home now.'

She stepped forward and put a hand on her mother's arm. Eleanor flinched slightly but managed a smile. Iris would have liked to hug her, but all her courage was gone.

'You've always been so much like him,' said Eleanor. She glanced up at Iris. 'I can see him now, in your face.' Her hands were shaking, but she carried on ironing, flipping the shirt over, making it neat and perfect, before hanging it on the rail. Then she paused. 'You know, I noticed when all the medicine was gone.'

Thunk, went Iris's heart. 'What medicine?'

Her mother didn't take another shirt from the basket, but kept her eyes on the ironing board.

'When you were unwell, when you were a teenager. I noticed. I saw all the packets in the bin.'

'And you didn't say anything?'

Her mother looked up, with tears on her cheeks, and swallowed. 'It was so frightening, Iris. I didn't know what to say. I didn't want to make it worse. I hadn't been able to help your father –'

'So you did nothing?' They stopped speaking and listened to the hum of the boiler. 'Does Jack know?'

Eleanor shook her head, wiping away her tears. 'No, I didn't tell him. I didn't tell anyone. I was completely helpless.'

Iris backed away from her, towards the door. 'How did you get like this?'

'You think I'm such a bad person, don't you?' Her eyes were flint-like. 'I'm not the one who walked out on the family.'

'Jesus, Mum. I'd hardly call what he did "walking out".'

Eleanor had no answers. There was no point in waiting for one. She was too far gone, too committed to turning away from life. Before she could say anything else, Iris walked up the stairs and left the house, knowing they would never refer to this conversation again.

✳

A week later, she was at the pond again, with Mona. The warm weather hadn't held up. It felt like autumn proper, and not one of those magical blue-gold days. Overcast and white – a typical English sky. The trees were red and brown. There was beauty in that, though. The water was dark and cold, not glimmering. Why hadn't they come when it was warm, when there was a heatwave? Still, it was good to be together, good to slice back and forth through the water, not talking too much. Don't stop moving or you'll get too cold.

This time they had come prepared, with towels, swimsuits and even suncream – Iris had been hopeful. They dried off and lay on the grass, huddled together, with one towel beneath them and another on top. Mona's body shivered against hers. Iris rubbed her sister's freezing arms. And then – a miracle: the white sky parted, revealing the sun, which briefly warmed them enough to throw aside the top towel. They sunbathed in silence, pretending to be on holiday, pretending their bodies weren't covered in goosebumps.

It had been a week of misery for Iris, ever since the conversation with her mother. A week of daily drinking, of internet marathons, of sweaty presentations, of crying and puking in the toilets at work, of ringing the GP and then hanging up, of having sex so wasted, she couldn't remember it the next morning. The pond washed it all away.

Mona leaned on Iris's shoulder. Iris patted her curly head, as if she were a sweet little baby. But no – thirteen. Not sweet any more. Almost a woman. Her body could bear a child. Still, they could pretend.

When they woke up, an hour later, Mona's skin had started to burn. Should've worn the suncream.

'Do you want to go in again?' said Iris.

'Nah,' said Mona, rubbing her eyes, stretching her skinny arms over her head. 'Too sleepy.'

So they changed into their underwear, under the towels, and into their clothes, and walked back towards their parents' house, where Iris would drop her sister off and then stroll blissfully to Gospel Oak Overground station and catch the train home, unaware that they would never swim together again, that they should've jumped in once more – even just for a minute, even if they didn't want to.

II

The Experiment

Kiran was going to Paris with her boyfriend, so Iris decided to embark on an experiment – to spend a week alone. She booked the same week off work, but didn't tell Kiran. There was a limit to their closeness. They had separate bones, brains, digestive systems and skins; this was what divided them. Kiran knew about Iris's sadness – she had noticed it over the years, though they never spoke of it – but she had no idea of its extent. She had her own secrets, too.

The experiment had six rules:

1. If someone contacts you, tell them you've gone away.
2. Follow your instincts.
3. Revel in aloneness and peace.
4. Do things that you would never usually do.
5. Live in the moment.
6. Don't rush.

It would be a holiday with no destination, a break from familiarity. Interacting with strangers was fine. Iris wanted to practise disappearing, to know how it might feel to leave every-one behind.

'I'm going to stay with some relatives in Cornwall,' she told her colleagues.

'I didn't know you had family there,' said Eddie, who had never met Iris's family and never would.

'Yeah, my great-aunt.'

'Where?'

He asked too many questions. The biological trick had worn off.

'St Ives,' she said, because it was one of the few Cornish towns she knew of. She had never been there.

Iris saw Eddie on Saturday night, just before the experiment began at midnight. They went to a restaurant in Soho that served delicious things on tiny plates, so they couldn't tell if they'd eaten enough. It was fine. They mostly talked about work. They were like veterans who can only talk about the war, except their most recent battle was a three-hour brainstorm to decide the tone of voice for a black Labrador called Hector, the star of an animal charity campaign, the nadir of which was Alison screeching, 'For God's sake, Hector would *never* say that!'

Eddie offered to foot the bill – which was sweet, since he earned less than her – but Iris insisted on going halves.

'Shall we go back to yours or mine?' he said, after they had paid.

'Oh, sorry,' said Iris, 'my train leaves really early tomorrow morning. It's probably best if we go our separate ways.'

'I can let myself out after you've gone.'

'I haven't even packed – I was planning to do that first thing. I'm waking up at, like, 6 a.m.'

He looked fragile, suddenly; his eyes downcast, his mouth serious. His freckles, which had been so adorable a few months earlier, made him look childish and vulnerable.

'What's going on?' he said.

'What do you mean?'

'You've been acting weird for ages.'

'It's nothing. I'm just tired.'

'It's not the ideal situation, us working together.'

'No.'

'Maybe we should think about next steps.'

'Next steps?' Iris laughed. 'That sounds like something Alison would say. Let's brainstorm our relationship, take this project to the next level.'

'You're so cynical.' Eddie looked at the table. 'Do you even like me?'

Iris reached for his hand, suddenly afraid. 'Of course I do! I like you *so much*, Eddie.'

This seemed to relax him. 'How about we both start looking for jobs? Whoever gets one first, leaves.'

'You wouldn't mind leaving Freedom?'

'Not really. Who hates it more – you or me?'

'Definitely me,' said Iris. 'I should be the one who leaves.'

Eddie shrugged. 'I don't mind leaving. It's not like I want to be doing this for the rest of my life.'

Iris was still holding his hand, playing with his fingers. 'Is there something else you want to do?'

Eddie shook his head. 'No. You?'

Iris thought of Nyx and its unchanging light; its deliciously vast distance from Earth, from life, from everyone, from Eddie.

'Not really, no.'

Afterwards he walked her to her bus stop on Oxford Street. Iris insisted, over and over again, that he didn't need to wait with her. Finally, he left. She watched as he walked to the Tube station. As soon as he disappeared into the crowd, Iris left the stop and walked back to Soho. Thus, the experiment began. It was just after midnight.

The slim pavements of Wardour Street were packed with people looking for a good time. Among them, Iris didn't stand out – a passer-by would have assumed that she was out on the town, on her way to a bar or a club. But she was not like the others, because she had no direction in mind. She'd only had two beers at the restaurant and felt spectacularly sober. The night-time streets sparkled with activity and light. She turned left onto another street, then right, then she walked further. She'd lived her whole life in London, but she could still get lost in Soho. All the streets were more or less the same. Nyx would be easier to navigate. She would never be lost again.

On some other busy street, people were queuing for bars and clubs, staggering, holding each other. Outside a newsagent, a girl with long dark hair and a pale round face was sitting on the pavement with her eyes wide open, catatonic, while her friends stood guard. A few metres away, a man pissed against a glossy black front door. Iris took a turn down a back street which, aside from a restaurant worker smoking a cigarette, was spookily empty – a rarity on a Saturday night in the West End. At the end of the street she turned right and heard, above her, a party; people talking over a glitchy, familiar pop song. She looked up to see a group of women in dresses and heels on a balcony, smoking cigarettes and shivering in the cold.

'All right?' one of them said.

'All right,' said Iris.

They waved as she went on her way. She had never known anyone who lived in town. Soho was for multimillionaires. In Nyx there would be no money, no divisions; everyone would be the same. She found herself back at Wardour Street, having walked in a circle. She turned left, back onto Oxford Street, and passed a homeless man in his fifties with two pretty Jack Russell terriers, their white coats gleaming in the night. Iris dropped a two-pound coin into his paper cup.

'Bless you,' he said, and kissed one of the dogs.

Just then, Iris saw a flash of red in the corner of her vision – her night bus was passing by. She thought of running, but then remembered the sixth rule: Don't rush. Never mind, another one would come. She had been walking for an hour and was feeling weary.

That night, Iris lay awake in bed for several hours, wondering whether the experiment was evidence that she had lost her mind. She reasoned with herself: People do all kinds of weird things – they kill each other, start wars, keep snakes as pets. By comparison, this is nothing. Some people even abandon their children, like Robert fuckface Cohen. She never thought of him as 'Dad' any more, because most of the Dad-like memories had long ago decamped to an obscure, hidden part of her brain. Only tiny, nebulous glimpses remained: Robert Cohen reading her a story, tucking her into bed, the feel of his stubble against her cheek – pain and joy. That was it. The Smog wiped out the rest.

Was I already so dreadful, she thought, even at the age of five?

How did you know that I was dreadful? What were the signs?

Iris lay awake until she could see the sun peeking, bright and white, through the blinds.

At around midday, she woke to the sound of wind rustling through the tree outside her window. You could always tell the season by looking at the tree. Spring was the best, when it sprouted pale pink blossoms. Winter was the worst, when it became a stark, bare skeleton. Now, her tree was starting to shed its glowing yellow-brown leaves. Iris had always noticed these changes, but never fully acknowledged – till that moment – the feelings they inspired in her: hope, loss, admiration. These are the things I can appreciate, she thought, now that I'm alone. But then she lay back in bed, took her phone from its charger and proceeded to waste two hours looking at shit on the internet.

She spent most of the day in a funk, switching between reading things on her phone, reading things on her laptop and half watching things on television. She didn't shower until 4 p.m., and when she did, she felt ashamed, thinking about all the people who by then had gone on ten-mile runs, had brunch with their friends and made Sunday roasts with all the trimmings. Those people, the good ones, were now kicking back and relaxing, while Iris had barely woken up. They would upload photos of their achievements to Instagram – their happy, attractive friends and relatives, having a wonderful time – and tag them: #sundayvibes, #fam, #besties.

She didn't leave the flat all day. There wasn't much food in the kitchen, but she made do with odds and ends. A fried egg with stale toast for lunch. Some slices of cucumber on the side, sprinkled with salt. Peanut butter on a spoon. For dinner, she made egg-fried rice. Her stomach wasn't full, but it was OK. It was good training for Nyx. The terms and conditions said:

While we aim to provide three delicious, nutritious meals per day to all cast members, these will be somewhat limited compared to what they are accustomed to on Earth. There will be no animal products available. All meals will be vegan and organic, with most ingredients grown on our community farm.

Well, at least she would become smaller and worthier. Buddha-like. A vegan! She could never be vegan on Earth.

She turned the lights off.

Tomorrow I must buy food.

One night, she couldn't sleep, so she decided she would walk to central London. She had never done this before, not from Clapton. She checked her phone – Oxford Circus was just over five miles away. Doable. Follow your instincts. She put on some thick socks, an old pair of trainers and a padded jacket over her pyjamas.

The street was dark and empty, but alive with birdsong. Iris made her way towards Lower Clapton Road, where humans could already be found: driving past in cars, sitting placidly on buses, on their way to jobs that started far too early. Two people passed her in the street: a labourer in overalls and heavy boots, and a madwoman, muttering to herself. Rule 4: Do things that you would never usually do.

'Hello,' Iris said to the woman.

The woman stopped walking and widened her eyes, amazed that someone had willingly spoken to her. She was wearing many layers of clothes, all different colours and textures. She was sixty per cent textile, forty per cent human.

'It's coming, it's coming,' said the woman, looking straight into Iris's eyes, though her own eyes were elsewhere, beyond the moon.

'What is?' said Iris.

'You know, you know it. The end.'

'The end of the world?'

'Nah, mate. Don't be silly. The end of the night.'

'That's true. Have a good day.'

'You too, my love!'

Iris carried on walking down a residential road, where a fox casually crossed her path, then past Hackney Downs. She crossed through Dalston, where the shops were shut, though some still shone their neon lights. The sound of cars kept her company. Usually, whenever she walked alone, she would listen to music or a podcast, but now she just listened to the world. Each bird sang in its own particular pattern. It was amazing that they chose to live there, in the city, and not in a nice green field. They were used to it, like Iris.

She crossed from the borough of Hackney to Islington and walked down Balls Pond Road and Essex Road, where the streets were cleaner, the smell of money more palpable. Hackney smelled of money, too, but it hadn't been completely cleansed – almost. The entrance to Angel Tube station was surprisingly busy. Bankers in exquisitely cut suits were making their way into the City. Early risers make the most money; early risers make the least money: bankers, builders, bakers and cleaners, and nothing in between, apart from Iris.

Clerkenwell was dead. All the architectural practices and design shops were closed. The neighbourhood's residents, people with harrowingly good taste, were just waking up. One of them ran past – a blonde woman in black athletic gear. She was so clean that you would eat from her hands without a second thought. Imagine being so saintly that you would go running before the sun came up. Iris had colleagues who did such things. Even if they were mean or took drugs at the weekend, they were inherently superior.

By the time she reached Holborn, there were a few more people in the street, but not as many as there would be in an hour, when life really began. Her feet were starting to feel hot between the toes, her underarms damp, but she wasn't tired, just thirsty. Near Tottenham Court Road, she bought a bottle of water, downed its contents and carried on, past Oxford Circus, into Mayfair, one of the richest parts of the city. Who the hell lived here? People for whom money was like tap water – plentiful and cheap. People who didn't drink tap water.

By the time she reached Grosvenor Square, the sky was a pallid, dreamy blue. The square was silent. There were no more birds singing – even the footless, diseased pigeons weren't making a sound. Iris stood at the entrance of the old American Embassy, which was now closed and patrolled by security guards.

Just then, she heard the sound of hooves approaching, too many to count. Horses entered the square from the opposite side, driven from behind. Their smooth bodies glowed silver in the morning sun. They were all the same colour, the same shape, almost naked, but tied together by their bridles. They trotted two by two, rows and rows of them. Twenty or thirty, each one a replica, as pretty as the last. Iris looked around, but the security guards were nowhere to be seen. There was no one else there to witness it, unless someone was peeking out of a window. She had so many questions, but then she remembered Rule 5: Live in the moment. The horses disappeared down the street.

Iris bought a coffee and caught the bus home, where she managed to sleep for a few hours. After that, she spent the rest of the day scrolling for clothes online. It was amazing how quickly the hours passed. She bought three items, but knew she would return them. Later, in bed, she could still see the scrolling dresses, even with her eyes shut. She wished she had made a video of the horses. Not to put it on social media, but because she was afraid she had imagined them.

On Friday night she walked to Hackney Central just after ten. She was nervous of running into people she knew. This was the problem with London – familiar faces everywhere. That guy over there, smoking outside a pub, had the same denim jacket as Eddie and the same wavy blond hair. But he turned and it wasn't him. The girl at the bus stop – was it her ex-friend Beth? She had the same evil blue eyes. No, not her. But it wasn't safe out there. Someone would spot Iris and know that she had lied about going to Cornwall. She started walking home.

On the corner where Mare Street meets Narrow Way, Iris saw a figure, draped in clothes. Another madwoman. She wore a pink hijab and stared fixedly at the street. Iris passed her and looked back. The woman was completely still. Iris wondered if she was a statue – some kind of art project.

But then the woman finally moved, pointed at Iris and said, 'You.'

A double-decker bus went past. Iris glanced up at it, catching sight of a man on the top desk, dressed in black, with a long beard. She looked back at the woman.

'Yes,' she said, 'it's me.'

Iris went to bed and slept peacefully, at last, until her phone alarm woke her at 6.30 a.m. She put her coat on, over her pyjamas, and walked towards Walthamstow Marshes. The streets were fairly empty, but Friday night was still alive, just about, for some. She passed a block of flats where a party was going on. Two or three people were singing along to Stevie Wonder's 'For Once in My Life' – a strained, lonely sound. She tried not to feel afraid as she walked into the marshes. The tall grass tickled her ankles. There was no need for a torch, because the city maintained a permanent blue-green glow. Birds sang a chaotic symphony above her head in a dark cloud of wings. If someone murdered her, no one would hear her scream – she would be drowned out by the birds. In the middle of a field of dying wild flowers, she lay down with her arms and legs outstretched, looking up at the sky as it lightened. If she went to Nyx, she would never see birds again. At least not these birds, this sky, this sun. She closed her eyes as it warmed her face.

'What are you doing?' said someone. 'Are you all right?'

She raised her head. An old woman was looking at her with a

worried expression. A Border terrier waited patiently behind her, showing its pink tongue.

'I'm fine,' said Iris.

'Do you need an ambulance? Are you on drugs?'

'No, I'm just listening to the birds.'

'Huh?' The woman drew her head back in surprise. Her dog barked in sympathy.

'Honestly, I'm fine.'

The woman walked on. Iris lay back and closed her eyes again. She didn't wake up until noon, shivering and covered in dew, something wet and pungent on her cheek. She opened her eyes and laughed – a black and white collie was licking her face. Its owner, a man, was looking down at her with pity and fear.

'Oh, thank God!' he said. 'You're alive.'

'Yes,' said Iris, blinking her eyes, laughing and stroking the dog. 'Sorry to scare you. I was just communing with nature.'

It was the middle of the day, unmistakably. The sun was high and bright, the sky so blue – an impression of a fine day in a foreign country, but with an English bitterness in the air.

'OK,' said the man. 'Just checking.'

Kiran returned the next day, looking gloomy because her boyfriend had admitted, right at the end of their trip, that he wasn't ready to leave his wife. Iris told Kiran that she'd had an OK week at work.

12

Interview #3

The final interview was not like the others. Iris realized this as soon as she walked into the black room and saw Edie Dalton, her ex-girlfriend, sitting at a table with an empty chair opposite her. There was a hopeful smile on her face.

'What the –?' Iris remembered that she was being filmed. She returned the smile. 'Edie. What are you doing here?'

'Surprise,' Edie said mildly, raising her eyebrows.

Iris hadn't seen her in a decade. Edie's hair was still short, but no longer golden – it had darkened to mousy brown. Her pale cheeks had a new, unhappy softness. When she stood up, she seemed shorter than she had been, though that couldn't be right – she wouldn't have shrunk, not yet. They hugged. Iris could feel sweat on the back of Edie's checked shirt. Her heart felt wild and feral, something that couldn't be tamed. She breathed shallowly and tried to focus on the moment. What would the Dalai Lama do?

'What is this?' she said. 'What's going on?'

'Welcome back, Iris,' said Tara. 'Congratulations on reaching the final stage of the *Life on Nyx* recruitment programme. Please take a seat.'

Iris sat down opposite Edie. The light on the ceiling seemed stronger and more focused, like a spotlight. Everything else was dark. It felt like an interrogation scene from a cop show.

'In the final stage of the recruitment process,' said Tara, 'we invite a person from the applicant's past to take part in the interview.'

'Is Edie going to interview me?'

'It'll be more of a conversation. I'll return at the end. Edie will guide you through the rest of the process.'

The room went silent. There was nothing to signify Tara's departure, no *click*, but her absence seemed to change the texture of the air. Iris was alone with Edie. She hadn't been alone with her – or seen or spoken to her – since they broke up, though they had never truly broken up; Iris had simply stopped returning her calls. Their twin-like closeness had started to feel repulsive. She hadn't known that it would echo through her life.

They looked at each other and flinched. It was too much – being there, in the same room.

'Why did you agree to this?' said Iris.

'I don't know.' Edie shrugged. 'I was intrigued.' She scratched the back of her neck and smiled.

'You look different.'

'It's been a while.'

'I heard rumours about you.'

Edie laughed. 'You shouldn't believe everything you hear. Well, some of them might have been true.'

'What do you do, these days?'

'I'm a landscape gardener.'

Iris pulled back in surprise. 'Wow, that sounds nice.'

'It is. I really love it.' It was obvious that she meant it.

Edie's voice was unrecognizable. Ten years ago, she had the poshest accent Iris had ever heard. The glitter had been rubbed off and replaced with rougher inflections. It made her seem pretentious, a rich girl playing a role. Iris's stomach pulsed with pain. Inside it, the eternal Edie Dalton, beacon of love and hope, was crumbling like a blown-up building.

'So what are we supposed to talk about?' said Iris.

'Anything you want.'

'What did they tell you?'

'They told me that you want to go and live on another planet. That's a bit nuts, isn't it, Iris?'

'Are you here to talk me out of it?'

'Yeah, kind of.'

'Why did they ask you? Why not one of my friends?'

'Why did you stop speaking to me?'

'Oh Jesus.' Iris buried her head in her hands. 'I was eighteen. I didn't know what else to do. I did love you, Edie. I can't explain it.'

Edie looked down. Her hands were on the table, spread out. Her fingers were still long and refined, like a pianist's, but sprinkled with small tattoos – dots, triangles and other geometric shapes. There was dirt under her fingernails.

'They didn't give me much information. They just said that I was the person most likely to convince you to stay.' She looked up. Her eyes were different from how Iris remembered them – dull brown, rather than hazel. 'Is it true, that you loved me?'

It didn't seem true now. This version of Edie, with her plump cheeks and mockney accent – she wasn't the girl Iris had loved. Bold, boyish, sharp – that girl was somewhere else. Perhaps she had been a performance.

'Yeah, it's true, I did.'

Edie breathed deeply, her hands still on the table. 'Why do you want to go to this planet, then? What's wrong with Earth?'

They're watching, Iris remembered. 'It seems like an amazing thing to do with my life – instead of, you know, staring at a screen all day. Have you seen the pictures?'

'Just briefly. I don't spend much time online.'

'It's beautiful, up there. They have this incredible indoor farm.'

'We have farms here, too.' She smiled. 'You would never see Earth again.'

'It's such a great place, Earth.'

'It's not a joke. What about your friends and family – you're going to leave them all behind?'

'People do it all the time, even on Earth, and they get over it.'

Edie opened her mouth to say something and then changed her mind. Instead, she said, 'How's your family?'

'They're OK. Mona's thirteen now.'

'Thirteen, wow.'

'Yeah, she goes to my old school. She's a complete nerd.'

'What about your mum?'

'What about her?' said Iris, irritated by the question.

'Did you ever get the chance to tell her about –'

'About what?' Iris kept her voice calm, but anger was rising in her chest, hot and glistening. It was obvious, what she was referring to. She was the only one who knew. Edie was trying to expose her, to sabotage her application.

'Nothing, it's nothing.' Edie shook her head. 'Sorry, I got my wires crossed.'

Iris clenched and unclenched her hands, and leaned back on the chair. She had a tendency to lean forward – always too eager. Edie looked at the wall with interest and Iris followed her gaze, but there was nothing there. How do you run out of things to talk about with someone you've dreamed of so often, someone you've yearned for? But Edie wasn't the person from Iris's dreams. They just had a similar face.

'Any more questions?' said Iris.

Edie pursed her lips, a little smugly. 'You're disappointed with me.'

'That's not a question.'

'*Are you* disappointed with me?'

'I . . .' She looked away from Edie, at the table. 'I suppose we all grow up with this idea that love is the answer, that it can save you from yourself.'

'And I wasn't the answer.'

'I'm not the answer, either. No offence.'

'None taken. I'm definitely not the answer to anyone's problems.'

'But, if I can be completely honest?'

'Yeah.'

'The way I felt about you was insane,' said Iris. 'It was literally sickening. I was so thin when we were together and after we split up, too, because you made me feel too ill to eat. I was disappearing, but I got so many compliments. I remember you loved it, actually.'

'Hmm. I don't remember that.'

'You told me my body was perfect, but I was so fucking unhealthy. It was like you satisfied my hunger. I felt I could *live* on you. I've been chasing that feeling ever since.'

'Right.'

'But it's just biology, isn't it? This explosion in our brains. With each relationship, it feels weaker and weaker, till one day, I'll probably find a guy –'

'A guy?'

'I'm not really gay, you know that – and I'll think, Oh, he's honest and kind and would be a good dad, but at the back of my mind I'll always feel like it was the realest with you. But now –'

'The fantasy has evaporated, now that you can see me.'

'That sounds harsh.'

'Have you considered that I feel the same way about you?'

Iris didn't respond.

'Well, I do, I feel the same way. The feeling is mutual. Since we're, you know, being honest. I've thought about you a lot, but now that I'm here –'

'What?'

'This whole thing, of going to space – it's a mistake, Iris. It's worse than anything I ever did. I fucked up my life, but I'm here, now, and my parents have forgiven me, more or less, and I have good friends. You seem . . . completely different.'

'I was a kid.'

'And now you're so jaded you want to step off the planet for good.'

'I'm not jaded. I just want to do something special.'

'No one's special. *No one.*' Edie held her gaze. She was completely still. Her eyes, too, barely blinked. It seemed as if she was trying to communicate something with them.

Iris felt a sick shiver in her stomach, a tiny echo of love. Edie smiled.

'Do you want to get a drink afterwards?' said Iris.

Edie finally looked away, up at the ceiling, at the wall, then back at Iris. 'Oh, uh, I can't, you know. I don't drink any more.'

'We could get a coffee.'

'I don't think that's a good idea.'

Just then, Tara's voice returned to the room. 'Edith, thanks for helping us with the recruitment process. You may now leave.'

Edie stood. Iris stood, too, thinking they were going to hug.

'Let's not,' said Edie, putting her hands up.

'But why?' Iris was still standing.

'Just because. No hard feelings, OK? Take care, Iris.'

Edie took one step towards the door and did a little wave with her right hand. Iris remembered how they would say goodbye to each other ten times on the phone, before one of them could bear to hang up.

'Bye,' said Iris.

But Edie didn't say it back. She nodded, opened the door and walked out.

'Thank you for taking part in the *Life on Nyx* recruitment programme,' said Tara. 'We hope you found it an enjoyable and interesting experience. We will be in touch soon to let you know about the outcome. Have a nice day!' She sounded more like a robot this time. Not like in the first two interviews, when she had seemed almost human.

Iris's exchange with Edie hadn't shown her in the best light – too much baggage. She was sure she would be disqualified. Oh, well. She left the room and quickly walked down to the ground floor, thinking she might catch up with Edie, but the building was empty. Outside, the street was crammed with people. No sign of her.

As Iris stood in the Tube carriage, pressed up against strangers' bodies, she thought of the eternal Edie Dalton, her favourite version of Edie. The eternal Iris Cohen, too. On another planet, in another universe, we're still kids and it's summer, and it always will be. That was the planet she wanted to go to.

13.

Goodbye Pie

On a Sunday afternoon in January, Eddie arrived at Iris's flat with a bunch of tulips wrapped in brown paper. He had cycled there with snowflakes biting his face. It rarely snowed in London, so Iris took it as a good omen. It was her last winter on Earth.

'Fuck, it's cold,' he said as he walked into the flat, rubbing his cheeks. 'I can't feel my face. These are for you, babe.' He handed her the flowers and smiled.

By then Eddie had left Freedom & Co to work for another agency. In recent weeks they had started talking, vaguely, of moving in together. But that wasn't going to happen any more – not since Thursday evening, when Iris had received a phone call from Los Angeles. They had given her two weeks to think about it. Since then, she had felt deliriously light and free, demob happy.

'That's so sweet of you,' she said. She took the tulips, turned away before he could kiss her and marched to the kitchen to put them in a vase.

Tulips – she can still picture them. Their petals glossy and pink, a few shades darker than the sand on Nyx.

Eddie knew her flat as well as he knew his own. He knew where to leave his bicycle in the corridor, out of the neighbours' way; where to hang his helmet and coat; where to find coffee, sugar, spaghetti, salt and moisturizer. But soon it would be over. Soon he would forget these things, and then relearn them at some other woman's flat.

Like many of their friends, he had recently taken to wearing glasses; their eyes gently declining after years of staring at screens. They suited him. He looked more like a sexy, young academic than a marketing man. Iris had showered before he arrived, but she was already covered in an oily film of sweat. Maybe it would make it easier for him to let her go – seeing her in this dreadful state.

'You all right?' he said, tenderly.

'Yes.' Iris snipped the ends from the tulips and put them into a glass vase with tap water.

'You don't seem all right.'

She grinned. 'I'm fine!' Perhaps the smile was too much, a bit deranged. 'Do you want some coffee and pie?'

'What kind of pie?'

'Pecan.'

'Yeah, OK.'

If she'd had a living room, she would have asked him to wait there, while she made the coffee, sliced the pie and performed a final, whispered dress rehearsal of her crazy admission, but she didn't have a living room, so she turned the radio on to cover the silence. Eddie sat at the table. West African music, something pretty and soulful, filled the kitchen. White, snowy light beamed through the windows. The heating was on too high. Iris placed two cups, a cafetière, a bottle of milk and two slices of pie on the table, and sat down.

'You made this?' said Eddie.

'Yes, this morning.'

'To sweeten the pill?'

'What do you mean?' She laughed, but he didn't.

'You never bake. What's going on?'

Iris poured the coffee and then the milk, and stirred both cups. 'OK, I do have something to tell you. It's a bit mad.'

'You're not pregnant, are you?'

'It's weirder than that.'

'You're becoming a man?'

'Eddie –'

'Sorry.'

'You know *Life on Nyx*?'

'Yes,' he said, slowly. His mouth hung open but he was smiling too, as if it were impossible – the thing she was about to say.

'I'm going, Eddie. I'm going to live on Nyx.'

He didn't speak. He looked into her eyes, searchingly, waiting for her facade to fall, for her to laugh, as if it were a joke. Iris's hands began to shake. She squeezed them between her thighs.

'I'm leaving London in June.' She looked at the table. 'First I'm going to California for training, but I won't be back after that. I'm going to Nyx in September. But you can't tell anyone. I'm only allowed to tell the people closest to me.'

She glanced up. Eddie still wasn't speaking. He was frozen, but not smiling any more, not even looking at her.

'Are you joking? You are, aren't you?'

'No.'

'I don't believe you.' He shook his head.

Iris had never seen him look so serious and confused. It didn't make sense. Everything was easy for Eddie, everything was logical, there was always a solution – right?

'You're the first person I'm telling. Even my parents don't know. Even Kiran.'

'Where is she?' he said quietly, looking at his pie, which he hadn't touched. His eyes were shining and red-rimmed, as if he might cry.

'She's at her parents' house.'

'So this is your goodbye pie.'

'No!'

'Sure.' He stood up and walked out of the kitchen, without looking at her.

'Eddie.'

He hurriedly took his coat and helmet down but didn't put them on, because he wanted to get out as quickly as possible. Iris watched him from the kitchen door.

'Eddie, please.'

'What?' he said, looking away from her.

'I thought you would –'

He turned. 'What? You thought I would beg you to stay?' His voice was hard and furious, all the sweetness gone.

'I have two weeks to decide.'

'But you've made your decision, haven't you?'

Iris didn't reply.

'What do you want from me?' he shouted.

Iris flinched. 'Don't shout at me.'

'Go and live on the fucking moon, if that's what you want to do.'

'It's a planet.'

Eddie dropped his things on the floor, walked back into the kitchen and grabbed Iris by her wrists.

'Ow, that hurts!' she screamed, though she was exaggerating – it didn't hurt. She tried to squirm out of his grasp, while hoping he wouldn't let go. Tears began to fall down her face. 'Don't hit me!'

'Jesus Christ, I'm not going to hit you,' he said, moving his hands from her wrists to her shoulders. 'What the hell is going on?'

Tears were dripping from Iris's face to her T-shirt, soaking through to her skin. Snot began to pour from her nose, but she couldn't wipe it away because Eddie was standing too close. She was sobbing heavily, with no control over herself, making animal-like noises. It was the first time she had cried in front of another person in years.

'Tell me, Iris. Please tell me.'

'I – I – I – I can't speak.'

'Just breathe. I'm not going anywhere. Tell me what's going on.'

'I can't, Eddie, I can't.'

'You can't what?'

'I can't, I can't, I can't tell you.'

He let go of her. Iris wiped her face with her hands and then rubbed them on her jeans. Eddie's tenderness seemed to ebb away. He sighed like an irritated parent.

'Why are you doing this?' he said, looking away from her.

'Because I want to. It's my life.' She could feel tears on her face hardening into salt.

'Do you actually care about anyone?'

'What kind of question is that?'

'Do you, though?'

Rage began to shimmer in her chest, rage against everyone and everything: Eddie, her mother, her father, herself, the planet, this dreadful planet.

'You have no idea how much I care.'

'Bullshit.'

'You barely know me.'

'You're right.' He almost laughed. 'I really don't.' His eyes were wet, just a little.

Why? thought Iris. Why would he cry over me?

Eddie turned away and started walking towards the front door. Iris followed him and put her arms around his waist. His muscles jerked away, repulsed by her touch.

'Don't touch me.' He held his hands up, as if she were arresting him.

She let go. He didn't look back.

'Please don't go,' she said. 'I'm a terrible person, I know I am.'

'I don't want to talk any more.'

'Please don't tell anyone. I'm supposed to send you this form –'

'Iris, just stop talking.'

Eddie took his things and walked out of the door, down the stairs, out of the building with his bicycle, and didn't look back. Iris went to the kitchen, drank both coffees, ate both slices of pie, and then burst into tears again – with relief, as well as sadness.

When Kiran came home that evening, she went straight to Iris's bedroom and lay down on the bed, beside her.

'How are your parents?' said Iris.

Kiran rolled her eyes, but they were full of love. 'Crazy as ever.' She had a huge family – an endless network of aunts, uncles and cousins all over the world. Kiran would never leave Earth. She would never consider it, not even for a second.

'Do you want some pecan pie? I made some.'

'Hell yeah!' She was still wearing her coat and leather boots.

Iris went to the kitchen and returned with a slice of pie and two glasses of Beaujolais, Kiran's favourite.

'You made this? said Kiran, impressed.

'Yeah.'

'What's it in aid of?' She sat up. 'Wait, let me guess.'

'I don't think you can.'

Iris sat next to her, propped against some pillows, and drank her wine.

'I know – you're pregnant!' said Kiran. She studied Iris's face and sipped her drink. 'No, no, you're drinking. You're engaged to Eddie? Yes, that's it.'

Iris kept her face blank. Kiran tried again.

'You've got a new job?'

Around midnight, at the end of the second bottle of wine, after they had both cried and smoked a dozen or so cigarettes – skinny ones that Kiran had brought back from Paris and forgotten about – they were still lying on the bed, staring at the ceiling in silence, in the gloom of the bedside lamp.

'Don't go,' said Kiran.

'You already said that.'

'I'll say it over and over again, till you change your mind.'

'I'm not going to change my mind.'

Finally Kiran got up. 'I've got work tomorrow.' Her long black hair was hanging in front of her face and her clothes were creased. She picked up her coat and bag from the floor. 'I don't know how I'm going to sleep,' she said, as she walked to the door.

'I'm so sorry.'

'I feel like I don't even know you.'

Before Iris could reply, Kiran walked out of the room and slammed the door behind her.

That night, when Iris was lying in bed, she couldn't feel the presence of the Smog, not even a tiny, microscopic speck. She opened her eyes, sat up and looked around. Her eyes quickly adjusted to the darkness. She could see her desk, the chair piled with clothes, and the wardrobe, but no Smog.

'Where are you?' she said.

No one answered. She lay back down and closed her eyes. Outside the window, a fox started crying like a baby, but Iris didn't hear it because she was already asleep.

The next day, Iris told Alison that she had been headhunted for a new, top-secret job.

Alison seemed disappointed but impressed. 'I don't know how we're going replace you,' she said.

Easily, thought Iris.

'Honestly, you've been such a great asset to Freedom & Co. I'm not surprised you've been snapped up. You have such an amazing future ahead of you.'

'Ah, thanks.'

'Can I ask, though?' Alison stared into her eyes and leaned forward. 'Is it Google? I won't tell anyone.'

'You'll know soon enough.'

She grinned. 'It is, isn't it! I knew it.'

In the team meeting, Iris shared the news with everyone else. Jenny and Rich glared at her, as if she were a murderer. Had Eddie already told them the truth? Never mind. None of it mattered.

Iris told her family last. She considered various options. A restaurant would be too public, her flat too claustrophobic, an email anticlimactic – she wanted to see their reactions. She called her mother and invited herself round, telling her she had some news.

'Can't you say it over the phone?' said Eleanor.

'I want to say it in person.'

'Are you engaged? To your colleague Edmund?' Eleanor had never met Eddie, but there was a smile in her voice – the idea of a wedding delighted her.

'Edward. You'll have to wait till Sunday.'

'That's it, isn't it!'

Iris's heart felt like it was being squeezed by a giant hand. A montage flipped through her mind: the engagement party, the hen do with her BFFs, the fairy-lit wedding, her mother in her best blue dress, proud of her at last, and then a baby – job done. All these achievements would be posted on the internet and everyone would be so very happy.

When Eleanor opened the front door on Sunday afternoon and saw Iris standing alone, no fiancé in tow, she stretched her smile to conceal her disappointment. They went to the dining room, where she quickly dismantled the fifth place-setting on the table. For lunch they had takeaway sushi with Prosecco – her parents had been preparing to celebrate.

After Iris declared her plans, Mona was, unusually, the first to speak. She dropped her chopsticks and said, 'What the hell?'

Jack White boomed, 'You're doing *what*?' He glared at Iris with confusion and disgust. 'Are you fucking insane?'

Eleanor flinched at his swearing. Iris did, too.

'Jack,' said Eleanor. She shook her head like a schoolteacher, but kept her eyes on the table, busying herself with the food – moving tempura rolls from the plastic tray to her plate, mixing green wasabi into a dish of soy sauce. Her pale hands shook as she did these things. Finally she put a piece of sushi in her mouth and chewed slowly, avoiding everyone's eyes.

'You're not going,' said Jack.

'I've signed the agreement.'

'I'm sure it's not too late to back out.'

'I don't want to back out.'

Iris picked up a piece of sushi with her fingers, dipped it in soy sauce and popped it into her mouth. Its texture was gluey and disgusting, like an old piece of gum. She forced herself to swallow and shivered as it went down.

'Why the hell would you want to live on another planet?' said Jack.

'It'll be interesting.'

'Learning a new language is interesting.' His face was a red, blotchy mess. 'This is just . . . suicide. Why don't you take up a hobby or something. Go fucking sailing. Adopt a dog!'

'It's not suicide. It's a really wonderful opportunity.'

Her mother said, 'Hmm,' and carried on rearranging bits of food on her plate.

Once more, the giant hand squeezed Iris's heart.

'Why are you doing this?' said Mona, her voice trembling. 'You'll never see us again.' Unlike Eleanor, she was looking at Iris, with pleading eyes.

'I know it's a sacrifice, but –'

'Shut up!' Mona shook her head. Tears began to fall down her face. 'You're crazy.'

The hand squeezed harder on Iris's heart. Mona stood up.

'Where are you going?' said Iris, trying to massage away the pain.

'Mona, sit down until we've all finished,' said Jack.

'No,' said Mona. 'Bye, for ever.'

'I'm not leaving London till June.'

'Whatever, I don't care.'

Mona left the room and ran up the stairs, taking two steps at a time, then slammed the door to her bedroom. All throughout this, Eleanor had barely said a word. Iris wondered whether she cared at all. Her mother was so good at keeping difficult things locked away, like wild, sedated animals in a cage. If Jack dropped dead at that moment, which was possible, because he was a fat workaholic, Eleanor might have just said, 'Oh dear,' and carried on eating. Iris had memories of her mother being more expressive, but she wasn't sure if she'd made them up. Both her parents had vanished: first Robert, then Eleanor.

'Mum?' said Iris.

'Yes?' Eleanor glanced at her daughter for a fraction of a second, then looked back down.

'What do you think?'

'I watched a documentary about it a few months ago,' said Eleanor, her voice almost inaudible, 'this . . . *planet*. It looked like a fascinating place.'

'I was chosen out of half a million applicants.'

'That's very impressive.' She nodded.

Ask me not to go, thought Iris. Please, just ask.

Nobody spoke for several seconds. Rain began to tap against the windows.

'It looked very beautiful,' said Eleanor. 'In real life, it must be dazzling. Do you think you would be happy there?'

Iris cleared her throat and sipped some water. She had a sudden urge to cry.

'Yes, I really do.'

'We would miss you, Iris, so very, very much. But if you think you would be happy . . .' She let the sentence trail off.

'Eleanor, are you serious?' said Jack.

Iris only realized, in that moment, that she had wanted her mother to become angry, to shout at her, to behave as Jack had done, to forbid her from going. She hadn't signed the contract yet. She had been waiting.

Her parents didn't ask for more details, but Iris told them anyway. She described the interviews in the black room, without mentioning Edie – they had never known about her. She explained that she would be teamed up with three other people at the training camp in California – two men and one woman – and that they would live together, like a family. Her parents listened, mostly in silence.

'What about Edward?' said her mother, towards the end of Iris's monologue. 'Is he going, too?'

'No. We've split up.'

'Oh, that's a shame. I was looking forward to meeting him.'

Iris turned down her stepfather's offer of coffee. It was time to go. As usual, she didn't hug her parents or kiss them goodbye – just gave them a little wave as they stood up to see her out. It was 3 p.m. She had lasted two hours at their house. The sky was grey; the sun was going down. When I leave Earth, she thought, I'll never see a darkening sky again. But it was OK. How many sunsets does a person need to see, to carry on living?

She didn't feel like going home, so she walked towards the Heath. The snow had melted by then, and the cold had lifted. She wasn't wearing gloves or a hat. She remembered the winters of her childhood, when it seemed to snow heavily every year; when her feet would go numb even when she wore two pairs of socks. Maybe the apocalypse will come soon, she thought. The ice will melt, everyone will die. There'll be a nuclear war. I'm making the right choice. Everyone will know that, someday, and they'll wish they had come, too.

The Heath was comforting and familiar, as ever. Iris had known it since she was born, from different vantage points. Before her mother remarried, she had been most familiar with the Heath Extension – the flat, pristine part of the park that seeped into suburbia. There was something melancholy about the Extension. It was always so quiet and still, apart from the odd dog walker and jogger. But this, the main part of the Heath, was its heart, and always busy. She listened to music as she walked up Kite Hill – that dreamy Frank Ocean song 'Pink + White'. At the top, she looked down at London. She could see the Gherkin, the Shard and the other steel and glass skyscrapers, most of which hadn't existed when she was born. She could also see the pale dome of St Paul's Cathedral, dwarfed by the skyscrapers and cranes. Once it had been the tallest building in London, but now that was hard to imagine. In two months she would turn twenty-nine, her last birthday on Earth. Three decades from now, the view would have changed again.

Nearby, some kids were sitting on a bench, passing around a spliff. When I was their age, thought Iris, it felt like London belonged to me.

Everywhere around the country, other people were enjoying this natural spectacle, the appearance and disappearance of our star, the birth and death of each day. Somehow, after thousands of years of human advancement, this everyday occurrence was still the loveliest thing on the planet. There would be no sunsets on Nyx. Iris took a photo of it, uploaded it to Instagram and waited for someone to like it.

14.

Say Something, Anything

The night before Iris flew to Los Angeles, she said goodbye to her family. Eleanor insisted on going to a fancy restaurant in town, to make it special. Iris suspected that this was a way of containing their emotions. Saying goodbye in public ensured that no one could become too hysterical, though Iris thought she could see tears glistening in her mother's eyes, over dinner. Eleanor looked like she wanted to say something. Several times, she opened her mouth, took a breath, changed her mind and closed it again. Say it, thought Iris. Just say it. Iris would rather have eaten at their house in Tufnell Park, watched an old film and slept on the floor of Mona's room, listening to her breathing in the night. Perhaps they could have driven her to the airport the next day. But no, they didn't offer to do this. Iris would spend her last night in Clapton, in her empty bedroom. She had given away most of her clothes and belongings. Kiran's new flatmate would arrive a few days later.

After dinner, Iris hugged all of her family in the street. She made the first move. Jack was surprisingly warm and bear-like. Mona squeezed her in a life-or-death clench, her arms tugging painfully at Iris's long, loose hair. When she pulled away, Mona was crying. Iris wasn't, because the situation was too bizarre to feel real. And then Eleanor stepped forward. She held Iris, but didn't speak and wouldn't let go. Iris eventually had to take a step back. She could still change her mind, but how awkward would that be? It would be even more awkward than her failed suicide attempt, because everyone would know. What would she do if she changed her mind – go back to Freedom & Co? To Eddie? To her parents' house? What would she do with her time on Earth? She didn't have any ideas.

Finally, her mother said something, her voice barely audible: 'Jack, please.'

Jack stepped forward and took Iris by the shoulders, gently. 'Iris, we think you should stay.'

'Wh– what are you doing?'

'You don't have to go through with this.'

Iris looked at her mother. She still didn't speak, but her face trembled, as if on the verge of collapse. Say something, thought Iris. Anything.

'What is this?' said Iris. 'An intervention?'

'You can move back in with us,' said Jack, 'and we can work through this together. You can get another job or you can just . . . rest for a while, and think about what you want to do next.'

'This is what I want to do next.'

'Iris,' said Eleanor, and everything seemed to go silent – the people around them, the honking cars. She put a hand on Iris's arm. '*Iris.*'

Mona pushed Eleanor out of the way and grabbed both of Iris's hands. She was crying freely with snot running from her nose into her mouth.

'Iris, what are you doing?' she sobbed. 'Don't leave me, Iris. Don't go.'

The silence had dissipated. Passers-by were looking at them. Cars were speeding by. Eleanor was looking at the ground. *Say it!* Iris waited another minute with Mona in her arms, so close she could feel her battering heart, but Eleanor didn't speak. Iris decided that she had to walk away, to make it easier for everyone.

'I have to go.'

'Iris!' screeched her sister.

'Iris,' said Jack, holding her arm, 'please consider it.'

'I'll call you from LA. We can talk every day until I start training.'

'Fuck you,' said Mona. 'Fuck you, Iris!'

Iris had wanted to watch her family walk away, turn the corner and disappear, but instead she herself walked away, with their eyes on her back, hearing Mona's voice become smaller and smaller, until it was swallowed by the night.

✳

Iris had just over £2,000 in savings. Money she had dutifully scrabbled to the side, for the future. In the morning, before she said a final goodbye to Kiran and caught a cab to Heathrow, she transferred the money to Mona's bank account and followed up with a text message. Mona didn't respond. Once Iris was in LA, she tried to contact her again, but she still didn't reply. Instead, Iris spoke to her mother every day before she went to the desert for training. They didn't have much to say to each other and Mona was seemingly never around. Despite that, Iris never wanted to end their conversations. There was still time for Eleanor to tell her whatever it was she had wanted to tell her. After saying goodbye, Iris would wait for her mother to hang up first. The last time they spoke, she listened to the crackling silence for five minutes, with tears running down her face.

On her last morning in LA, before she left the hotel, she received two messages from her sister.

> I hope it's everything you ever wanted.

> Please don't reply. It doesn't help. I love you & always will xx

Iris typed, 'I love you too,' but deleted it. Then she changed her mind.

I'm sorry – I had to reply. And I'm sorry for everything. I never wanted to hurt you. I love you more than anyone I've ever met. I hope you will grow and thrive and be happy. I love you, I love you, I love you, my dear Mona xxxx

She waited a few minutes for a response, but nothing came. Mona must be in school, or asleep, or doing her homework, or eating dinner. Iris couldn't remember what time it was in London. She was shaking all over. She removed the phone's SIM card, threw it in the bin, and left the handset on a table with a handwritten note for the chambermaid: 'Free phone – please take.'

15.

Departure

They posed for the world's media – smiling, thumbs up, giving peace signs like 1960s pop stars. Photographers were screaming, 'Look over here – no, over *here*, give us a smile!' The hubbub smothered all of Iris's doubts. She wondered who was watching her on TV – her mother, her sister, her friends, her exes? What a wonderful feeling, to be seen.

That day, five ships were launched into the Pacific Ocean, each carrying twenty people. Iris was on the second ship. She shared her quarters, Block G, with a woman called Abby and two men, Rav and Vitor. The women were separated from the men by a sliding door, which on Nyx would be fused shut. They would travel for seven days, mostly sedated, strapped to their bunk beds and fed through tubes.

It was a shame that Nyx could only be reached through the wormhole. Iris would have loved to see Earth from above, just so she could think: Wow, there it is. Earth would get smaller and smaller and smaller and, after a while, it would look like a blue plastic ball, something you could bounce against a wall. All the suffering. *Bounce.* All the wars. *Bounce.* All the suicides. *Bounce.* Someone being fired. *Bounce.* Someone being born. And then it would disappear. Abracadabra.

But it wasn't like that. She didn't get to see Earth. She didn't even see the wormhole. Six days passed in a haze of dreams. Another one about Edie, in which they found each other again, and were very much in love. Stress dreams about school exams, about Mona becoming a drug addict. In one dream, Iris was on the Tube in London when her train passed another going the same way, side by side. Her father was on the other one, dressed in black, reading the *Evening Standard*.

He looked up and said, 'Wake up!'

But she didn't wake up, because the drugs were too powerful.

SOMEWHERE

Seven Years Ago

16.

Floating

On the seventh day, Iris opened her eyes. The tubes had been taken away. For a minute she enjoyed feeling cosy and warm in her bunk, hovering between wakefulness and sleep. Then she remembered where she was and thought: Fucking hell, I actually did it. She unstrapped herself and floated towards the ceiling, then held on to the bunk and pulled herself towards the floor, stretching her limbs, one by one. Her hair and skin felt greasy. Abby still had her eyes closed. Iris somersaulted in the air, giggling.

'Oh my God,' said Abby, opening one eye. 'I can't move.'

They were called to the front of the ship, where the technical team worked. Everyone gathered together, rubbing their eyes, looking like shit, holding on to the walls and each other, so they wouldn't float away.

'We're nearly there,' said Johnny, an Australian technician, strapped into his seat. 'We didn't want you guys to miss this.'

He hit a button. A panel opened to reveal three large windows to the outside. Everyone breathed in sharply. It looked just like space did on TV – supernal and black – except they were there, surrounded by it. Johnny pointed out the debris floating around from the Pacific Ocean, things that had fallen through the wormhole: clumps of seaweed, a few fish, a shark, a huge whale covered in white splotches, floating in space for ever. Everyone cooed in amazement.

'That's our new sun,' said Johnny, pointing at an increasingly bright, orange star, 'but please don't look directly at it. And that over there is our new home, the planet Nyx.'

People whooped, applauded and hugged each other.

Nyx was a pink blob, the colour of poached salmon, still small and far away, in the future. Even further away were the millions of stars, everywhere, all around them.

NYX

Seven Years Ago

17.

Year 1

Every Friday at the farm, Iris's hands and nails became caked in dirt. After her shift, she would scrub and scrub in the shower, to no avail, until finally she decided that she liked it: this faint grubbiness, permeating her skin like a tattoo. Sometimes she would catch herself sniffing her fingers – deliciously bitter, organic, unclean.

She read for hours every day. She learned how to make soap, using fat from the kitchen and corrosive lye. Her cleaning shifts with Yuko and Stella were surprisingly satisfying. On Earth, she rarely cleaned – only when her flat was disgusting or when Kiran complained. She took photos of the Hub and the landscape outside, wrote pithy captions and clicked 'send'. She did more exercise than she had ever done on Earth, so that her body thinned and hardened, the way she had always wanted it to.

Iris's first year on Nyx passed slowly, delectably, like summer used to.

What was happening on Earth? Bad things, probably. Global crises, terrible new leaders, untold suffering, maybe World War III. Nothing of that scale ever happened on Nyx.

Iris didn't hear about any of these bad things, so it felt as if they weren't happening at all. It was relaxing, this state of ignorance. It helped to silence the hum of anxiety she had lived with for so long. This must be how it had felt in the past – each tribe only concerned with the goings-on of their own people.

But sometimes it was boring. Sometimes she missed hearing about the bad things.

A few months in, Hans had a huge row in the living room with Maya, a Canadian woman. It was a spectacle. He was a foot taller than her; quiet and passive, while she screamed. He was trying to shrug her off, after they'd had a brief fling. Several other people were sitting on the sofas, trying not to look.

'You can't treat people like that!'

'Like what, Maya?'

'Like shit! I'm not your goddamn whore.'

Someone let out a supportive murmur.

Hans looked pained. He hated confrontation. 'Come on, let's talk about this somewhere else.'

'I don't want to talk somewhere else.'

'Should we leave?' whispered Iris.

'Are you kidding?' said Abby. 'This is better than TV.'

After Maya had stormed out, Hans sat down with them and quietly admitted that, on Earth, he would've just blocked her on his phone and never seen her again.

The drama carried on for several weeks until, finally, he apologized to Maya.

There was no escape on Nyx. No ghosting. You can't ghost people when they're always there, sitting at the next table, eating lunch. You could blank them for a few days, but eventually you would have to let them back in. This was a good thing, thought Iris. Everyone would learn how to discuss their problems; to manage their relationships, rather than throwing them out and seeking new ones. On Nyx, nobody was entirely new.

There is good in everyone, she once muttered to herself, as she walked away from the farm. Sean had spent the whole shift tutting at her, telling her off – she couldn't do anything right. There is good in everyone, she repeated. There is good in everyone. There is good in everyone. There is good in everyone.

But as the months passed, she began to wish she could see someone new. Not even meet them – just see them. Glance at their face, notice their hair, the way they walked and talked.

More than that, she wished she could be alone, just once in a while. Like she used to be, on Earth. On a Sunday, when Kiran was with Ben, she would wake up, pull on a dressing gown, make tea and toast, watch Netflix in bed, scour the internet and maybe argue with a few strangers online, without having to smile or utter a single word.

Even Abby started to irritate her, at times, with her ironic tone of voice, the way she rolled her eyes. Even Rav, who smiled too much, and Vitor, who smiled too little, and thought he knew everything.

But this feeling never lasted long, not in Year 1. Iris would wake the next day in a better mood, go to breakfast, chat with her friends and love them again, and she would look out of the window, at the luminous pink sand, and think: *Yes.*

NYX

Present Day

18.

These Are the Things She Misses the Most

The sea. Any sea. Standing on beaches and waiting for cool water to lap against her feet. Rivers, streams, ponds and lakes. Bodies of water in general. The cold silk of the Ladies' Pond on Hampstead Heath. The glistening blue off the coast of West Sussex. The way cold water made her skin pucker and redden. From her bedroom window on Nyx, Iris can see New Lake Michigan, but she has never been there. Iris has never left the Hub. She's been here for seven years.

The sun on her skin. The real sun, not the Nyxian one. On Earth there was no better feeling than when the first ray of spring warmed her winter-white face. It made her feel new, like a polished diamond. There are no seasons here. One side of the planet always faces the sun; the other looks out to the abyss. The Hub is located a few kilometres from the Twilight, where it's neither day nor night. Everything is constant.

Mona. She was fourteen when Iris left Earth. Now she's a young woman. It's unimaginable.

Eleanor, despite the fact that she didn't fall down on her knees crying when Iris announced she was leaving the planet, like a normal mother might do. Iris misses her pale face. She misses the electrifying anger she felt towards her mother, which she held close to her heart. It has dissipated, leaving nothing in its place.

At least they have books.

In Year 2, Johnny started a weekly book club. Book choices were anonymously submitted through a specially devised app. At its peak, over thirty people took part and it could go on for hours. Watching people read and talk about books wasn't great for ratings, so in Year 3 the control room imposed a limit: one book per month, per person. In protest the Nyxians started reading super-long classics, such as *Middlemarch*, *War and Peace* and, currently, John Steinbeck's *East of Eden*. The latter was chosen by Iris, purely for its title. Now that she's reading it, the name of the club in London seems incongruous. *East of Eden* is an epic story with biblical undertones about warring brothers and crazy prostitutes in California – nothing to do with cocktails or rooftop swimming pools. The book makes her glad to be far away from Earth, from all those wild expectations people have of life. Up here, wild expectations can't be met. This is a comfort to her.

Iris's favourite thing about the book club is staring at her crush, Elias, across the circle of chairs in the living room. She never sits near him because her feelings are too strong. She fears that one look from him will cause her to faint, puke or shit her pants. She loves this feeling. Elias has long black hair and dark, doleful eyes. He's American, with Lebanese parents. Iris should have grown out of this by now – being attracted to unhappy, handsome men – but his beauty gives her hope.

After the cutback in books, people started having more sex. Some of them even moved to the family quarters, where they could fuck whenever they wanted. The first Nyxian baby, Norma, was born to Yuko and Carlos in Year 4. She was named in honour of Norman. When her name was announced in the cafeteria, Abby turned to Iris and rolled her eyes. Yuko and Carlos were on the podium, cheeks flushed and smiling, holding their little messiah, bundled in a white blanket. It was no surprise that Yuko was the first to procreate. In Tokyo, she had been a nanny. She missed the company of babies.

She was so damn cute, Norma, this human baby who would

never see Earth, but would instead learn her parents' customs through a haze of distance, like a second-generation immigrant. Norma had her mother's eyes and her father's golden skin and wavy dark hair. Everyone in the Hub went crazy for her. She was the first baby they had seen in years. When Yuko or Carlos entered a room, all eyes turned to check if they were carrying Norma. She was always trailed by fans – people wanting to hold her, squeeze her chubby cheeks, touch her dimpled hands, sniff her sweet-sour head or just gaze in wonder at her face. She was a drug, a miracle. Overwhelmed by the attention, Yuko would hide in her room to breastfeed in peace, often weeping with regret that she wasn't on Earth, with her mother. She finally understood what she had done.

Iris misses her old flat in Clapton. She misses Kiran. The idea of a best friend is so childish, but that's what Kiran was – the best one.

There was perfection on Earth, but only sometimes.

Who knows what became of Kiran. Maybe she's still with Ben. Maybe he left his wife and they're official now. Maybe she dumped him and married a nice Indian boy like her mother always wanted her to, and had a wedding that lasted days and days, and she didn't think of Iris, not even once.

She misses Orthodox Jewish families walking down the street in Upper Clapton, all in black, like visitors from another century. They were oddly reassuring, these people who clung to the past, refusing to change while the rest of the world refused to stop. They reminded her of her father. He must have dressed like that after his religious epiphany, but she can't remember.

She doesn't miss him. It's been too long. He's up in Jewish heaven. Do Jews believe in heaven? Iris can't remember. Everything she knows about Judaism was gleaned from TV and films: menorahs and skullcaps, matzo ball soup, Holocaust trauma, melancholic prayers in old dead languages. There are a handful of Jews on Nyx – like Abby. Her mother was Ashkenazi; her father was black. Both Iris and Abby are half Jew, half goy, but only Abby has the correct half.

Those earthly rules. She still doesn't miss them.

19.

No Place Like Home

Iris wakes with the taste of artificial cherries souring her mouth. She was dreaming about sweets. The automatic blackout has half lifted, giving the impression of morning sun, though the light is always like that – golden and soft, 8 a.m.-ish.

After the alarm turns off (a dawn chorus of birds, recorded in California eight years ago), she looks down at Abby from the top bunk and says, 'Did you have Haribo in the US? You know, those gummy sweets – the fizzy ones.'

'I can't remember,' says Abby, without much enthusiasm. 'I wasn't into sweets.' She looks like she's been awake for a while, sitting up in bed, her eyes crinkled and small. Insomnia is endemic on Nyx, contagious. Abby's long brown curls are shining in the light. Her pale brown skin looks yellow.

'I would cut off a finger for a bag of those sweets,' says Iris. 'I'm not even exaggerating.'

Abby flicks her eyes up at Iris, too tired to engage. She's playing with her gold wedding band, trying it on different fingers for size. Her ring finger is too thin these days. Recently she's taken to wearing it, but only in the bedroom, where there aren't any cameras. Outside the room, she keeps it in her pocket. She got divorced years ago, before she left Earth.

'Seriously,' says Iris. 'I hardly ever ate them, but I wouldn't think twice now. Any finger, even an index one. You could cut off the index finger of my right hand –'

'Dude, come on. I would cut off my fucking *head* for one bite of a cheeseburger.'

Abby's in a bad mood. Nyx is getting to her.

On Earth, seven years is long enough to fall in and out of love three times, switch careers, produce several new humans, become old. None of these things has happened to Iris and Abby since they started living in the Hub. They have grown a few grey strands on their heads and their skins have paled to queasy, unhealthy shades. They now possess the kind of easy, frank thinness they once dreamed of, though it gives them little pleasure, since they wear the same outfit every day. Their clothes are worn-out and shapeless.

Everyone has changed. Within a few years, Norman went from being everyone's favourite boss to practically a hermit, rarely seen. When he does appear in public, he has the faraway, preoccupied glamour of a CEO. It's been over a month since anyone saw him. Everyone assumes he's hiding in the control quarters, which Iris has still never visited. Abby has – they're on her cleaning rota. She says they're nothing special.

Iris leans out of her bunk with her tab to take a picture. Through the window she can see Annex 1, acres of peachy pink sand and, on lower ground, the indigo water of New Lake Michigan glimmering in the distance, surrounded by forest. Everything as it always is.

'Aren't people bored of seeing that?' says Abby. 'I know I am.'

People will get bored of anything, even living on another planet.

Iris writes on her tab:

Good morning, Earthlings! It's another beautiful, sunny day on Nyx. Hope you have a great Sunday, wherever you are in the universe 🚀 😊 #lifeonnyx #sundayvibes #iriscohen

And then she hits 'send'. She always tags her name, for a personal touch. There's a short delay while someone in the control room checks the post, then a blue tick appears. This means it's been approved and sent to Earth, where it'll be re-approved and then, hopefully, be seen by millions of people. Sometimes a red cross appears when the post is rejected, but this hasn't happened in a while, because Iris has learned to make them as bland as possible. She can't see the likes or comments, nor can she look at the posts themselves. All she can do is press 'send'. There is no interaction, no engagement, no scrolling, no desolate envy of other people's lives, no addiction to 'likes' – that bitter-sweet dopamine whisper, 'I see you.'

It's much easier than working at Freedom & Co. She doesn't have a boss, she keeps her own hours, she doesn't have to give presentations and very little is expected of her. If she stopped posting, she doubts that anyone would care.

She climbs down to Abby's bunk, as she always does in the morning, and lies beside her, top to toe. They talk about Elias, but Abby's heart isn't in the conversation.

She says, 'Just fucking talk to him, dude.'

'God, OK. No need to be rude.'

'I'm not being rude. Just giving you some advice.' Abby stares blankly, not quite meeting Iris's eyes. 'I'm getting up.' She pulls her legs from under Iris's head, picks up a greying towel and leaves the room.

Abby sticks to the Earth convention of showering every morning. Iris does it once a week. She feels like she doesn't smell as bad, up here. There's something about Earth that makes people reek. Plus, it means she can use her weekly ten-minute allowance (which was introduced in Year 5) in one go. She gets under the sheets and blankets, inhaling Abby's scent. They smell sweet and musty, like broken biscuits, but with a rank bitterness that Iris would have found disgusting on Earth. Here, she likes it.

No one on Earth is watching her now. There are no cameras in the bedrooms, though some people say that Norman sees everything – through hidden cameras, telepathy, omniscience. She puts her head under the covers, just in case. Here, in the dark, it's easy to pretend she's still on Earth. If she could snap her fingers and go back, she wouldn't think twice. Back to London, to her job, her unhappiness, her flat, her bed, to that Thursday night on Earth when Rich told her about *Life on Nyx*. If she could go back, she would, as easily as Dorothy clicking her ruby slippers. Iris closes her eyes and taps her bare feet together.

'There's no place like home,' she says. 'There's no place like home.'

Nothing happens.

Here it comes, here it comes. That feeling again – panic shimmering from her heart to her skin. She hugs her arms around her body and waits till it subsides, then pulls the blankets off her face and breathes the manufactured oxygen with her eyes still shut.

'Come back to Earth,' someone whispers in her ear – a woman.

'Abby?' She opens her eyes, looking around the room.

The voice was low, firm and oddly familiar. An English accent – London or the south-east. She can hear Rav and Vitor in the corridor, walking to the cafeteria, laughing at something. Iris has waited her whole adult life to lose her mind. Proper madness – the kind that melts reality. On Earth, it was always around the corner, waiting to pounce, but since she came to Nyx, the Smog has retreated.

'Oh, you,' she says, pretending not to be afraid.

Nobody responds. The room is empty.

✳

The cafeteria is busy this morning with adult chatter and the shrieks of children, excited to be alive and eating their terrible breakfasts – they don't have anything to compare it to. The food has taken a nosedive in the past year. Iris isn't sure why. She hasn't worked at the farm since Year 6, and neither have most of the Nyxians – the control room wanted to 'streamline' operations. The farm stopped opening on Sundays, too. She misses the heat of the sun through the glass dome.

Elias isn't working at the counter today, which is disappointing. Iris and Abby take their breakfast plates and join Rav and

Vitor at their usual table by the window. It is 8.04 a.m. in the Hub, Central Standard Time – the time zone chosen by Nyx Inc to maximize live viewing figures. After seven years on Nyx, they still follow the Gregorian calendar and behave as though there are twenty-four hours in a day, even though their planet doesn't turn. Like bad immigrants, they don't assimilate. It is also 8.04 a.m. in Chicago, Mexico City, the Galapagos Islands and Belize. People are having all kinds of breakfasts in those regions of Earth, but on Nyx, these days, they eat more or less the same thing every day: a single slice of bread with brown protein spread and sometimes, if they're lucky, a piece of fruit. Today there is no fruit. The farmers are struggling. The kitchen is running out of things.

'Hey!' says Rav.

'Good morning,' says Abby.

Vitor looks up. He is sponging the last crumbs off his tin plate with his fingers. Next to him, outside the window, pink sand dunes sit beneath a searing blue sky. It was such an exotic view when they first arrived, but now it's like a screensaver – unreal and easy to ignore. Iris sits next to Rav and Abby sits opposite.

'*Bom dia*,' says Iris, smiling at Vitor.

'*Bom dia*,' he says.

She has greeted him in Portuguese every morning for the past two weeks, since he told her he missed his native language. He's the only Portuguese speaker on the planet. Nyx Inc intentionally did not recruit two native speakers of any language other than English, for logistical reasons.

'How's it going?' says Iris. She takes a bite of her bread. It's chewy and gritty. The spread tastes like a watery combination of beans and cocoa.

Vitor rubs his face with his fingers. 'I slept so badly.' His eyes are wrinkled and bloodshot, encircled by shadows.

'Same,' says Rav, with a small grin, 'because I could hear you sighing and turning all night.'

'Sorry. It's not my fault.'

'I know, brother.'

Someone is watching us on the livestream, thinks Iris. Some-one who knows our faces better than their own. Once in a while, she tries to remind herself of this. What kind of celebrities are we? she thinks. A-list, B-list, C-list, surely not Z-list? On Earth, even Z-listers enjoy the benefits of fame: the passive love of strangers, emanating from their phone's notifications. For the Nyxians, fame is a matter of faith. There's not much evidence of it, but believing that they're well known and important makes everything worthwhile.

Iris rarely forgets that Norman is watching, but it's easy to forget about Earth, when it's so far away. Right now, someone is sitting on their sofa, tapping on their laptop between the Hub's different rooms and cameras until they pause, for a minute or two, on Block G's breakfast. Iris imagines a faceless, genderless viewer, their fingers encrusted with snacks, their mouth slightly open, staring into the blue light of a screen. They watch Abby eat her bread in tiny bites, to make it last longer. I wish I were on Nyx, thinks the viewer, because then I wouldn't have to be here.

'Why couldn't you sleep?' says Iris, just for something to say. She knows why Vitor doesn't sleep. Sometimes she stays awake all night listening to Abby breathing over the low metallic hum of the Hub.

'I don't know,' says Vitor.

He misses Earth, that's why. When Iris first met him in the Californian desert, Vitor was handsome and clean-shaven, but now he is diminished, like all of them. His olive skin and black hair have greyed, his body has shrunk. Like most of the men on Nyx, like Rav, he has a beard and long hair, which he wears in a bun. Same hair, same clothes, same underfed physiques.

'Did you take a pill?' says Iris.

'We're running out. You know that.'

Vitor can't do his job properly because of decreasing supplies. He's bored of them, these people who aren't his real friends. He misses the chaos of the hospital in São Paulo. He misses drinking beer on his balcony after work. He misses picking up men in bars, the anonymity of it. Maybe his parents would have accepted him, in the end.

'So hungry, man,' says Rav. 'Look at my arms. I'm a fucking skeleton.' He rolls up his tatty sweatshirt sleeves. Seven years ago, he looked like a boxer. Now, his muscled arms are as thin as a teenage boy's, with a greenish tint from lack of sun.

'It's not that bad,' says Iris.

'I don't look like myself.' He rolls his sleeves back down. 'It's better not to look.'

Nothing ever happened between Iris and Rav. Perhaps it would have, on Earth, but now they know each other too well.

'I've stopped looking at mirrors,' says Vitor.

'Tell me about it.'

'It's the opposite for me,' says Abby. 'I can't stop looking at myself in the mirror. Check out these cheekbones.' She turns her head from side to side.

'We should market it as a diet,' says Iris.

Abby puts on a deep voice: 'Leave your friends, family and life behind for ever. A small price to pay for the *body of your dreams*.'

They laugh for a few seconds, then stop. They have gone too far. Criticism of *Life on Nyx* is frowned upon, particularly in public areas, where Earth can see them. Iris has a strange feeling in her hands and feet, like pins and needles. Something foreboding. It's the panic again. She shakes her feet under the table, presses her hands together and waits for it to pass.

Looking as casual as possible, Vitor bites his left thumb. This is Block G's signal to request a meeting in one of their bedrooms, away from the cameras.

'Well,' says Abby, 'I'm done here.'

'Me too,' says Rav.

The four of them walk towards the exit. The cafeteria has mostly emptied out. Rav goes up to one of the tables and greets people, makes them laugh at something, while the other three carry on walking. Rav is so good at pretending that everything is fine.

On the way to Block G, the four of them chat awkwardly because the corridors are rigged. Someone on Earth is watching. Maybe Norman is watching, too – wherever he is.

They flash their wristbands at the door to Annex 2 and then Block G.

'Let's go to your room,' says Vitor. 'Ours is a mess.'

'OK,' says Iris.

They flash their wristbands again to enter Iris and Abby's bedroom. If they don't do this, an automatic sensor sets off an alarm, alerting the control room. There's nowhere to hide in the Hub – not for them.

'Good morning, Ravinder and Vitor,' says the disembodied voice – the same one that interviewed Iris in the black room, on Earth. Good old Tara, so cheerful and never-changing.

The four of them crowd the room. It's the size of a prison cell – the ones Iris has seen on TV. She and Abby sit on the bottom bunk, while Rav and Vitor hunker down on the floor.

'What is it, V?' says Rav, his eyes flicking around to check that there isn't a new device watching them. It's second nature, now, to doubt everything they've been told.

'I heard something,' says Vitor.

Everyone leans in, their interest piqued, like dogs waiting for treats. Gossip is even more precious on Nyx than it was on Earth. Lately people have been sharing a new conspiracy theory: they're not in space, they're still in California, it's all a hoax. But it's just wishful thinking. They're not in California.

'Someone who works in the control room told me this,' says Vitor. 'I swore I wouldn't tell anyone, but the show's doing really badly. They think Nyx Inc is going to fold.'

'What the fuck?' says Rav.

Iris's stomach lurches. She covers her mouth, afraid she might be sick.

'I knew it,' says Abby, shaking her head. She glances at Iris. 'Didn't you? I fucking did.'

Iris swallows, before speaking. 'What does it mean, though?'

'It means the show would be cancelled, the money would end. We would be cut off. Do you know how expensive it is, keeping us connected to Earth?'

'But we're self-sufficient,' says Rav. 'Even if the show finishes, it doesn't have to be the end.'

'Of course it does,' says Abby. 'No one is coming. No new people. No supplies. No communication with Earth. We're going to die.' She laughs unhappily, a small echo of her beautiful old laugh.

Rav shakes his head with a bemused smile. 'No, it's not possible.'

Iris doesn't understand why he and Abby are smiling. Fear and also excitement, perhaps, that something is finally happening.

'You read the contract, Rav,' says Abby. 'You read it and you signed it. We all did.'

'Your friend in the control room,' says Iris. 'Do they know where Norman is?'

'No,' says Vitor. 'Maybe he knew and wasn't telling me. He's probably just in the control quarters, don't you think?'

'I go there all the time,' says Abby. 'He's not there.'

The men leave the room. Iris and Abby remain sitting on the lower bunk, staring at the floor in silence, though the Hub is never truly silent. They can still hear the quiet, high-pitched buzz of solar-powered electricity, pumped oxygen, atmosphere control: the mysterious processes that keep the Nyxians alive. It's only when they stop speaking that they become aware of this, how silence doesn't exist in their lives any more, and it never will again. Did it exist on Earth? Not in London, but yes – somewhere. Whenever Iris went to the countryside, the heavy quiet in the middle of the night would thrill her. The weight of nothingness. Outside the window, the sky would be black, dotted with stars. Not the greenish, polluted night sky of the city. She misses stars. The sun never sets over the Hub, so they're not visible here.

'It was inevitable,' says Iris. 'People get bored of TV shows.'

'But it was the TV show to end all TV shows.'

Iris shrugs. 'No, that was *The Sopranos*, and even that had to end.'

Abby laughs, but her eyes are still blank. 'I never saw *The Sopranos*. I guess I never will.'

'What happens now?'

'Nothing happens. We wait.'

20

These Are the Things

Silence, stars, the night and so many other things.

Cigarettes. Mmm, *cig-a-rettes*! Even the word delights her. She had her last one in front of a hotel in West Hollywood, the night before she went to the desert for training. In fact, she had three in a row. They were deee-licious.

The smell of money. Weird, right? She didn't expect that. The other night, she dreamed she was in a corner shop, and as she unfolded a twenty-pound note it released a whiff of papery, cocaine bitterness. Did banknotes smell of cocaine, or did cocaine smell of banknotes?

Painkillers. Iris left Earth behind, but not her body, so she still suffers from horrendous period pain – an ominous trembling in her upper thighs that radiates into a stabbing stomach ache. On Earth she wasn't fully aware of its violence; she would swallow two ibuprofen and the pain would ebb away like a falling tide. But ibuprofen finished in Year 3. Paracetamol in Year 2. SSRIs and sleeping pills are running low. More people are coming, Norman used to say. They'll bring everything we need. At some point he stopped talking about them – the new arrivals, who would fix everything.

Sex and romance. Sure, she misses them. Privacy is hard to come by. Committed couples can live in the family quarters, but casual sex is limited to quickies, when roommates are elsewhere. Iris last had sex two years ago, with Jonah in the Annex 4 bathroom, out of boredom more than anything else. Since then – nothing.

And then she noticed Elias. Until three months ago, they had barely talked – beyond 'please' and 'thanks' at the cafeteria, where he works. But then she had a dream about him and woke at the end of a tender, throbbing orgasm. The morning after the dream, he was at the counter, serving grey, sticky mashed potatoes.

'Want some?' said Elias, blinking his sad, pretty eyes.

Iris opened her mouth, but couldn't speak.

Elias smiled. 'You all right, Iris?'

Her stomach pulsed when he said her name.

'Yes, please.'

'OK.'

He slopped them onto her plate and looked at the next person in the queue.

21

Cleaning

On Earth, Iris worked long hours and was always on call. On Nyx, time stretches around her like an empty room. Her social media duties take barely ten minutes a day. She cleans the Hub six days a week, for a few hours. Nearly everyone cleans. Iris doesn't mind it. It's repetitive and soothing; it's a chance to talk to Yuko and Stella for hours on end. She likes the vinegary smell of the cleaning fluid. She likes how her hands and arms have hardened. On Earth, sitting at her desk, she felt as fat and soft as a manatee.

This morning, on the way to her shift, she glances through a window at the farm, catching sight of luscious greenery and people working. It's hard to tell from here, but are the farmers really struggling that much? A minute later, she passes a window that overlooks the unfinished extension, Hub 2. It's a black skeleton of a building: a few walls surrounded by heaped rubbish.

Today, the team begins cleaning in Annex 5, in the women's bathroom. Most of the toilets are separated by flimsy cubicles, but a few of the walls have fallen down. The showers are communal. There are no cameras in here. The three women have stripped down to grey tank tops and shorts. Cleaning is sweaty work. As they scrub on their hands and knees, Vitor's secret fizzes on Iris's tongue like a pill. She wants to tell them so badly. When Yuko looks up, Iris opens her mouth but changes her mind.

'What is it, Iris?' says Yuko, in her sweet, flinty Japanese accent. 'You looked like you were going to say something.' She glances at her four-year-old daughter, Norma, who is sitting in the corner of the room, drawing something on Yuko's tab.

'Nothing,' says Iris.

'You know,' says Stella, from across the room, 'I got up in the middle of the night and went for walk, because I couldn't sleep, and I swear I saw Norman skulking around in a corridor.'

'No, really?' says Yuko.

'Yeah, he ran away like a frightened rabbit as soon as he saw me.' Stella throws her hands in the air. 'Who knows? I might've been dreaming.'

'Weird,' says Yuko. 'I wonder what he's doing.'

'He's probably locked in a room somewhere, pissing into bottles like a madman,' says Stella.

All three of them laugh.

'Hey,' says Yuko, 'do you guys know how to cut hair?'

'You want a haircut?' says Stella.

Yuko nods. 'Yes, it's been a while.'

'I can do it.' Stella rummages through the box of cleaning products and pulls out a pair of thick black scissors. 'Look! Could do it now, if you like.'

Yuko frowns. 'I want to go to my hairdresser in Tokyo, have one of those head massages and a blow-dry, and come out looking like a million dollars.'

'I can give you a massage,' says Stella, deadpan.

'Awww, thanks.'

'I'm serious!' It's hard to tell when Stella is being serious. She rarely smiles, but there's always a glint of silliness in her eyes. She's in her early forties, but looks older. Sometimes she alludes to her life in New Zealand, to difficult times, but Iris knows not to ask. Over there, she worked as a secretary, among other things. Over here, she cooks and cleans.

'Why didn't they bring a hairdresser to this fucking planet?' says Yuko. 'I mean, *God*.' She widens her eyes when she swears, delighted with herself. Her use of language has changed over the past seven years, taken on American inflections.

'So you want it cut or what?' says Stella.

'Have you done it before?'

'Sure, I used to cut my boyfriend's hair all the time.'

'Hmm, OK, then.'

Stella points at one of the toilets. 'Sit on there, facing away from me.'

Yuko screws up her face in disgust.

'I just cleaned it!'

'OK.' Yuko sits on the edge of the toilet.

'Try not to fall inside, OK? Or I'll have to flush you out to space.'

Yuko starts to undo her bun – a huge black puffball, tied together by hair alone. (All the hairbands were lost years ago.) Her hair falls thickly to several inches below her bum.

'Jesus, girl!' says Stella.

Iris walks over and stands beside Stella as she combs her fingers through Yuko's hair with great tenderness. It's wispy at the ends, with a few grey strands, but still shiny and thick. Seven years without earthly products and it looks just fine. It smells like soil and crushed leaves. Iris remembers the shelves in her bathroom in London, laden with potions. Even at the time, she marvelled at her own gullibility.

'How long has it been since you cut it?' says Stella.

Yuko laughs. 'Oh, you won't believe it.'

'Two, three years?'

'I haven't cut it since I left Earth.'

'Whaaat?!' say the other two, in unison.

'Do you remember my hair when we arrived?'

'Didn't you have a buzzcut?' says Iris.

'Yeah, I did it for the show. I thought it would be easier to look after.'

'It looked so cool.'

Yuko smiles. 'Thanks.'

Stella takes a handful of Yuko's virgin hair and lets it run through her fingers. 'Seven years of hair,' she says. 'So how do you want it?'

'Shoulder-length?'

Norma is not paying attention. She's still glued to Yuko's tab.

'Shoulder-length,' says Stella. 'OK.'

As she assesses the situation, they all stop speaking. Stella gently moves Yuko's head with her hands, checks that the hair is hanging straight and then, finally, scissors across in five thick snips. Thousands of black strands fall to the floor.

'Done!' says Stella.

Yuko runs her hands through her hair, widening her eyes in surprise when her fingers reach the ends. 'Wow, that feels so much better.'

'It looks great,' says Iris.

'It really does,' says Stella. 'Very chic.'

There's no mirror in this bathroom – it fell and smashed a while ago – so Yuko takes their word for it.

'*Okaasan*, I'm hungry,' says Norma in her hybrid accent, without looking up from her tab.

In a hundred years, thinks Iris, maybe there'll be a Nyxian accent. By then, all of the non-English speakers will be dead.

'OK, Norma,' says Yuko, sighing.

She sits on the floor in the corner. Norma sits on her lap, lifts Yuko's top and starts to suckle on her breast. It's partly why Yuko is so skinny – her daughter is sucking her dry.

Stella gathers the hair from the floor with her bare hands, rolls it into a ball and throws it in the bin.

'On Earth you could've sold this to a wig-maker,' she says. 'It's good-quality hair.'

'No,' says Yuko, 'there's too much grey.'

Norma stops suckling and looks up at her mother, whose hair hangs bluntly over her shoulders. Yuko does look chic. She could be an architect or a designer – someone who makes beautiful things.

'*Okaasan!*' shrieks Norma. 'Your hair!' Her mouth hangs open in shock.

'Stella cut it for me. Doesn't it look nice?'

'Noooo!' Fat tears begin to fall down her cheeks. 'It looks *awful!*'

'Sweetie, come on.'

Norma hides her face in her mother's breasts, wracked with sobs, unable to say anything more. Yuko smiles at Iris and Stella, and rolls her eyes. They turn away to give her some privacy, and carry on with their cleaning.

'Bloody hell,' says Iris, quietly.

'She didn't recognize her mother,' says Stella. 'That's all.'

Afterwards they clean the living room and a couple of corridors. The other teams will do the rest. At one point they pass Abby, carrying a bucket to the control quarters. Everyone says 'Hey!' to each other and carries on walking.

When Iris gets back to her bedroom, it's empty. Abby is still working. As well as cleaning, she holds classes for the Nyxian children – just a couple of hours a day. Most of the kids are too young for school, but they're getting older. Iris is glad to be alone, glad to hear the hum of the Hub, the almost-silence. When she climbs up to the top bunk, tiredness ripples through her body, like it did at the end of yoga classes, when she would lie down and think of nothing. On Earth, she rarely went to yoga, rarely did any exercise at all, but when she did, that was the best bit – when the work was done. When work finished at the office there was also a sort of joy, but alongside it, a gaping hole that could only be filled with alcohol. Iris looks at her tab. It's 11 May. Seven years ago, she had just left her job at Freedom & Co.

She lies with her palms facing the ceiling, her legs slightly apart, her eyes softly closed, her jaw relaxed. *Shavasana*. She thinks of nothing. Her muscles radiate peace. This is the highlight of her day, always.

22

These Are the Things

New music. They have their hundred songs, and that's it. Songs by Bob Dylan, Beyoncé, Mozart, Tinariwen, Gal Costa, Prince, Asha Bhosle, Bob Marley, LCD Soundsystem, the Notorious B.I.G. and others. Iris never imagined that she would one day become intimately familiar with George Michael's 'Careless Whisper' or Chopin's Ballade No. 1 in G minor, Op. 23, but she grew to love them both. Now she can't bear any of them, not even the song she chose. There are other songs in their heads, of course – the ones they can't forget – but the Nyxians aren't allowed to sing them in the Hub's public areas. The royalties would be too high.

There was one exception: when Hans died, Elizabeth sang Bob Dylan's 'To Ramona' a cappella at the memorial service in the cafeteria. The song was muted on TV and the livestream, so all you could see was people crying, holding hands. Elizabeth also cried as she sang, but she didn't miss a note. Her voice was clear and cool as a stream.

Hans isn't the only Nyxian who has died. There have been three others, all of natural causes. On Earth they would have lived.

Films and TV.

The internet. The ability to stalk people, look at clothes, photos of dogs, waste hours of her life in a vacant, meditative state. All she can do now is send her pictures out to the world. She knew it would be like this. It was in the terms and conditions.

*

Cocktails, beer and wine. All alcohol. Drugs, too. On Earth, oblivious, dumb joy was just a couple of phone calls away. Iris had taken it for granted.

Sometimes they make moonshine up here. It isn't allowed, but it happens. Abby managed to get some once. It tasted like bin juice. They drank it quickly in their bedroom, laughed for hours and talked about how they would literally kill someone in order to hear one song that wasn't on the playlist. Something with a beat, something you could dance to. They sang the songs themselves – Rihanna's 'What's My Name', Carly Rae Jepsen's 'Call Me Maybe', Michael Jackson's 'Billie Jean' – and forgot most of the words. Abby tried to moonwalk in her bare feet, but the room was too small and she couldn't do it. The hangover the next day was mild and also pleasant, somehow. Iris had forgotten how sweet and soft a hangover could be, like a blanket draped over your body, telling you: *Slow down.*

When Iris is asleep she can go anywhere she wants, eat and drink anything, hear any song – and everything tastes and sounds exactly like it did on Earth. Other than sex dreams, her favourites are the ones in which she eats Earth foods. Sometimes something extravagant, like duck pâté or oysters. Sometimes a McDonald's cheeseburger or a chocolate biscuit. Then she wakes up with her mouth full of saliva, wanting to scream, but thankful for the dream.

23.
Elias

The following Saturday, after her shift, Iris goes to Rav's exercise class in the living room along with twenty or so other Nyxians – mostly women. She and Abby always stand at the back because their giggling puts him off. Everyone wears the same tank top and shorts, barefoot because their shoes are falling apart. They run, they squat, they do burpees, press-ups, sit-ups and stretches. Rav does the same moves but barely sweats, while shouting instructions:

'Five more!'

'Three more!'

'Don't forget to *breeeathe*!'

He laughs along with them at the strain and effort of it all, even though it's easy for him. Iris used to see men like him in London parks, training rich people to be better versions of themselves.

Their arms are shiny and slick, their mouths gasp for air. On Earth someone would say, 'Can you crack open a window?' but they can't crack open a window, because the atmosphere would kill them, so nobody says this. Breeze on sweat, thinks Iris. That was a good feeling. The room becomes hotter and hotter, permeated with the smell of humans, exerting themselves.

As always, Iris leaves early so she can enjoy a few minutes alone in the shower – her weekly cleanse. The soap is scent-free and barely lathers, but it works – she can smell dirt disintegrating on her body. With her eyes closed, she pretends she's at home in Clapton, rubbing lavender shower gel over her skin, hearing the distant sound of a radio, Kiran knocking on the door.

'You almost done?' she would say.

But then, suddenly, her body goes cold – the shower has switched off. Her ten minutes are up. She dries off with a semi-clean towel.

Kiran probably left the flat years ago. Strangers live there now.

After lunch, fifteen or so Nyxians gather in the living room for the book club. Interest has waned since Year 3. The funky smell of the gym class lingers in the air, and a humid, tropical warmth, but neither of these things bothers the Nyxians. The air is always stale; they're used to it. They sit on chairs in a circle, like a support group, clutching their tabs, waiting to talk about *East of Eden*. Iris sits across from Elias, far enough for his presence to not overwhelm her, but with a good view of his pretty face. He rarely catches her eye. He looks at the floor, he looks at the ceiling, he looks more or less in the direction of whoever's speaking, he nods and shakes his head. Like Iris, he mostly listens. He sits next to Sean.

'Hi, everyone. Thanks for coming,' says Johnny. Outside the book club, Iris doesn't know him very well. He's a technician, and therefore superior. 'So, *East of Eden*. Great choice. I'd never read it before. I'd never read any Steinbeck at all, actually. How about you guys?'

'I read *Of Mice and Men* in high school,' says Elizabeth.

'Yeah,' says Abby, 'me too.'

'Well, whoever suggested it – thank you. It's an incredible book.'

Several people look around to see if they can tell who chose it. Iris tries to look casual, but her face burns. Elias rests his gaze on her. She feels her face go redder and redder, till the warmth spreads to her throat, her chest, her fingers. He raises his eyebrows and smiles. Iris's face spasms. She looks away. She has to.

'What did you guys think of it?' says Johnny.

Sean and Abby both open their mouths, ready to talk, but then Elias puts his hand up.

Johnny nods at him. 'Yes, mate.'

Elias shifts in his seat. 'I thought it was amazing,' he says, looking at Johnny and then at the ground. 'Truly. I was intimidated by its length, though we've read a lot of long books. There was something about –' He pauses and looks up. 'I'm from California. Not from Salinas, not even close, but still . . . I guess that's what spoke to me the most – the love that Steinbeck has for California. The love we all have, maybe, for the place we're from. And yeah, the other themes – good versus evil, the destructive power of love, sibling rivalry – they were all interesting, too. It made me think –' He nods and leans back in his chair, deciding against whatever it is he was going to say. 'Nothing. I don't know. I loved it.'

Iris has been holding her breath. She exhales. Elias looks at her again and smiles, but he doesn't look happy. His shining dark eyes give it away. A sense of . . . resignation. The discussion continues, but she doesn't take part. She thinks of the book's namesake, the club in London. Maybe people are there right now, drinking cocktails by the pool. Life going on. Elias doesn't say anything else.

When the book club ends, there's a sudden hubbub as everyone starts speaking at once. They stack the chairs and put them in a corner. Some of them leave, while others sit on the threadbare sofas, talking about other stuff. Iris hears little snatches of conversation.

'Did you . . .'

'Well, I'm . . .'

'Oh, really?'

It's meaningless noise. She doesn't try to talk to anyone and no one tries to talk to her.

'Come back to Earth,' she whispers to herself. It's been two weeks since she heard the voice. Obviously it was some kind of dream or hallucination, but she wishes it would return. Someone new to talk to, even if they don't exist. Someone who misses her, who wants her back.

Abby walks over and nudges her arm. 'You picked it, didn't you? The book.'

'What?' says Iris. Had she ever mentioned the members' club to Abby? 'How did you know?'

'Because of your face.'

'Oh.'

'Why don't you go talk to him?' Abby nods at Elias, who is sitting on a sofa, looking at something on his tab. 'I'm going back to the room. *Go talk to him.*' Abby smiles, showing her straight, white American teeth. The smile doesn't reach her eyes, but Iris knows she means it.

Once Abby has left, Elias looks up and starts walking over. Iris fights an urge to flee the room, to avoid talking to this man she has admired for months. She realizes, in this moment, that she enjoys the infatuation as it is; that it relies on the distance between them. The distance is the whole point and now he's going to ruin it.

But when he says, 'Hey, Iris,' she feels pleasure sparkling in her veins.

'Hey.' Her voice sounds like someone else's – embarrassingly low. She coughs.

'Thanks for suggesting the book.'

'How did you know?'

'Oh, I dunno. I could just tell.'

'You're welcome.' Iris realizes she has never really talked to him, not properly. 'I'm glad you enjoyed it. I did, too.'

Someone on Earth is watching, she thinks. They're probably laughing at my awkwardness, at my love-struck face. Elias looks at her with a wry smile. His eyes are dark brown, flecked with gold. He lightly touches her arm for a second and it's the greatest thing she has experienced in years. A wave of joy ripples from the touch. It feels better than drugs, music and alcohol, and all the other things she misses.

'So?' says Elias, cocking his head.

'Yeah.' She laughs. 'OK.'

He begins to walk towards the door and she follows.

In the corridor, as they silently walk towards Annex 3, where he lives, Iris glances up at a camera above their heads. Its red LED is switched off. A few metres on, she looks up at the next camera – it's also off. Huh, strange. But when she turns to Elias – who is looking ahead as he walks, with purpose – the strangeness is quelled by excitement. They flash their wristbands at the entrance to Annex 3, Block L, then again at the door to Elias's room.

'Good afternoon, Iris,' says Tara.

'Good afternoon, Tara,' says Iris.

'Tara?' says Elias.

'Yeah, that's her name.'

'I didn't know that.'

It looks much like Iris's room, but smells strong and pungent, like men. It's not a bad smell. Iris doesn't know who Elias's roommate is. She wonders whether anyone saw them, on Earth or on Nyx, walking into his room, but the thought is brushed away as soon as he pulls her towards him and kisses her mouth. Both of them sigh with relief. It feels unreal.

'How did you know?' says Iris.

He pulls off her top and kisses her neck. 'How could I *not* know? You're like my little stalker.'

Iris laughs. 'Well, that's embarrassing.'

'We don't have much time. My roommate will be back soon.'

They separate, undress quickly and then lie on the bottom bunk, skin to skin. He enters her almost immediately, which hurts a bit, but it feels good to hurt this way. They barely kiss, because that, too, would be a waste of time. His lovely mouth stays mostly on her neck, his right hand between her legs.

'Let me,' says Iris, removing his hand, because she will do it better than him. On Earth, she often held back from doing this, for fear of seeming too sexual, too aware of her own body, but now it doesn't matter.

He says, 'OK,' and she replaces his fingers with her own.

Several minutes later, when Iris starts to moan, Elias says, 'Shhh,' with his breath still on her neck.

Nearly there, nearly. Elias begins to whimper. Here it comes: a crescendo, a blur, a tsunami of pleasure, the world disappears.

But this isn't the world; it's far, far away.

Iris faces the metal wall, with Elias behind her. She would like to lie here for a while, feeling the aftershocks, but she can't. As she turns to look at him, this near-stranger, he averts his eyes. Damn, she thinks, I forgot how weird this could be. She stands and dresses. Elias finally looks at her for a moment, but his eyes are unfocused. It's as if he can't see her. He reminds her of Abby.

'I'm sorry,' he says, covering his face.

'What for?' She can feel his semen soaking through her underwear.

'I barely know you.'

'That's OK, isn't it?'

Elias stares at the wall, behind her. 'I'm sorry,' he says again.

'You don't have to apologize.' He wants her to leave, she realizes. 'I should go. Send me a message, sometime?'

'They'll read them.'

'Who will?'

Elias doesn't respond. He closes his eyes.

'OK, I'm going,' says Iris, as she leaves the room. 'See you later.'

The feeling of bliss has already evaporated. Even so, she can feel new paths forming in her brain, turning Elias from a person into a promise. That old biological trick. Iris looks up at the camera that hangs over the entrance to Annex 3. A red LED beams out from a dark corner. It's still filming. She sighs with relief. Someone is watching. She still exists.

The next day, when Iris approaches Elias in the cafeteria, he looks the other way and leaves the room. Tears prick in her eyes, but she holds them off by blinking several times. Did anyone on

Earth see that? she wonders. Did anyone tweet, 'Wow, what an arsehole'? Did they notice her dejected face? Rejection feels just the same up here. Like you've suddenly regressed to being a child, an idiot who knows nothing.

Later, in the privacy of their bedroom, Iris and Abby analyse the situation to shreds, like teenagers. The conversation seems to break Abby out of her gloom, momentarily, but the topic quickly wears itself out, even for Iris. Elias is undeniably beautiful, but her feelings for him are an echo of something else.

They stop talking and go back to reading their tabs in silence – Zadie Smith's *NW*, the latest book club choice. The novel is so vivid, so quintessentially London, that Iris can almost smell home in its electronic pages: traffic fumes, weed smoke, desperation, fried chicken. At times, while reading it, she forgets she's not in London and never will be. How can that be possible? Every time she looks up from her tab, she feels devastated.

After a few minutes of silence, Abby says, 'Must be weird for you to read this, huh?'

'I don't know if I can carry on.'

But she will carry on. She can't stop. All of those humdrum places and things – Willesden, Golders Green, Poundland, kebabs – make her want to puke with longing.

'You OK?' says Abby.

'Yeah.' Iris changes the subject. 'Can I take a photo of you? For a post.'

'I look so bad, though.'

'You never look bad.'

'Hmm. OK.'

'Just sit there, pretending to read.'

Iris stands up, takes the photo and puts a warm filter on it. Abby's eyes are downcast, but there's a small smile on her face. Her dark ringlets are tied up, sprouting from her head like the leaves of a pineapple. Next to her, outside the window, is that same old view: the eternal 8 a.m. sun, the pink sand, and the indigo lake, so far away.

Here's Abby enjoying our latest book, #NW by #zadiesmith.
Have you guys read it? What did you think? 📚 #nyxbookclub
#bookstagram #lifeonnyx #iriscohen

People are probably commenting, saying they love the book or don't love it, recommending other books they think the Nyx-ians will enjoy, saying that Abby's hair looks great, that she's one of their favourites. Iris can't see the comments, but she still asks questions in her posts. That's something she learned at her old job. People love to be asked what they think, even if no one is listening to their answers. Iris once mentioned this in a social media presentation at Freedom & Co. All her colleagues laughed, as if they were superior to such people.

24.

These Are the Things

Grass. Swans. Cygnets in the spring. The last time Iris heard the word *cygnet* was when Mona reminded her of it, when they went swimming in the ponds.

Mona's curly auburn hair. Mona in a bad mood, eating dinner in silence. Mona putting her thumbs through the wrists of her jumpers. Mona and her wire-rimmed glasses and her cute little nose. Mona, who was born when Iris was fifteen – too old to be her friend, too young to appreciate babies, too busy counting the years till university, when she could finally leave home. Mona, whom she barely knew – not like most siblings know each other – but whom she loved more than anyone on Earth, instinctively. Mona swimming in the pond, in her underwear, and laughing because the water was so cold.

Sometimes, Iris tries to imagine Mona's face as it might be now. She rarely looks at the photograph she brought to Nyx, of Mona with Eleanor, but she can picture it exactly. The garden in Tufnell Park. Yellow sunshine on the grass. Mona's childish white teeth. Their mother looking polished and beautiful.

Mona would have lost her puppy fat by now. Maybe she dyed her hair, straightened it and cut it short, and Iris wouldn't even recognize her in the street.

What else, what else? Think of something else.

Robins, magpies, sparrows, geese, ducks.

*

Parakeets flying over the Heath, their high-pitched screeching. When Iris was a kid, she hardly ever saw them – they were almost an urban myth, these foreign lime-green birds, living in the centre of London. By the time she left Earth, they were everywhere, all over the city. There were several theories about their origins: they were descended from escaped pets; they were released by Jimi Hendrix in Carnaby Street; they were leftovers from a film shoot; they flew all the way from Africa and Asia, in search of a milder climate.

There are animals on Nyx, apparently – small ones – but no one ever sees them. They live somewhere else, far from the Hub.

She even misses pigeons.

Foxes.

Dogs in parks running ahead of their owners. She will never see a dog again, not even a photo of one.

The Heath, Regent's Park, Springfield Park, Hyde Park; Hackney and Walthamstow and Tottenham Marshes.

Lipstick. Foundation. Blusher. New clothes.
    She doesn't miss removing her body hair, though – such a chore. They ran out of razors in Year 2, but she had stopped using them long before. All the Nyxians are hairy, both women and men. Iris's legs are covered in dark fuzz, her pubic hair is luxuriant. It makes her feel warm and cosy. It must be what Eve looked like.

25

Silent Night

Over the next few weeks, the texture of Iris's mood shifts from low-level panic to high-level nausea, like a constant hangover. She retches into the toilet, but nothing comes up. At night, she passes out as soon as the lights switch off – a sweet, heavy slumber. She keeps her sickness to herself. She doesn't even tell Abby, who has become increasingly distant and strange, as if she's trying to delete herself from her own life. At mealtimes, she barely speaks. Most mornings, when Iris climbs down to the lower bunk, Abby stands up and walks out. Sometimes she'll say something, like:

'I need the bathroom.'

'I'm going to shower.'

'I have to meet someone.'

But often she'll leave the room before Iris has even woken up. It makes her feel needy, like an unwanted child.

One night, when they're lying in bed, Iris asks, 'Are you OK?'

The blackout is down and the lights will soon switch off.

'Am I OK?' Abby says slowly, as if she is asking herself the same question.

'You don't seem –' The lights go out. The room is so dark that Iris can't see her hands, but she can still hear the hum of the Hub, its mysterious processes. 'You don't seem yourself,' she says.

Abby doesn't reply. The hum seems to be getting louder. Iris wishes she had some earplugs. Her eyes adjust to the darkness. She props herself up on the bed, on her elbows. When she turns, she sees a faint line of light tracing the edges of the window. The eternal light, the eternal hum. Her skin prickles with embarrassment. She hates difficult conversations. She's like her mother, in that way.

'Sorry,' she says, 'this is a stupid conversation to be having in the dark.' No response. 'Abby?'

Iris hears a sharp intake of breath. On Earth she would clamber down the ladder and turn on the light and talk about it, but she can't turn on the light – it's out of her control.

'I'm just tir–' Abby's voice catches in her throat. 'I'm tired of all this. Goodnight.' She sounds like a stranger.

Iris wakes in the middle of the night. The room is still black. For a few minutes, she listens to Abby's slow, heavy breathing, and the hum. She begins to fall back asleep, the darkness of the room dissolving into a deeper, blacker darkness; the hum dissolving into silence.

A woman's voice, bright and soft, breaks through the quiet. 'Silent night, holy night,' she sings, into Iris's ear.

Iris opens her eyes. 'Abby?' she whispers.

The singer, who is not Abby, continues: 'All is calm, all is bright . . .'

Iris can feel someone's breath on her cheek, she can even smell her light, grassy shampoo, but she can't see her.

'Round yon virgin mother and child . . .'

Iris remembers Christmas on Earth, years ago, just after her father died.

'Holy infant, so tender and mild . . .'

Her mother had appeared at the door, wearing a white cotton nightgown. Her long blonde plait shone in the light of the corridor like wheat in the sun. She came and knelt by Iris's side and sang till she fell asleep. Her breath smelled sweet and sour, like hot milk. Iris has no other memories of her mother doing this.

Her eyelids are heavy. The singing continues.

Sleep in heavenly peace,
Sleep in heavenly peace.

189

I'm just dreaming, she thinks.

Iris wakes up before the alarm-birds. The blackout has half lifted. A poor simulation of dawn. She looks down at the lower bunk, but it's empty – Abby has already left the room – so she lies in bed for a while, reading her tab. Within a few minutes she becomes distracted and starts taking selfies instead. In the pictures her face is grey, with fine lines around her eyes, which will only get deeper. She's still young, more or less, but her skin doesn't have the easy glow of genuine youth. Thirty-five? she thinks. No, I'm thirty-six. It's easy to forget. The nausea comes and goes, and then it just comes. There's a tang of acid at the back of her throat and she begins to gag. Iris swallows and closes her eyes, takes sips from her water bottle, but it's too much, too late. She leans her head over the side of the bunk and a cascade of sick falls to the floor. *Splat.* She lies back for a few minutes and relief rolls over her body.

Iris gets up and cleans the vomit with a towel, which she throws into the laundry room on her way to breakfast. Abby is sitting at their table. Elias is at another table, on the other side of the cafeteria.

'Hey,' says Abby.

'Good morning.'

Iris sits and begins to eat. The bread and paste tastes like mould, shit, sick and other bad things, so she pushes it aside. She looks over at Elias, eating alone. He concentrates on his food as it if were very interesting and complicated – grilled lobster rather than a nasty piece of bread.

'You OK?' says Abby.

He won't talk to me, Iris wants to say. *Why won't he talk to me?* But she can't say this here, in front of the cameras. Everyone would see.

'Yeah. You?'

Abby stares at Iris. 'I'm fucking *fantastic.*'

26.

Things

Iris doesn't miss her job one bit. No way, José.

Good dark chocolate. Shit milk chocolate. Mediocre chocolate.

The taste of meat. Specifically a medium-rare steak, dripping with salty blood, with triple-cooked chips, which she would dip in mayonnaise. Maybe a little green salad on the side. Jesus Christ, what she would do for a fucking steak.

Sitting on the Tube or a bus in London, waiting for her stop to arrive. Just being taken, passively, from one place to another. Alone, but surrounded by strangers.

OK, sometimes she misses work. The yearning catches her off guard, for those static hours sitting at her desk, staring at a screen, not speaking; for zoning out of meetings and thinking, instead, about sex; for taking notes she would never read again; for the moment on Friday evening when she would turn off her computer and already feel the glow of alcohol in her chest.

27.

Wake Up!

Iris zones out as she cleans the bathroom floor. But then she hears Stella say 'Elias' and her stomach lurches. There are rumours going round. Elias has gone missing.

'We haven't seen him in the kitchen in two days,' says Stella, 'and he hasn't been to his block, either. People are saying things.' She throws her hands up. 'It doesn't make sense.'

'Oh no,' says Yuko. 'Has this ever happened before?'

Iris stays quiet. She's afraid that if she talks, her voice and manner will reveal everything.

'One time I couldn't find Elizabeth,' says Stella. 'Turned out she was lying under our bed.' She laughs. 'For *three days*!' Her eyes become moist, with laughter or something else. She wipes them with her hands.

'Wow. That's crazy.'

Iris swallows before speaking. 'What was she doing?'

'Having some sort of crisis. I guess she wanted to be alone, for once. She stayed there in silence, not eating. Maybe she moved around when I wasn't in the room. She had some water. It was just after Hans died. She was so upset.'

'I never heard about that.'

'Me neither,' says Yuko.

'They kept it quiet. Sometimes people just need space. I sure do.'

'Is she OK now?' says Yuko.

'I don't know.' Stella shrugs. 'She's all right.'

Yes, perhaps Elias found a hiding place, and just wanted a break. If Iris found such a place, she would probably do the same.

'I hope they find him,' she says, mopping the floor.

'Me too,' says Stella. 'He's so cute, Elias.'

'Yes, he is!' Yuko giggles.

Iris's stomach goes, *Ungh*. Will I be sick? she thinks. No. It's just fear and love – intertwined, indistinguishable – for the tiny, helpless thing that's growing inside her.

✳

A week later, five minutes after the alarm-birds sing, comes an announcement through the loudspeaker – not from Norman, but Peter, the Hub's chief technician. Iris doesn't know what he looks like, but he has an American accent. Like a lot of the senior technicians, he stays mostly in the control quarters, away from the cameras.

'I'm sorry to announce,' he says, 'that our friend Elias Haddad, a very special member of the Nyxian community, has died.' His voice is low and sad, like a politician talking about a tragedy.

Iris and Abby are still in bed. They both say, 'What?!'

'Elias escaped the Hub and was suffocated by the atmosphere,' says Peter. 'Thankfully it was all over in seconds, so he didn't suffer too much. I am so sorry to share this terrible news. Please join us now in the cafeteria if you wish to say goodbye to Elias.'

In the cafeteria, there's no breakfast. There's no memorial. Nobody makes a speech. Peter doesn't show up. Nor does Norman. There is only Elias's body, lying on a table, wrapped in a white sheet like a mummy, with just his lovely face showing. People are crying and shouting and murmuring in disgust. Lots of them walk out. It's a silent warning to the Nyxians: stay inside, or die. This does not appear on television or the internet. For one hour, the livestream is shut down and replaced with a respectful message about Elias's death.

Iris has never seen a dead body before, let alone a body she's had sex with. To the best of her knowledge, none of her former lovers have died, but of course she can't be sure. She remembers watching a wildlife documentary on TV in which a dead baby elephant was prodded by its friends and family with despairing tenderness. 'Wake up, little one,' they seemed to be shrieking, in their elephant language, 'wake up!' Iris wants to touch Elias; she wants to shake him awake. She wants to comb her fingers through his shining black hair and smell the crown of his head. She wants to flutter her fingertips against his long eyelashes and stroke his uneven beard. But people would judge her. They would think she was a freak, touching a corpse like that, so lovingly, when she wasn't his mother, sister or partner. Elias's body, emptied of his soul, now seems both precious and cursed.

Her mind is wandering. Focus, focus. Elias is dead, she thinks. He's dead. This is real. She looks at him. He looks like he's just sleeping, though his skin has a glossy, unnatural pallor. It seems like a joke. This lifeless thing isn't Elias. It's his shell. He's somewhere else. Iris's mouth feels as though it could almost curl into a laugh, but nothing's funny, not at all. She puts both hands over her face until the feeling passes.

Later, when Earth is watching, the Nyxians gather again in the cafeteria. This time, Elias's face is covered. Sean makes a short speech – it turns out that he was his roommate. Iris didn't know this. She didn't know him at all. All the women cry. A few of the men do, too, but less dramatically. They're so lucky, thinks Iris, to be capable of such repression. But mostly she isn't thinking. She doesn't even listen to the speech. It sounds like a jumble of words, spoken in another room. She feels crazed and inconsolable, crying for more than just Elias, this man she didn't know, this father of her unborn child.

Iris imagines that millions of people on Earth are watching them live on the internet, with cathartic tears in their eyes. Crying over the death of a handsome man on another planet is easier than crying for themselves. Maybe his name is trending on Twitter. In San Diego, California, Elias's parents might also be watching, surrounded by family, weeping. And surely his mother would notice Iris, crouched in the cafeteria, covering her wet face.

'Who is that stupid girl?' she would shout. 'Why is she crying for my baby?'

28.
Things

Light rain, normal rain, torrential rain, falling from the sky, wetting her hair, soaking her clothes, making things grow.

It rains the day after Elias's funeral, but Iris doesn't get to feel it on her skin. She lies in bed, hearing it tap against the window. It sounds just the same as it did in London.

The moon. There was something so reassuring about it. It was always there: circular and white, waxing and waning.

Mona. Mona. Mona. Mona.

29.

All This Longing

Abby raises her head and narrows her eyes at Iris.

'Can I ask you a question?' she says.

Iris looks up from her tab. 'Of course.'

'Why did you come here?'

'Huh?'

It's Sunday evening. They're lying in the bottom bunk, top to toe. A month has passed since Elias died. Iris's belly has started to grow, but it's still hidden by her baggy clothes. In the northern hemisphere of Earth it's the height of summer – August. Those sweet, slow-moving weeks when nothing seems to happen.

'What kind of person moves to another fucking planet?'

Iris shakes her head. 'We've talked about this a million times.'

'Yeah, but have we been honest with each other? Not the same old, "Oh, I thought it would be such a great opportunity for mankind" bullshit.'

Iris doesn't say anything. There are so many things she doesn't tell Abby. There are things that Abby doesn't tell her, too.

'Were you, like, incredibly unhappy?' says Abby. 'Because I was.'

'Yeah.' Iris can feel tears pushing against her eyeballs. She blinks several times and opens her mouth, but she can't say it.

'What?'

She moves to the head of the bed and whispers in Abby's ear because it's the only way she can be sure that no one else will hear: 'I tried to kill myself, once.'

'Oh, wow.' Abby puts an arm around her. 'When?'

'It was . . . shit, it was twenty years ago. It doesn't feel that long.'

'But why? Why did you do it?'

Iris looks around the room. 'I – I can't talk about it.'

'Sure, Big Brother's always watching. You can tell me some other time.' She adds, under her breath, 'When we get out.'

'When we get out?'

'I found a way out.'

Iris looks around the room again, to check she hasn't missed anything. She can feel her heart beating all over her body. There's a sudden thickness in her throat. Abby's eyes lose their blankness for the first time in weeks. Her gaze is unwavering.

'That's impossible. There's no way home – you know that.'

'I'm not talking about going home. I'm talking about *going*. I found a window in the control room, when I was cleaning.' She speaks quietly, her lips barely moving, her face still.

'A window?'

Abby nods. 'A glass window, under the control panel. It had a handle. I opened it a bit, just for a second. I could feel the breeze.'

'No way.' Iris sits up straighter. She hasn't opened a window since she left Earth. None of them has. 'How did you not notice it before?'

'It's not in an obvious place. My ring fell out of my pocket and rolled under the desk. I got down on my knees to find it and crawled as far as I could go, under the controls. God, it was disgusting down there. So much dust and dead bugs – these huge blue flies. I'd never seen them before. I got covered in crap.'

'Gross.'

'I found my ring, but then I noticed –' Abby stops herself and lowers her voice. 'Right at the back, on the left, there was this tunnel. I crawled through it and at the end of that, there was the window.'

'Jesus.'

'I'm going to leave the Hub.'

Iris feels the same spasm in her stomach she felt when Elias went missing. She groans a little at the pain.

'You OK?' says Abby.

'But you'll die if you do that.'

'Some people think it's all fake, like *The Truman Show*. Maybe we're still on Earth.'

'And you believe that? Elias is dead. That was real.'

Abby sits up and stretches her arms over her head, a falsely relaxed movement, before lying down again, next to Iris.

'It's suicide.' Iris can feel Abby's tangy, hot breath on her mouth, as if they're lovers, about to kiss.

'I can't stay. I can't, Iris.'

They breathe into each other's mouths. Iris strokes Abby's face, taking in her freckles, her large brown eyes – trying to remember them, to keep her in her mind. They've slept in this room every night for seven years. They've eaten every terrible meal together. They've listened to each other masturbating in the dark, and pretended they couldn't hear.

'Come with me,' says Abby. 'We'll do it together.'

'I can't do that.'

'You'd rather live your whole life like this? That could be another fifty years. Fifty years of being told what to do, when to eat, when to go to bed.'

'We chose this.'

'I know, but *why* did we choose it? I don't even remember.'

✳

Iris wakes up feeling sick again. In a rush to get up, she jumps from the top bunk to the floor, landing awkwardly on her feet.

'Ow,' she whispers, 'fuck.'

In the dark, she staggers to the bathroom and pukes into a toilet. There's no one else around – it's too early. If she were on Earth, the sun wouldn't even be up. Abby sleeps through the whole thing. Afterwards, Iris climbs back to her bunk, feeling weak. I know what would make me feel better, she thinks. The breeze against my face. A lungful of fresh air. She adds them to her list of things she misses: wind, air. She remembers a weekend on Earth, many years ago, when she visited Eastbourne with an ex-boyfriend, the one before Eddie. One night, as they walked on the seafront from a pub to the B&B, the wind went 'Wooooo!' and pulled Iris's hair up high on her head. They both laughed, even as they were battered with rain. Once they were inside, in their warm, dry room, they kicked off their wet clothes and went to bed. His name was Sam. They were only together for six months. She had almost forgotten about him.

Iris would do anything for a slight breeze, like the one that brushed her face when she opened her bedroom window in Clapton. She would do anything to see the tree that lived outside, the one that sprouted blossoms every spring. Jesus, she thinks. All this longing for unreachable things.

She lies with her eyes open in the dark, listening to Abby's heavy breathing.

'Don't go,' she whispers. 'Please don't leave me.'

Still sleeping, Abby says, '*Shhhh.*'

30

Do People Still Care about Kim Kardashian?

The room is bare, aside from a plastic chair and a large screen on the wall, currently blank. Iris sits alone, feeling jittery, waiting for her annual psychological check-up – the only time she ever speaks to Earth. The speakers go *Ding!* and a woman with big blonde hair appears on the screen, her head and shoulders against a white background. She wears heavy make-up and a blue blazer. Iris feels ecstatic – she's meeting a new person, an adult human being, for the first time this year.

'Hi, Iris,' says the woman. 'My name is Rachel Kern. How are you?' She has one of those flat American accents that turns 'you' into *'yeaow'*.

'I'm fine, and you?'

'I'm good,' says Rachel, in a flat, mechanical tone. 'Thanks so much for talking to me.'

'No problem.'

'Can you s–s–see me?' Rachel's face freezes and splits into shards and pixels. Her mouth becomes a black hole.

'No, the connection's gone.' Iris starts counting to twenty: 'One, two, three . . .' This is what the control room advises: if the connection fails, sit tight and count to twenty. She keeps her eyes on the frozen, distorted image of this stranger in Los Angeles, the last city she visited on Earth.

'. . . four, five, six . . .'

It had been her first time in LA, as well as her last. She spent three days sightseeing alone, before going to the training camp in the desert.

'. . . seven, eight, nine . . .'

They were three of the best days of her life. She ate all of the city's famous tacos, hot dogs and cheeseburgers. She went to Venice Beach, swam in the sea and fell in love with the tall palm trees and the hazy light, like something from a dream or an advert. The jet lag made those days seem even softer and more indistinct.

'. . . ten, eleven, twelve . . .'

But then the three days ended. As Iris waited outside her hotel for the cab to pick her up, she realized that she would rather spend a few more days exploring LA than go to the desert. Afterwards, she could catch a bus to another city, then another, and never stop. She could call Nyx Inc, send them an email and cancel the whole thing, but damn it, it would've been too embarrassing for words. She wasn't a quitter.

'. . . thirteen, fourteen –'

The pixels melt back together. Rachel reappears.

'Can you see me?' she says.

'I can now.'

Iris can also see herself in a smaller window at the bottom of the screen – her pale face, her grey top, the metal wall behind her. Everything here is so plain and simple, in contrast to Rachel's garish make-up and big hair.

'How are you feeling, Iris?'

'I'm fine.'

'How would you describe your mood?'

'Good.' Iris rubs her eyes. 'I'm tired, but I feel fine.'

It isn't a lie. Something has shifted in her. She still misses Earth. She would still do anything to go back. She still wants to eat a medium-rare steak, still wants to go swimming with her sister, to see the moon and stars, to sleep in her old bedroom with Kiran close by. But beneath all this yearning, there's a new undercurrent of hope and serenity. It's clearly irrational, but that doesn't detract from how good it feels. Is it just the hormones, helping her to stay alive and well? If she'd known that this is how it would feel, she would've got pregnant years ago, on Earth.

'How are you feeling at the moment, about being on Nyx?'

'I feel OK about it.' Iris is so used to lying about her state of mind that it comes naturally. She doesn't think twice. 'I miss things about Earth, of course, but I'm still happy to be here.' She nods.

'No depressive thoughts, no suicidal ideation?'

'No.'

Under her thick make-up, Rachel looks tired, bored and surprisingly young. Iris wonders what her qualifications are, if she has any. She seems different from the previous psychologists – less engaged, somehow.

'Are you sleeping well?'

'Yes.'

Rachel looks down at something – perhaps her own tablet. 'Have you been sexually active since we last spoke to you?' She's reading from a script.

'No.' Iris exhales deeply. She thinks of Elias, wrapped in the white sheet. His closed eyes, his bluish mouth. A rush of heaviness comes over her. She bites her lip to distract herself. Say something – anything.

'How are things on Earth?'

Rachel furrows her brow. 'What do you mean?'

'I dunno.' She shrugs. 'Is there peace in the Middle East? Who's the prime minister of the UK? Do people still care about Kim Kardashian?'

Rachel laughs. She can't help herself. 'Wow.'

'And, like, what's in fashion now? Has Twitter gone dead, like Myspace did? Is everyone still becoming a vegan?' Iris doesn't say it, but she also thinks: Is my family OK? Has my mother died of repressed sadness? Did my prodigal sister fulfil her promise? More importantly, is she happy? Does she think of me?

'Iris,' says Rachel. 'You know that I can't –'

'I know. I can ask, though, can't I?'

'Of course. You can say whatever you want. This session is for *you*.'

'Sure.'

'How are you feeling, now that the seven-year anniversary is coming up?'

'It doesn't feel that different from six years. Sorry, I know that's not an interesting answer.'

'That's OK.' Rachel smiles. 'You don't have to be interesting. Not to me, anyway – just to the viewers.'

'I've heard they're not that interested, either,' says Iris. Her heart goes *boom*. The words slipped out. She hadn't meant to say them. 'I mean, that's the rumour.'

Rachel shakes her head. 'I can't talk to you about that.'

'Yeah, I know.' Iris leans in and tries to study Rachel's face. The connection isn't great. Her features are indistinct. 'I get it. People have been watching us for years. They're bored.'

'Um . . .' Rachel looks down at her notes and reads, in a whimsical, high voice, 'If you could go back in time, would you still leave Earth and live on Nyx?'

'It's kind of monotonous up here, but I wasn't that happy on Earth.'

'Really? Why?'

'I was amazingly depressed.' Iris closes her eyes. She didn't plan to say this, but what does it matter – now that she's pregnant, now that nobody's watching. When she opens her eyes, Rachel is staring out of the screen, blinking, her face stuck between expressions. 'I hated myself. I hated my life. That's why I came here.'

'So you lied on your application?'

'Yeah.'

Rachel takes a breath and runs her fingers through her hair. Iris notices that the bottom half of her scalp is shaved and tattooed with a swirling pattern. It seems incongruous with her TV anchor-style outfit. Fashion has evidently moved on. Iris doesn't understand it.

'Tell me more,' says Rachel.

'I was just sad. It's nothing special. I've always been that way.'

'Did you get any help?'

'No, I felt I could handle it myself.'

'Why did you think that?'

'I don't know. Because of my mother, maybe. She always handled everything herself. She didn't like talking about difficult things. Even my decision to come here – we barely discussed it. Who knows, maybe she watches me on the livestream every day.'

'But it's not running any more.'

'What?' Iris suddenly feels cold. The nausea returns. 'It's not running?'

'Oh, God.' Rachel covers her mouth with her hands. 'I said it without thinking. I wasn't supposed to talk to you about that. I'm sorry.'

'The livestream isn't running any more?'

'I can't talk about this.'

'What about the TV show? Is it still running?'

'I can't say anything.'

'Are we going to be cancelled?'

Rachel looks to her left. 'Hi,' she says to someone off-camera. 'I'll just be a minute.' She turns back. 'I need to go. Thanks so much for speaking to me.'

'Come on, you can't give me that information and not say anything else. When did it stop running? A long time ago?'

Rachel stares into the camera. 'I have to go.' Her eyes are wide and anxious. She reaches a hand forward and the screen goes blank.

The idea of the livestream has always been a comfort to Iris, the way God must be to other people – the knowledge that someone, somewhere, is always watching. She decides not to tell Abby, at least not for now. She doesn't want to lose her.

31.

No One Is Watching

One evening, over dinner, Abby bites her thumb. Rav nods, while Vitor pretends not to notice. Iris feels her heart lurch, but she doesn't say anything. They finish their last mouthfuls of the chewy meat substitute, take their plates to the counter and walk to Abby and Iris's room.

'Good evening, Ravinder and Vitor,' says Tara.

'I found a way out.'

'*Abby*,' says Iris.

'A way out?' says Rav.

'To Earth?' says Vitor, his eyes full of hope and disbelief.

'No, a way out of the Hub.' Abby glances at the window. Outside, everything is pink and still. 'I'm leaving.'

Vitor's face crumples. He presses his fingers to his eyes. 'What does that mean? You're going to kill yourself, Abby?'

She shrugs. 'You don't know that for sure. I'm going. I thought you guys should know, in case you want to come with me. Iris won't, so –'

'What do you want, a suicide pact?' says Rav.

'I don't care any more.'

Iris wants to tell them about the livestream shutting down, that no one is watching, but she's afraid of what they might do. It would push them over the edge. If the Nyxians don't exist on Earth, they might as well not exist at all.

'Count me out.' Rav holds his hands up.

'Seriously? You're not sick of this?'

'There's being sick of it and there's killing yourself.'

'I dunno,' says Vitor, quietly. 'Maybe it's worth the risk. I'll come with you.'

'Are you serious, V?' says Rav.

Iris puts a hand on her stomach. It's firm and warm with the heat of a brand-new, untarnished life. None of them has noticed her expanding belly.

'Iris?' says Vitor.

She shakes her head. 'No. I don't want to die. I . . .' She doesn't finish the sentence. She was going to tell them that her body is no longer her own, but it feels good to keep a secret, to have the baby to herself. The one thing that is hers alone.

Iris and Abby get under the covers and hold each other. They inhale the scent of sweat, skin and dirty hair. It soothes them, like children sniffing favourite old toys.

'We chose this,' says Abby. 'We have no one else to blame.'

Iris feels tears dripping onto the crown of her head, through her hair, to her scalp, wet and tickly.

'I miss my husband.'

'I'm sure he misses you, too.'

'I bet he remarried years ago. He probably has kids and a dog and a house – everything we nearly had. What's wrong with me? Why didn't I want it? He was such a good person.'

'It's OK not to want those things.'

'It's not OK to walk out on your life. *It's not OK.* We're bad people.'

'Shhhh.' Iris strokes Abby's head. She doesn't disagree, though.

'I'm losing it. I'm losing my mind.'

It's strange to be the one who hasn't lost hope – a new feeling. Iris likes it. It makes her feel strong. She holds Abby super-tight. She wishes she could squeeze their bodies together to become a single, heaving, breathing mass: Iris, Abby and the baby. Then they might be able to survive.

'You shouldn't go,' she says. 'I need you.'

Abby doesn't reply. Iris remembers standing with her family on a street in central London, waiting for her mother to say those words.

32.

Someone Is Watching

Iris dreams that she's making breakfast with Eleanor, Jack and Mona at their house in Tufnell Park. Jack and Mona are the same age they were when Iris left Earth, but Eleanor is younger – even younger than Iris – with peachy skin and a long plait. She wears the same white cotton nightgown she wore when she sang 'Silent Night' to Iris, and keeps reaching for her, patting her reassuringly. It feels natural, somehow, to be older than her mother.

Together, they toast the bread, butter it, fry the bacon and poach the eggs. Everything is slow and close-up, like one of those pornographic cooking programmes that are designed to make you hungry. No one talks. They're smiling peacefully and enjoying each other's company – more than they ever did in real life. The stodgy, salty smell of bacon and eggs, and delicate Earl Grey tea, fills the air. They lay the table and start to eat. God, it's delicious.

Someone is knocking on the glass door to the garden – *rat-a-tat-tat* – but when Iris turns, there's no one out there. She can hear a voice saying, faintly, 'Iris . . . Iris . . . Iris.' The garden is perfect and still, with green grass and red roses, like a CGI garden from a property brochure.

'Iris,' says Eleanor, 'I'm so glad you decided to come back to Earth.'

'Me too,' says Iris, and she genuinely means it. She looks around the table, nodding at each member of her family. What a relief. 'Thanks for having me back.'

'Of course, darling. This will always be your home.'

'I knew you'd come back,' says Mona, chewing some bread.

Out in the garden, dozens of birds begin to fly around,

crashing into the plants, singing like crazy. Shut up, thinks Iris. Let me concentrate on the crispy bacon salting my tongue, cracking between my teeth. She looks around the table at her family again. There's a Christmassy feeling in the air. They're so happy, their faces bright and rosy – even her mother's, which is usually colourless and translucent, like tracing paper – but outside the sun is shining and there's blossom on the trees. Is it winter or spring? It's hard to tell. The birds are too loud. Iris puts her hands over her ears. Shut up, shut up, shut up. Her family disappears and the kitchen fills with birds, flapping their wings, knocking things over, singing.

Iris opens her eyes. Oh, it's the bloody alarm-birds. The dead, recorded animals continue to sing. She sees the metal ceiling. Her mouth is full of saliva. She adds these to her list: bacon, eggs, butter, toast, tea – how did she forget tea? Then she closes her eyes and transports her mind back to Tufnell Park, to the butter melting on her tongue; the creamy, salted egg, dripping with hot yellow yolk. Her pretty young mother, dressed in white. Mona. She opens her eyes. But I'm here, she thinks. I always will be. What day of the week is it? Who knows, who cares. The walls feel closer together than usual. The image of the dream breakfast flashes in her mind again, but her family aren't smiling any more, not rosy-cheeked and glad, but gurning and sweaty, under harsh yellow lighting, like people in a soap opera. Iris laughs, even though she knows it's coming. All over her body, her hairs stand on end. Her skin feels cold to the touch. Her blood, her organs and her bones – they all know that someone is watching. Not someone on Earth, but here, on Nyx. It's been so long, but it's coming.

Go away, she thinks. I don't need you any more.

She tries to distract her mind by wondering what Mona looks like now. Her parents, she can more or less imagine – heavier, greyer, slower – but she can't picture Mona. People change so much between fourteen and twenty-one. They start to become themselves. She might have graduated from university by now.

Or did she rebel and skip university altogether? Unlikely. Has she been in love? Does she love women or men, or both, or neither? Does she still hate me? What is she doing with her life? This is pointless, thinks Iris, rubbing her eyes.

'Morning, Abs,' she says.

Abby doesn't reply.

'Still asleep?'

Silence. Iris looks over the side of her bed at the bottom bunk, but Abby isn't there. She must be in the bathroom. Her grey blanket is scrunched up and there's something sitting on top of it. A piece of paper, folded in two? She goes down the ladder, picks it up and unfolds it. It's a photograph of Abby and her husband, Joe, on their wedding day. It's weird to see Joe's face at last, after years of hearing about him. Iris realizes she doesn't know him at all. He's a stranger – stocky, with brown hair, pale skin and kind eyes. He wears a black suit and a kippah on his head. Abby is more recognizable – several years younger, plumper, darker and happier, wearing a modest white dress with lace sleeves. Both of them are full of joy, smiling wide with their American teeth. The photo is creased all over.

Iris waits a few more minutes, but her stomach is growling, so she goes to the cafeteria. She feels self-conscious walking in on her own, like a friendless kid at school, but thankfully Rav and Vitor are already there.

'*Bom dia*,' she says, sitting at the table.

'*Bom dia*,' says Vitor, looking up. 'Where's Abby?'

'I think she's showering.'

He cocks his head. Iris tries to look bland and unassuming.

'So what's for breakfast today?'

'Avocado on sourdough with smoked salmon,' says Rav.

'That's what I thought.'

Iris goes to the counter and brings back the usual: a slice of bread with protein spread, plus a small, soft pear. This makes her happy – they haven't had pears in a while. When she returns to the table, Vitor looks up, catches her eye and turns away, looking exhausted. His eyes are bloodshot, surrounded by creased, sallow skin. He stands up.

'Can I come see you later?' says Iris. 'I have a medical question.'

'Yeah, I'll be there all day.'

He leaves the cafeteria. Rav soon follows. Iris eats alone, saving the pear for last. She waves at Stella across the room, then picks up her tablet and sends Abby a message:

> Hey. Where are you?

While she waits for a reply, she takes a bite of the pear. Its sweet, ripe deliciousness catches her off guard. For a moment, she forgets about Abby. Damn, she thinks, I hardly ever ate pears on Earth. I should've had one every day. She takes another bite, closes her eyes and keeps it on her tongue as it dissolves, before swallowing the sugary pulp. She remembers Abby and silently counts to twenty, hoping that a reply will appear by the time she finishes. It doesn't appear. She finishes the pear.

Iris goes for a walk around the Hub, looking out of the windows – in the bedroom, the cafeteria, the living room, the corridors. If Abby escaped and was suffocated by the atmosphere, her body would be lying just outside, dead on the sand. But she's not there. Maybe they took her away before anyone could see. *They.* Maybe she held her breath and ran away from the Hub until she was out of sight. Was that even possible? Iris imagines Abby sprinting, her bare feet flicking sand into the air, hair flying, her lungs feeling like they could burst. Freedom. And then she remembers, for the first time in years, the gymnast Ella Williams, who swooped off a building in London like a wild, exotic bird.

On the way to her shift, Iris is stopped in the corridor by Maya, carrying a box of cleaning products. She looks wide-eyed and a little frantic.

'Have you seen Abby?' she says.

'No. You haven't seen her?'

'She hasn't shown up for her shift.'

'Yeah, I don't know where she is either.' I'm saying this too calmly, thinks Iris. I should be panicking. It's just the hormones, the hope and serenity, fooling her.

'OK, thanks,' says Maya. 'I have to go.' She walks away briskly, struggling to keep hold of her heavy box.

Would Abby leave without saying goodbye? thinks Iris. This can't be it.

For most of her shift, Iris doesn't mention Abby. The cameras would pick it up. She and Yuko clean the cafeteria floor on their hands and knees with disintegrating bits of cloth cut from old sweatshirts. They tie rags around their knees to stop them from hurting, but still they ache, like old women. The cleaning cloths are filthy, so nothing gets truly clean. The dirt just gets moved around, displaced. It gathers in dark corners, where no one can see it. Their hands become caked with grime. Every few minutes, they stand, stretch and grunt. Stella is older, so she gets the easier jobs – wiping down the tables, counters and chairs. Today, Norma is somewhere else, with her father.

During one of her stretches, Iris feels the baby move for the first time – a slight, balletic twist – and she yelps in surprise.

'You all right?' says Stella.

'Yeah.' Iris realizes she's rubbing her belly, and immediately stops – it would give her away. 'I, uh, hit my elbow.' She massages her right arm, unconvincingly. They get back to work.

Five minutes later, Stella whispers, 'Look at that.'

'What?' shouts Yuko from across the room.

'Shh!' Stella motions for them to come over to where she's standing, by the counter, and nods towards a corner of the room, near the ceiling. 'Look,' she whispers, 'that camera isn't filming.' The machine's LED is switched off. It's black where it should be red. 'That one, too.' Stella points at the next camera along.

'I've noticed a few others,' says Yuko. 'In the corridors and living room.'

'Why are we even whispering? If the cameras are broken, the microphones probably are, too.'

'I don't know,' says Iris, 'but now I feel too self-conscious to raise my voice.'

The other two laugh quietly in agreement.

In one of the bathrooms, they can talk more freely. Within a few minutes, all three of them are sitting on the floor with their backs to the walls, resting and chatting. Cleaning has always been exhausting, but it's getting worse as they age, as their muscles wither from malnutrition, as their rags fall apart and the cleaning products become ineffective. It would be easier to let the dirt thrive, to let it fester and destroy the Hub. This is what Iris thinks, anyway.

When she tells them that the livestream has been shut down, they widen their eyes, but their surprise is somewhat mild and jaded.

'It's only a matter of time before it's all over,' says Stella, rubbing her tired, blotchy face. 'Well, it was fun while it lasted.'

'Was it?' says Iris.

'Maybe not *fun*,' she concedes, 'but it was different. I have no regrets. Do you?'

They don't reply. Yuko looks pained, while Iris's regret is too gargantuan, too monstrous, to face. It's better to push it away, cover it up, make it small and manageable.

'I think Abby has left the Hub,' she says. 'I think she's dead.'

'No!' says Yuko, reaching for her. 'Why?'

'I haven't seen her all day. She's not replying to my messages.'

'Abby wouldn't do that, would she?'

'Yeah, I think she would.'

'You never know,' says Stella, 'she could just be hiding somewhere, like Elizabeth did.'

'Yeah, I suppose so.'

Iris and Yuko stand up and carry on cleaning. Iris can hear her own bones creaking, protesting, as she moves.

'If you don't mind, girls,' says Stella, 'I'm going to stay down here a bit longer. I'm so exhausted.'

'Of course we don't mind,' says Yuko.

The hairs in the shower are super-long. With her bare hand Iris swirls a cobweb of different-coloured strands into a little ball. This would disgust her on Earth; here it doesn't bother her at all. In fact, it feels kind of nice – soft and springy. She stands up and chucks it in the bin.

'What if she doesn't come back?' she says. 'What if she's gone for good?'

'But where the hell could she have gone?' says Stella.

'Out there,' says Iris, pointing at the window. The sun shines, soft and golden, on the pink sand. 'Do we even know what's out there?'

'Death,' says Stella.

'Yeah.'

'But you know what?' she adds. 'A quick death is better than a slow one.'

The three women agree that they have finished for the day, even though the bathroom is only marginally cleaner than it was before. It smells faintly of old piss, but it's OK – everyone's used to it. Iris's eyes droop with fatigue. She would like to take a long, hard nap, to dream about Earth and escape this planet for an hour or two, but first she has to see Vitor.

As they leave the bathroom, Stella says to her, 'You're looking good, Iris. You're glowing.' Her blue eyes are clear and bright, but there's sadness beneath the surface – something that can't be hidden.

'Thanks.'

The baby is fattening Iris up with optimism and love, even as she starves. Instinctively, her hand goes to her belly. Stella doesn't notice.

★

Vitor's consulting room is tiny, with two chairs, a sink and a bed with a thin mattress. There's no computer, no printer for prescriptions. Medication is doled out from a large plastic box, which Vitor is rifling through when Iris walks in.

'Hi,' he says, 'what's up?'

He probably thinks I can't sleep. He probably thinks I'm just feeling sad, I'm missing Earth and I want some pills. He's probably thinking, How am I going to tell her that we don't have any left?

Iris sits on one of the chairs. 'Weren't you supposed to go with her?'

'Huh?' Vitor raises his eyebrows. He's still standing with his hands in the box.

'With Abby.'

'Oh, shit. You think she's really gone?'

'I haven't seen her all day.'

'She never mentioned it to me again.'

'It's only been a few hours. That's not why I'm here.' She shifts in her seat. 'I have something to show you.' She lifts her sweatshirt and shows her pale, protruding stomach. 'It's been around four months, maybe longer. I'm not sure, to be honest.'

Vitor opens his mouth to say something, but stops himself.

'It was Elias. If that's what you were about to ask.'

'You had sex with Elias?' He almost looks impressed. If Elias weren't dead, Vitor might have congratulated her. But then his face changes. He closes his eyes and shakes his head. 'Oh my God, Iris.'

'You didn't notice?'

'No. I did think you looked different the other day, but . . . I didn't think it was anything.'

'Can you give me a test? I mean, I know I am, but I just want to be sure.'

Vitor finally sits on the other chair, and sighs. 'You should've come to me earlier. It's too late now.'

'Too late for what?'

He blinks, slowly. 'This isn't a good time to have a baby.'

'But I want it, V. I've never wanted anything so much.' She touches her belly. 'Can I have a test?'

'Of course, but I'll have to put it on your record.'

She shakes her head. 'I don't want them to know.'

'People will notice.'

'I don't care. They can notice when they notice.' She stands up and walks towards the door. 'You still haven't heard anything about Norman?'

'No, I –' He winces a little, rubbing his head.

'Are you OK?'

'Yeah. It's nothing, just a headache.' He stands up – her cue to leave.

Iris carries the test up her sleeve to the bathroom and pisses on it. As she waits, sitting on the toilet, she notices the best-before date on the packet – four years ago. Oh, well. When the result comes up and confirms what she already knows, she feels the purest joy she has felt in years – the kind she experienced at her birthday parties when she was a child. She doesn't remember much about the parties themselves, but she remembers the feeling of being special, chosen, the centre of attention. This is mine, all mine.

Later, she remembers that she, too, was once a cluster of cells, an embryo, a foetus, but more than that, a promise of love, growing inside her mother. Of course she has always known this, but not truly.

She wishes she could tell her mother, *I know how it feels, now.*

33

Call Me Maybe

Iris and Vitor eat lunch, mostly in silence. Rav is elsewhere. Iris takes a photo of her half-eaten fake-cheese sandwich and, beside it, a pale green pear. She doesn't know how they make the cheese and she doesn't really care. It looks like the kind you'd get in a cheeseburger on Earth – square and luridly yellow, but with none of the salty, fatty goodness. The sandwich looks even more unappetizing in the photo than in real life. She picks up the pear and photographs it against the window, to capture the pink landscape. Better.

A Nyx-grown pear – delicious and sweet 🍐 What are you eating for lunch today? #lifeonnyx #lunchinspace #health #selfcare #iriscohen

Are people still into 'self-care'? she thinks. Probably not. She wonders what the commenters are saying.

you poor souls

#prayfornyx

RIP :(

Something like that. She bites into the pear and almost gags with disappointment. It's watery and bland, with none of the sweetness of the one she ate a week ago. Did I dream it? she thinks. Does it even matter? She closes her eyes and tries to conjure up the taste of the previous pear: sugary and juicy, with a tang –

'What are you doing?' says Vitor.

'I'm imagining I'm eating something else.'

'Sounds like torture.'

'It's the only pleasure I have in life – allow it. Have you noticed,' she says, pointing towards the corners of the room, 'that none of the cameras are filming in here?'

'Yeah, I know.' He carries on eating, looking at his food, as if it doesn't bother him.

Iris spends a lot of time lying on Abby's bed, basking in the musty, pickled scent of her absent friend. She sends her countless messages.

> Hey

> Where are you?

> Are you dead?

> It doesn't feel like you're dead

> What's it supposed to feel like, tho?

> I haven't even cried yet

> Are you living in the sand dunes?

> Or by the lake? It looks nice over there

> I'm having a baby!

> Abby Abby Abby

Iris tries to remember their last conversation, but she can't. Since getting pregnant, she often forgets things: words, memories, names. What was the name of her boss at Freedom & Co – Andrea? No. She picks up Abby's wedding photo and studies it again. The Abby she didn't know. Earth Abby. She's freckled and luminous, thinking – no, *believing* – that she would spend her life with this kind-eyed man; that he was the answer, The One. But no, a person is never enough.

How does it feel to die? How does it feel to leave your body behind like an empty cardboard box? Did Abby regret it at the last moment? Did it hurt? Iris listens to the faint hum of air conditioning, the oxygen being pumped into the room. She squeezes her eyes together, willing herself to cry, but there's no one around to see her suffering, so she gives up.

'Same old Iris,' says a voice from the top bunk – a woman.

'Abby?'

No reply. Iris slaps herself on the face. Her cheek and palm both tingle. I'm not dreaming, she thinks. This is real. I've gone insane.

'Who are you?' she says. 'What do you want?'

The woman doesn't reply. Iris's heart pounds so hard she can hear it in her ears and feel it in her fingertips. She wants to hear the voice again, like a child lying in bed at night, terrified of monsters but willing them to exist.

In the afternoon, Iris cleans some rooms and posts pictures online – smiling selfies with Yuko and Stella, Norma looking extra cute.

While they're cleaning a bathroom, Yuko catches her humming a tune and says, 'What's that? I recognize it.'

Iris laughs. She hadn't realized she was humming.

'It's "Call Me Maybe" – do you remember it?'

'Yes, of course,' says Yuko.

They sing the chorus together and shimmy from side to side, doing the phone sign with their hands. It's OK to sing in the bathroom because there are no cameras or microphones, no royalties accrued. Norma claps her hands with glee and prances around them, showing her small white teeth. Stella doesn't join in – maybe she doesn't know the song or can't muster the energy, since everything is falling apart.

They clean for five more minutes before giving up out of boredom.

Iris is walking down a corridor when she hears the voice again.

'Look up,' it says. 'Look up, Iris.' It's the same voice as before – well spoken, a bit old-fashioned.

Iris looks up at one of the cameras and notices that its red light has gone out. She carries on walking, studying each camera that she passes. All of them are switched off. Nobody is watching.

Dinner is quite good – a vegetable curry that tastes more or less like something you would eat on Earth, though the portion would be suitable for a toddler and it's served with stale bread. Iris, Vitor and Rav eat quickly and retreat to Vitor and Rav's bedroom, which smells sour and skanky. It reminds her of Elias's room.

Tara the AI doesn't say anything when they walk in.

'Huh?' says Vitor. 'That's weird.' He lightly punches the loudspeaker with his fist.

'We need to talk about Abby,' says Iris.

'It's been a week,' says Rav.

How did time pass so quickly? Iris has been working too little and sleeping too much – always in Abby's bed, where she can smell her.

'We have to report it,' she says.

'I'm sure they already know,' says Vitor.

'But there hasn't been an announcement, there's been nothing. We can't just pretend that she's disappeared into thin air and that we're OK with it.'

'Why are you both looking at me?' says Vitor.

'Come on, Vitor, you have special privileges. Get us a meeting in the control room.'

'Norman isn't there.'

'So what? We'll speak to whoever's there.'

'OK.' He picks up his tab and taps it several times, requesting a meeting. 'This fucking thing. It barely works any more.' The tab pings. Vitor looks up at them, surprised. 'Oh. We can go see them.'

'Now?' says Iris.

'Yes – right now.'

The doors to the control room slide open three inches and then pause – a glitch – before someone shouts, from inside the room, 'You have to push 'em!' Vitor prises them open with his hands. Iris hasn't been in the room since the welcome tour, seven years ago. She feels thrilled and intimidated, unsure of how to behave, as if she's about to meet the Queen. The room looks much the same as it did before, but with a staleness acquired over the years. It's one of the oldest parts of the Hub. There are dozens of screens, covered in dust. Most of them are switched off. A couple of them are smashed. Four people sit facing the control panel, two men and two women. One of them is Amanda, who led the welcome tour. Iris hasn't seen her in years. She glances at them, smiles and returns to her work. A man in his forties with red hair spins on his chair to face them. He nods but doesn't smile. Iris has never seen him before.

'Are you Block G?' he says. He has an American accent. Iris recognizes his voice from announcements.

'Yes,' says Rav. 'Who are you?'

The other people turn as well, briefly, then continue hitting buttons, twisting knobs and tapping their fingers on their tabs.

'I'm Peter,' says the man.

'We've never met,' says Vitor.

'I'm the Hub's chief technician.'

'I know who you are. We've just never met.'

'Where's Norman?' says Iris.

Peter turns to her with a jolt, as if she's suddenly appeared in the room. He stands and walks towards her. His face is so still. It makes him seem imposing, despite his physical slightness.

'Norman is taking a break. Is that why you're here?' He stares vacantly into her eyes, as if he's thinking of something else.

'No, we're here about Abby,' says Vitor.

'The one who escaped?'

'Why haven't you made an announcement?' says Rav.

'We're planning to do that later.'

'Why are all these screens switched off?' says Iris.

Peter looks at her mildly. 'What's your name?'

'Iris.'

'Oh, yeah. You're the one who lied about your medical history.'

'I –'

'The screens just need to be fixed. It's nothing serious.'

'What about the cameras?' says Rav. 'How is the show still running if the cameras aren't working?'

Peter shakes his head and ignores the question. 'I'm afraid that your friend is dead. She left the Hub and suffocated in the atmosphere. You can organize a memorial, if you like.' On the surface he's still calm, but red patches are blooming on his face and neck.

'Where's her body?' says Iris.

'Oh.' Peter turns to one of his colleagues. 'Nancy, can you get the, uh?'

'Sure thing,' she says. Nancy is short and strong, with mousy hair. She looks like a police officer, someone who enjoys following orders. She reaches under the panel and brings over a small black plastic box.

Iris takes it. It's heavier than it looks. 'What is this?'

'Her ashes,' says Nancy.

'What am I supposed to do with them?'

Nancy shrugs. 'Whatever you like.'

'Thanks for calling by,' says Peter, smiling as if they had popped round for tea. He realizes this and rearranges his features into something more suitably mournful. 'I'm so sorry about your friend,' he adds, before turning back to the control panel, 'but we have a lot of work to do.'

'Has the show ended?' says Rav.

Peter sits on his chair, facing away from them. 'Forget about the goddamn show.'

'Are we going to die?' says Iris.

He turns back and laughs. His face is red and moist, like raw meat. 'What did you think you were signing up for? *Dancing with the* fucking *Stars*?'

34.

A Ghost? A Vision?

Iris lies on Abby's bunk, holding her ashes.

She whispers, 'We're going to die, we're going to die, we're going to die.' Then she corrects herself, rubs her belly and says, in a loud voice, 'Don't worry, baby. Everything's going to be just *fine.*'

Her skittering heartbeat tells the truth.

She taps a message on her tab and sends it to everyone in the Hub:

> Does anyone know the words to the Kaddish, the Jewish mourning prayer? I'm looking for someone to recite it at Abby's memorial. I would really appreciate it. Thank you x

Iris has heard the Kaddish recited just once in her life – not at a synagogue, but at a theatre in London, during the play *Angels in America*. She didn't understand a word of Aramaic, a dead language, but somehow her body did. Her hairs stood on end, her hands shook and she began to cry – profoundly, but quietly, so that Kiran wouldn't hear. She was grateful for the darkness of the theatre.

She lies back and waits for a response, absent-mindedly sniffing Abby's blanket, but her friend's smell has faded, replaced by her own humdrum rankness.

Jonah responds:

> I can do it. I remember most of it. I'm so sorry about Abby.

Iris writes back:

> It's OK if you don't remember all the words. Thank you x

As she hits 'send', she hears something shift on the top bunk, like a person turning in their sleep. Her skin prickles with fear.

'Hello?'

The voice begins to sing, from the top bunk, *'Silent night, holy night . . .'*

'No,' Iris whispers, 'no, no, no.' Her limbs go cold, she begins to sweat and her heart beats hard and fast, like a mad, galloping horse. 'What do you want from me?'

'All is calm, all is bright . . . Oh good, it finally worked. I'm here. I'll come down.' Someone moves around on the mattress above Iris's head. 'Sorry it took me so long. I was having, uh, technical issues. I haven't been dead for very long. Ha ha! This is all new to me.'

Iris closes her eyes and smacks herself on the head. 'Wake up,' she says, 'wake the fuck up.' When she opens her eyes, a pair of bare feet are walking down the ladder, followed by a body clad in a long white cotton nightgown. Iris pulls the blanket over her head. 'Please go away. Don't hurt me.'

The woman walks around the bed and stands over Iris. Through the blanket, Iris can see her vague, familiar shape.

'Please,' says Iris, closing her eyes again.

'I know this is all very strange, but of course I'm not going to hurt you, darling. Why would I do such a thing?'

Iris pulls the blanket from her face and inhales the stale, oxygenated air. A sense of calm envelops her when she sees her mother's worried face, her long plait, her smooth, blue-white skin. Her fear vanishes like smoke. Eternal Eleanor Cohen, thirty-one years old, the age she was when Robert died, younger than Iris is now.

'Mum, you look so real.'

'I *am* real.'

Iris sits up. 'Hey, I've gone insane,' she says, doing jazz hands. 'Woohoo, mad at last! What are you – a ghost? A vision?'

'I told you, Iris, I'm dead. I had cancer. They didn't catch it in time.'

'What kind of cancer?'

Her mother shakes her head. 'That's not why I'm here,' she says, primly. 'I don't want to talk about it.'

'Why?'

'Iris, I –'

'Wow, it really is you. Only you could be embarrassed about having cancer.'

'If you wanted to know how I died,' says Eleanor in a flat, patronizing tone, 'you should've stayed on Earth – then you would know.'

'I don't believe you.' Iris turns away and curls into a ball. Her mother sits on the edge of the mattress. Iris feels it dip. She can feel the heat of her mother's body, as though she is really here. 'How is this happening?'

'I don't know how it works. Does it matter?' Eleanor lays a hand on her head. Iris flinches, but her mother continues to lovingly stroke her greasy hair. 'Do you want me to sing to you, darling?'

'I'm not a child any more,' says Iris, though she very much wants it. 'You're getting it all wrong. You're nothing like my mother.'

Eleanor takes her hand away. She sounds like she's going to cry. Ghosts can cry? 'Iris, it's me. I've missed you so much.'

'You never said anything like that to me.'

'That doesn't mean I didn't feel it. I wasn't perfect, Iris. I never knew the right thing to say.'

'Why are you telling me this now? Why didn't you say this when I was on Earth?'

'Everything's easier when you're dead.'

'What were you –' The words stick in Iris's throat.

'What is it, darling?'

'You never called me "darling".'

'I did when you were a child.'

Iris swallows. 'What were you going to say to me, the last time I saw you?' she says quickly, then closes her eyes and waits. Tears stream from her face onto the dirty blanket. She wipes her nose with her hands. She feels like a deranged baby with no control over her emotions. If her mother answers her question, she might just die of sadness and regret, just like that: *pouf!* 'Wait,' she says, 'don't tell me. I don't want to know.'

'I –'

'Please, don't.' She turns to lie on her other side, facing Eleanor. 'I can't handle it.'

'Iris,' says Eleanor, smiling. 'We've missed you terribly.'

'You have?'

'Of course we have. You look lovely. So grown-up.'

'That's not something you'd say.'

'But I'm saying it now.'

'I look terrible. I know I look terrible. You're going to be a grandmother, by the way.'

'I know,' says Eleanor, before adding, 'but I'm already a grandmother.'

'What, Mona has a baby? Are you serious?'

Eleanor closes and opens her eyes, slowly. 'Yes, a son. A beautiful boy.'

'Is she OK? Did she go to university?'

'She took some time off. She's a wonderful mother, she really is. Do you need to know more than that? Do you want to know everything?'

Iris turns her head slightly, so she can't see the look on her mother's face. She hankers, suddenly, for not knowing; for imagining that Mona is really fine. So what if she had a baby young? People do it all the time.

'Maybe later,' she says.

'Fine, but think about it first. Think about what it would mean, to know what's going on over there.'

'On Earth?'

'Mona's fine – you don't need to worry.'

The ghost of Eleanor Cohen doesn't eat or drink, but for some reason she sleeps. She lies flat on her back on the top bunk, in her nightgown, with her hands resting on her stomach. After the lights go out, Iris says goodnight to her mother for the first time in years. She can't remember the last time they slept in the same room – perhaps it was their first night in Tufnell Park, when all the other rooms were full of boxes. Or was it because Iris was scared to be alone in a new house?

'Goodnight, Iris,' her mother murmured back then, just as she says it now. 'Sleep tight.'

Iris waits a few minutes until Eleanor's breathing becomes heavy above her. She breathes loudly, skittishly, as if panicked. Iris remembers that she always breathed like that in her sleep. Her mother drowns out the clinical hum of the Hub, for which Iris is grateful, though she can still hear the wind whipping sand against the window. Some kind of storm. It's been years since she last shared a room with someone other than Abby, even if it's someone who doesn't exist. She closes her eyes and falls asleep.

35.

Kaddish

They gather in the cafeteria the next day to remember Abby. It still doesn't feel like she's dead, but perhaps, Iris thinks, this is how mourning always feels. It's the first time that she has lost a friend to death, rather than to her own terrible behaviour, and it feels like a bad joke, as if Abby is hiding somewhere – under a bed, like Elizabeth – waiting to jump out and scream, 'Surprise!'

Iris stands on the podium – the same one Norman used to stand on, when he made his speeches – and scans the crowd. Almost the entire population of Nyx is here, give or take a few. Jonah is standing a couple of metres away, waiting for his turn. She almost regrets volunteering to speak. There are no drugs to help her cope with the attention. Peter and his team aren't here, and she's grateful for that, but there's no sign of her mother, either. When she woke up, Eleanor wasn't around. Iris can smell her own BO, spicy and pungent, permeated into her clothes. She'll never be clean again – not Earth-clean. She glances up at the cameras. Three of them are switched on. So they weren't broken after all – just turned off. Death is good for ratings.

The room quiets down, even though she hasn't made a signal to speak. She takes it as her cue.

'Hi, everyone,' she says, swallowing the last syllable.

'You'll be fine,' whispers Eleanor, into her ear.

Iris looks to her side. Her mother is there, standing next to her. She puts an arm around Iris and taps her back, reassuringly. She feels so real. Iris looks up at the crowd. They are in silence, waiting, their faces blank. They don't seem to have noticed the ghost.

'This isn't like work,' says her mother. 'They're not waiting for you to fail.'

How would Eleanor know how she felt about work? They rarely talked about it. Iris can feel her breath on her face, can even smell it – milky and warm.

'They can't see me. Don't worry.'

Iris clears her throat, and begins: 'Abby is – was – my best friend. I'm not sure if that's because we were thrown together into this strange situation or because she genuinely was my soulmate. I like to think that it was both. We were so lucky to find each other, to be roommates on Nyx.'

She stops and looks around. Around a hundred people are watching her, like a field of meerkats. Her mother's bony hand still rests on her shoulder, lightly.

'I can't believe she's gone. My life will never be the same again. She was the first person I spoke to in the morning; she was the last person I spoke to before closing my eyes at night.' She pauses, noticing that people are starting to whimper and cry. 'Abby was incredibly kind, generous and clever, and in many ways felt more like a sister than a friend. We knew each other so well that I find it hard to describe her. She was just Abby. She was important to me because I loved her. I loved her completely. I know she felt the same.'

Her voice is flat and calm.

'I didn't know Abby on Earth. I can't represent her as she was, there. I don't know what her favourite drink was, I don't know how she liked to dress, I don't know if she wore lipstick or perfume. These are all things that people might know, on Earth, about a friend. They were some of the ways in which we defined ourselves, down there. Her family and friends on Earth would have a lot more to say about the things she liked. I know that, like many of our families, they found it hard to accept Abby's decision to come here. And who could blame them? It was a crazy thing to do. But it seemed like a shortcut to an extraordinary life.'

Iris sees some people nodding and hears them go, 'Hmm.'

'I know about some of the things Abby missed. I miss many of them, too. Things we all took for granted, like sunshine and swimming and having a meal with your friends. Those things were often overshadowed by everything else on Earth. This is why Abby left the Hub, I think. She missed Earth too much.'

Iris hears a clear, high sound, like tinnitus, bearing down on the room, but she can sense that it is in her head.

Her mother whispers, 'You're doing so well.'

Iris nods. 'Jonah is going to say a prayer for Abby. It's called the Kaddish.'

There's a heavy silence as she steps down from the podium and is replaced by Jonah.

'Hi everyone,' he says. He holds up a rag – a circle of grey material, cut from a sweatshirt – and places it on the crown of his head. 'I haven't done this in a long time, so I might forget the words. No, I *will* forget the words. When I pause and nod, please can you say "Amen"? I know most of you aren't Jewish or don't believe in God, but please do it anyway, if you can.'

Abby herself had lost her faith a long time ago, before she left Earth. It doesn't matter. She would have wanted this. The high sound in the room has morphed into a low buzz, like the air conditioning at Freedom & Co. Iris thinks of her desk there, piled with pieces of paper, of Eddie next to her, with his impish smile and blue eyes. She can't remember the bad feelings. They have shrunk over the years. Life was both simpler and more complicated, back when the future was unknown. What happened to Eddie?

'Listen,' says her mother, as if she can read her mind. She holds on to Iris's hand.

Of course she can read my mind, thinks Iris. She's my hallucination.

Jonah takes a breath and begins to sing, in a wavering, minor-key voice:

Yitgadal v'yitkadash sh'mei raba.
B'alma di v'ra chirutei,
v'yamlich malchutei –

'Um, wait a second,' he says, 'OK.'

– b'chayeichon uv'yomeichon
uv'chayei d'chol beit Yisrael,
baagala uviz'man kariv. V'im'ru –

Jonah pauses and nods. His face is damp and flushed with the stress of remembering.

Thirty or so people say, 'Amen.'

Y'hei sh'mei raba m'varach
l'alam ul'almei almaya.
Yitbarach v'yishtabach v'yitpaar
v'yitromam v'yitnasei,
v'yit'hadar v'yitaleh v'yit'halal . . .

To Iris, it's just gobbledegook; the ancient gobbledegook of her long-lost father. It reminds her of the Lord's Prayer she learned by heart at school. She didn't believe a word, but she always enjoyed reciting it.

'Um . . .' Jonah looks at the floor, moving his head from side to side, trying to shake the words out, but they won't come. Instead, he skips several lines, but nobody notices. Sweat is dripping from his hairline, down the sides of his face. 'OK,' he says, and continues to sing:

Oseh shalom bimromav,
Hu yaaseh shalom aleinu,
v'al kol Yisrael. V'im'ru –

He pauses and nods. Everyone says, 'Amen.'

36.

The Ecstasy of Approaching Death

Iris lies in bed. Her stomach groans. Their meals are smaller every day. Better to live on air alone. Hunger makes her feel sad and helpless, yet exultant and energized, all at once. She remembers a brief internet craze, several years before she left Earth, of attractive young women sharing photos of themselves looking thin and ecstatic, preparing colourful, low-calorie meals with esoteric ingredients. This must be how they felt: thin, saintly and unencumbered. In her early twenties, Iris wasted hundreds of hours looking at those women, tapping her thumb on their hashtags – #eatclean, #wellness, #yum – thinking they were morons, but also wondering if their souls were purer than hers. Now, she feels as pure and clear as an icicle. A martyr. The ecstasy of approaching death, the end of things – perhaps that's what those women were feeling.

But when Iris remembers the baby, thoughts of martyrdom evaporate. This isn't the end. She forces herself out of bed and goes to the cafeteria.

She wishes she could speak to Mona, just once.

The cleaners mostly work in silence, out of respect for Abby.

Stella says to Iris, 'Your speech was really special. The prayer, too. I didn't understand it, but it sounded nice.'

'It did, didn't it.' Iris's stomach rumbles. Breakfast wasn't enough. She puts her hand under her sweatshirt and tries to massage away the hunger. Her belly is round and hard, like a ball, but easily hidden. She has developed a way of walking hunched over, so that it doesn't stick out. Or maybe everyone's noticed and hasn't said anything.

'You're hungry, huh?' says Stella.

'Yeah.'

'Me, too.'

After a tiny lunch, Iris lies in bed again, feeling depleted. The hunger pangs have gone for now, but the emptiness remains. She cried for Elias, she cried for her mother's ghost, but she still hasn't cried for Abby. Her death doesn't feel real – it's as if she's just on annual leave. *Limited access to email, but you can text me if it's urgent!* Iris holds the box containing Abby's ashes, shakes it and listens to the remnants of her friend, rustling like sugar.

'Is this you?' she says. 'It doesn't sound like you.'

She takes a picture of Abby's wedding photo and writes:

In memory of our dear friend Abigail Johnson, pictured here on her wedding day in San Francisco, on Earth. We love you, Abby 🖤 #iriscohen

She writes the hashtags #lifeonnyx, #outerspace, #RIP and #inmemoriam, before deleting them and hitting 'send'. Five seconds later, a red cross appears. Huh. She tries to resend it. Red cross again. Either the app isn't working or her post was rejected.

She looks out of the window at the pink wilderness and the lake in the distance. The air shimmers in the heat, just like it did on Earth, on hot days. Iris never understood the physics of it; she never bothered to look it up. Outside the Hub, it seems to be shimmering in one particular place – a circle of dancing light, hovering in the air. Iris hears a noise outside, like a frantic, muffled voice. The circle continues to glow – angrily, faster. She looks away.

I'm just seeing things.

Her eyes are getting heavy. What day of the week is it? What month, what year, what decade? It's the constant daylight, meddling with her sense of time. Her bedroom window blacks out every evening, but she hasn't seen a sunset in seven years. It has been one long, never-ending day. Does that mean I'm still twenty-nine? she thinks. Yes, even as my body continues to age, I'll be twenty-nine for ever. She checks her tab. It's Friday, 25 September.

Her tab beeps. It's Rav.

> Vitor's gone. Can't find him anywhere

She's too tired to be surprised, too buoyed by the hormones in her body. She thinks of the foetus pulsing inside her, the first person in the universe who truly needs her. A skull, a spine, hands and feet, a brain. Eyes that have never cried. A tiny pink tongue.

Iris doesn't want to die, not even a bit.

37.

The Missing

Rav leaves the next day without saying goodbye. It's so unlike him, Iris thinks, but perhaps she didn't know him at all. Two days later, Stella disappears. Then Yuko, with Carlos and little Norma. All of them gone, within a few days. All of her close friends. Other people follow.

The Hub should be surrounded by dead bodies, but it isn't. Perhaps everyone melted into the air as soon as they left. Though the pink sand looks more disturbed than usual because of all the footprints – like a beach in the summer.

News about the missing spreads through word of mouth – whispers in the cafeteria, carried from table to table. Messages via their tabs. All the technicians have left. Norman must have gone, too. Perhaps he was the first to leave. Most of the kitchen staff have disappeared, so other people take over, cobbling together whatever they can. Several Nyxians find themselves eating alone, because all their friends have gone. For a few days they appreciate the novelty of eating, chewing and swallowing in silence. But then they realize that this makes the food taste even worse. A bland Nyxian apple is twice improved by conversation.

Three weeks have passed since Abby's memorial service, but it feels like ten years. They don't talk about her any more. People leave every day. There are no more memorials.

★

Iris doesn't cry over any of the missing. She feels cut off from reality. She wonders if this is how her grandfather Otto, Robert's father, felt at Auschwitz. No, he must have felt miserably, utterly alive. By comparison, this is nothing. This is of my own making.

Nobody cleans any more. The social media app still isn't working, so Iris gives that up, too. Nearly everyone stops doing their chores. The Hub becomes coated in a thick layer of dust and grease. Iris touches the walls and leaves black smudges. When she walks past the farm, she can see through a window that the crops have drooped and yellowed.

She starts to find dead insects scattered about. They are pearlescent blue, two or three inches long. Natives of Nyx – perhaps they can't survive in the oxygenated Hub. 'Insect' is the wrong word, since they have five pairs of legs. They must be the ones Abby was talking about, when she first discovered the way out. Iris has never seen one outside the Hub, through a window. Not once, in seven years.

She spends a lot of time wandering around aimlessly, talking to people she never got to know very well. They gently ask her, with a touch of horror in their eyes, 'You're not . . . pregnant, are you?' Iris tells them that she is, indeed. None of them knows how to respond. A few people say 'Congratulations' and then blush, embarrassed.

One night, she thinks she hears someone walking outside the Hub. She gets up and puts her ear to the blacked-out window. She can't see outside. The blackout is automated; she has no control over it.

'Hello? Who is it?'

Iris hears a voice, unmistakably human, but she can't make out any words through the thick glass and metal. 'Uh-uh-uh-uh.' It sounds like a woman.

'I can't hear you,' says Iris. 'I can't hear you, I'm sorry!'

The person stops speaking. Did she run out of oxygen and die? Iris stays at the window, sitting on Abby's bunk, for two hours, till the blackout lifts halfway at 6 a.m., Central Standard Time. There's no one there. There's no body.

Iris makes new friends. One of these is Maya. They talk for hours about the men they loved on Earth, mildly aroused by their own descriptions of various shoulders, arms, eyes and sexual techniques, and revelling in the warm buzz of a brand-new friendship. The two women start living together in Maya's room, in Block Q. Iris sleeps on the top bunk, just as she did in Block G. When she wakes briefly in the night, half dreaming, her brain tricks her into thinking she can hear Abby's breathing. Such sweetness.

Someone breaks the door down to the control quarters. There's nobody in there. Iris and Maya wander from room to room. Abby was right – it's nothing special. A few dark, dingy bedrooms. An open-plan living room and cafeteria. In the men's bathroom, someone has written 'FUCK YOU' on the wall, in shit.

One morning, she wakes to find that Maya has left. Iris returns to Block G.

Her tab stops working. She loses track of the days. If she had a pen, she would record them with tally marks on her arms. At first she asks other people, but then she stops. It's nice not to know. It reminds her of being a kid during the summer holidays, when she seemed to exist outside time. Who cares what day it is on Earth?

It is . . . November-ish.

One afternoon, there's a message on the cafeteria door written in a black, dripping substance: 'No lunch today.'

There are thirty-three people left. The figure is exact because Sean keeps a list on his tab – one of the few that are still working. Every time a Nyxian goes missing, someone tells Sean and he adds another name. This nod towards bureaucracy has a calming effect over the Nyxians. Lists are a sign that everything is in order – or, at least, something is.

Iris's tracksuit hangs off her shoulders and hips, while clinging to her belly. Not enough farmers, not enough cooks. The baby sucks all the nutrients out of her. My dear little parasite, you'll be the end of me.

Two days later: 'No breakfast.' Iris goes in anyway, because she can see half a dozen people through the door, milling around, sitting at tables. She sits next to Sean and Jonah.

'Hey, Iris,' says Sean. 'You all right?'

His breath smells foggy and rancid from hunger. Iris tries not to gag. Sean rolls up his sleeves, showing his jumble of old tattoos: mermaids, skulls and roses. One of them says, in smudged green letters, 'Free Ireland'. She never noticed that one before. It looks homemade. She wonders if he's ever been to Ireland.

'I'm so fucking hungry,' she says.

'Try the farm,' says Jonah. 'I've just been walking in and eating whatever I can find.'

Iris looks at Sean. Officially, he's still the head gardener.

He nods. 'Knock yourself out.'

'But my wristband won't let me in.'

'Oh, it will.'

The door to the farm opens easily. Inside, everything is wilting. The sun is warm and delicious, magnified by glass, and the air is heavy and damp. Iris closes her eyes and enjoys the heat on her face. Then she walks among the dying produce: fallen fruit, greenery gone brown, everything close to death. Her stomach rumbles with hunger and her baby kicks, flooding her with love and desperation, a sickly warmth that spreads through her torso to her hands and feet. It's the same feeling she had when she was in love with Edie Dalton. What's Edie doing now? The baby kicks again. *Who gives a shit?* it seems to say. *Eat something, for God's sake!* Iris thinks about a bloody steak covered in salty, creamy Béarnaise sauce. The baby stops kicking and enjoys the mutual reverie.

A bright red dot stands out against the decay. Iris walks overs and bends down. It's a tiny strawberry, an inch long, dotted with yellow seeds, just like the ones in good old England. She pops it off the plant. On Earth it would be mediocre, but here it's sweet enough. She carries on like this, eating random bits and bobs, never fully satisfied, until she is too tired from crawling on the ground.

At least once a day she thinks: Where is my goddamn mother?

Iris thinks Norman is dead, but Jonah and Sean disagree. They reckon Norman is still in the Hub, hiding somewhere.

'He's one of those noble captain types,' says Jonah. 'He'll go down with the ship.'

'Like that Dido song,' says Sean.

'Yeah.'

The two men sing the chorus in a strangled, high-pitched tone. Iris has never liked this song, but she enjoys hearing them sing. Nobody is watching, so they can flout all the rules and sing all the songs they like.

Sean stops. 'Holy shit. Look at that.'

He points at the air. One of the blue bugs flies past, very much alive, sparkling with light and buzzing like a tiny chainsaw.

The control room is empty whenever Iris passes it, but some-how the Hub is still working, the lights switching on and off, the oxygen pumping, water running, keeping them alive. These processes will cease when the Hub falls apart or when the sun stops shining or when someone hits the 'off' switch, if there is such a switch – whichever comes first.

Iris begins to see the fire-bugs on a daily basis, alive and crackling. She takes them as a good sign.

Sean goes missing. No one takes over his list.

38.

Tweet-Tweet-Twoo

Iris dreams that she is lying in bed, weak with hunger and cradling her enormous belly. Her tab beeps. It's a message from her sister.

> Hey Iris, how are you? xx

Dream-Iris is too happy to wonder how the message got through. Mona's love pulled the words from London to the Pacific Ocean, through the wormhole, to Nyx, to the Hub, to Iris's broken tab. *Beep!* She immediately calls her sister. Mona appears on the screen, sitting in front of a window. The sky is bright and white behind her, shadowing her features. The awful, glorious London sky. Mona wears a green sweatshirt and glasses, half her hair pinned back. She's still a child.

'I'm so sorry,' says Iris.

'For what?' says Mona, mildly.

'For being a selfish cunt.' She begins to cry. 'It was a mistake. You were right. I miss Earth so much. I miss all of you, so much.' Her face is wet with salty tears and snot. 'What's wrong with me? Am I a monster?'

'No, you're my dear sister.'

Iris opens her mouth to speak, but nothing comes out. She is swamped by a wave of love so large and powerful, it feels as though it could stop her heart.

'I forgive you,' says Mona. 'I love you. We all do. We love you very much.' She wears a blissful, affectionate smile.

'I wish I could meet your son. I don't even know his name.'

'It's –'

'Tweet-tweet-twoo!' sing the alarm-birds.

'No!' says Iris. 'I have something else to tell you.'

Mona continues smiling as the screen gradually fades to black. 'What is it?' Her face disappears.

'Tweet-tweet-twoo!'

Iris opens her eyes.

Hunger moves beyond the pain barrier. For a couple of days Iris feels clean and free, as if the need to eat had been a shackle, weighing her down. She goes to the farm, lets the sun shine on her face and wonders whether she could live on light and water alone, like a plant. She feels ecstatic and deranged. The baby kicks and the pain returns. She realizes she isn't alone – Jonah is combing through half-dead plants at the other end of the farm.

They nod at each other and shout, 'Hey!'

Iris pulls a half-grown potato out of the ground and eats it, raw and muddy – not too bad – and then munches a few random, bitter leaves. As she rakes the ground with her fingers, looking for more potatoes, she remembers eating a 'chocolate soil' dessert at a restaurant in London: crumbs of cake with crystals of sea salt, served on a garden trowel. It was so dumb, so delicious. She takes a crumb of soil between finger and thumb, checks Jonah isn't looking, and places it on the tip of her tongue. It melts in her mouth, just like it did on Earth. She takes a fistful, gulps it down, and wipes her face with her filthy sleeves.

'What are you doing?'

Iris looks up. It's her mother, standing over her and shaking her head, still barefoot, in her white nightgown.

'Mum!' Iris smiles, her face dirty like a child's.

Eleanor gestures at the ground. 'Has it come to this, darling – eating mud?'

'No, it just looks like mud. Where have you been?'

'There was some kind of . . . glitch.' Eleanor bends down, takes a fistful of soil in her pale, bluish hand and lets it fall to the ground. 'It's soil. You're imagining things.'

'I'm imagining *you*,' says Iris, laughing.

'Iris,' says Jonah, from the other side of the farm. 'Who are you talking to?'

'No one! Just talking to myself.'

'Oh, OK.'

Dignity. Always dignity.

Iris sleeps as much as she can, at odd hours, like a cat, because it makes hunger easier to cope with. When her body can't sleep any longer, she haunts the empty corridors and rooms of the Hub, sometimes with her mother by her side, though she comes and goes. They don't talk much. They just walk. The hem of Eleanor's nightgown becomes grubby with dirt; the soles of her feet are almost black. There are grains of pink sand everywhere, piling in corners, spiking Iris's face on her pillow. More fire-bugs, buzzing around. In the cafeteria, she sees something move from the corner of her eye. When she turns, an animal the size of a chihuahua scurries behind the counter – a shiny red blur, too quick to see. She runs after it, but it's gone. Again, she wonders: Why have I never seen these creatures through the windows? Have I not been looking hard enough?

The outside is coming inside. The real Nyx, not this poor simulacrum of Earth.

At night, she hears distant sex sounds – laughing, sighing, moaning, teetering between agony and pleasure. It makes her smile, the idea that imminent death hasn't entirely destroyed everyone's spirits.

She looks through a window at the ruins of Hub 2. Its walls have now fallen and are buried in sand. Just the black frame still stands. A scrap of plastic hangs from the frame, flapping in the breeze. She envies the scrap. She wishes she could go outside, feel the wind on her face, and not die.

Her arms, in the mirror, are like stalks in contrast to the luscious roundness of her belly. Maybe the little parasite will survive, she thinks, even if I don't. Maybe she will crawl out of my vagina while I'm dying and be adopted by an alien – one of those red chihuahua things. They will keep her safe, like the wolves in *The Jungle Book*. Maybe she will be happier with them. Maybe, maybe, maybe.

For some reason, she assumes that the baby is a girl.

All the cameras are off. Iris checks each one as she passes. No one is watching. When she ceases to exist, no one on Earth will know. Does it matter? She's already dead to them. She ceased to exist seven years ago. They've probably mourned and grieved and got over it. Though she still wishes she could talk to her sister. What would she say? 'Life is worth living, yada yada yada. I love you.'

Millions of people are starving on Earth. People are fighting wars and dying for their idiotic countries. People are drinking champagne in hotel rooms, getting married and making love. People are learning to walk and talk; learning to shit in a toilet. People are standing on bridges and thinking of jumping. Poor old Earth.

If Iris were there, she would walk away from the bridge, catch a bus to Clapton, slump into bed, under the duvet, and listen to the radio – the same old voices debating the same old issues. No, it would be a Sunday. On Sundays she listens to the music station. They're playing a song she's never heard before – something gorgeous and melancholic from Brazil, Mali or Angola, somewhere she's never been. She can't understand the words, but they seem full of yearning. A car goes past. The birds sing. Kiran is sleeping in the next room. Her phone beeps.

> **Eddie: Morning, beautiful. Hungry? Brunch?**

> **Iris: Yesssssss xxx**

✳

Iris doesn't see anyone for two days. A dream fulfilled. She is alone. She wants to lie in the centre of a car-free Oxford Circus, inhaling the pollution, then go to Topshop to buy a dress. She wants to see twenty pretty silver horses trot through Grosvenor Square. She wants to free the animals from London Zoo, so that tigers, giraffes, tarantulas and gorillas can take a walk down Regent's Canal. She wants to see the sunset from Parliament Hill and then roll on her side from the top to the bottom, like she did when she was a child. She wants to stroll through the secret Edwardian pergola in Golders Hill Park, near where she lived when she had a father. With the gardeners all gone, the vines and flowers would grow around the structure, engulfing it in soft, colourful, fragrant walls. They would think: Ahhh, our time is now.

Perhaps in two hundred years, when Earth is finally ravaged by its inhabitants, humans will make another attempt to colonize Nyx. Maybe they'll find Iris and her baby buried in the pink sand, rubbed away to skeletons, one inside the other like Russian dolls. A mother and her unborn child. How sad and fascinating! It will be like when those terrified corpses were discovered in Pompeii, cast in volcanic ash. Perhaps their skeletons will be displayed at a museum – the first one on Nyx.

No, this isn't our time, thinks Iris. We won't end up in a

museum. My baby will be born. She will survive, just like the babies who were born on Earth before doctors, midwives and hospitals existed. She will never see Earth, but she will live. She will never eat a cheeseburger and fries, a pizza, a curry, a lamb shawarma with pickles, a steak, fresh pasta, oysters or even a boiled egg with salt – even that was heaven itself. She will know other things. She will live.

39.

This Is Where It Ends

In the middle of the night, Iris stands in her bedroom looking out of the window. The blackout has stopped working, so she can see outside. The sun is bright and soft, like always. She doesn't know what time it is, but the shape and feel of her exhaustion seems 4 a.m.-ish. That means it's also 4 a.m.-ish in Chicago, Mexico City, the Galapagos Islands and Belize. Most people in those places are sleeping now. Maybe not the animals in the Galapagos, but they're not people. Iris looks out at the scenery and clicks her bare, dirty heels.

'There's no place like home,' she says. 'There's no place like home.'

'That won't work,' says her mother, standing behind her. 'This isn't a film.'

Iris presses her nose against the glass. 'I'm going to walk to the lake.'

'That sounds dangerous.'

'It's dangerous in here.'

'You should think of your child.'

Iris turns to face Eleanor. 'You should've thought of *your* child.'

'I thought of you a million times a day.'

Iris turns back to the window, to the pink sand. 'I came here because I wanted to be reborn, but I just carried on living.' She rests her hand on her belly. 'Maybe it's time to live out there.'

Her mother says nothing.

'I should go,' says Iris.

'Do you forgive me?'

Iris turns. There are new wrinkles on her mother's face. She still wears her nightgown and plait, but her skin is papery and thin, like it was when Iris left Earth.

'Forgive you for what?'

'For not being a better mother.'

'It doesn't make sense, forgiving my hallucination. It would be like forgiving myself for something I didn't do.'

'What if I'm not a hallucination? What if it's really me?'

'Yeah, of course, but only if you can forgive me for leaving.'

Her mother doesn't reply, but she smiles. Perhaps she doesn't forgive her, but that's all right. Iris can handle it. Eleanor holds her arms wide. They hug. Iris can smell her mother's clean, grassy shampoo, the one she used back then, when Robert died. Everything had ended – her marriage, her family – but Eleanor still managed to wash her hair, she washed her daughter's hair, she fed her and took her to school, went to work and made money and paid the bills, even as she disappeared, bit by bit.

Eleanor touches Iris's cheek and kisses it. 'Goodbye, Iris.'

'Bye, Mum.'

'I love you.'

Iris blinks and she's gone. The smell of shampoo lingers. She fills her lungs with it.

She puts her shoes on, leaves the room and goes for a wander, saying her silent goodbyes to the Hub. Seven years – that's as long as she spent at St Peter's Girls' School. The windowless corridors are dimly illuminated, but the rest of the Hub is flooded with sunlight. Iris walks slowly. No one is watching her. Not in Chicago, Lima, Moscow or Bangkok. Not in London, nor at the Nyx Inc headquarters in Los Angeles. The cameras are off; the TV show is history. The Wikipedia page was probably updated a while ago: 'Life on Nyx was an American reality TV show.' Was, not is. Iris wonders whether the date of her death has already been written on the internet. Iris Cohen was a British reality TV star. She was born, she lived, she died on another planet.

250

She can still hear the hum of electricity, the Hub's mysterious processes. How much longer will it run for? Since it's solar-powered, perhaps for ever. No – human creations don't last as long as stars, moons and planets. The Hub will disintegrate, through lack of use. All the walls will eventually fall down. Alien moss and mould will grow in the Nyxians' dirty sheets. By the time humans return to the planet, there will be complex ecosystems thriving in the building. The Hub will have taken on a faded grandeur, like those ruins in Detroit everyone went crazy for. Oh, what dreams they had, when they built this opulent theatre, this proud mansion, this state-of-the-art human colony on another planet. There's nothing more poignant than the remnants of hope.

The control-room doors slide open with a gentle push. Iris is momentarily dazzled by the light from the curved panel of windows. The room looks like it's been empty for years, not weeks. Or has it been months? She can't remember. Two chairs lie on their sides on the ground. There is sand everywhere. A fine dust hangs in the air. The control panel is filthy, the buttons covered in smudges. Half a dozen fire-bugs fly around, their buzzing twice as loud as the hum of the machines. This is where it ends.

She crouches down under the control panel and crawls on her hands and knees as far as she can go, with her enormous belly brushing the floor. There it is, swerving to the left, as Abby described it: the mouth of a black tunnel, just big enough to squeeze through. Iris drags herself, gathering dirt from all sides. The heat of her body warms the tunnel, making her feel sweaty and claustrophobic. What if I get stuck? The only way to pass would be to give birth. But she doesn't get stuck. At the end, she stands up in a small chamber. There's a window to the outside, around five foot high, covered in fingerprints and grime from all the people who have stood there, bracing themselves, before stepping outside. She bends down and looks through the glass at the pink haze, blurred by dirt. This is where it ends. Or maybe it doesn't. Her baby moves.

'I'm sorry,' she says. 'We have to do this.'

She hears someone sighing close by, but there's no one around.

'God's sake,' she hears him say, through the wall on her right.

It's just another metal wall, nothing special about it. But then something goes *Bleep!* and the wall slides open to reveal a tiny room full of electrical equipment – machines, wires, lights; beeping, humming, ticking. On the floor, a thin mattress is piled with blankets and dirty plates. A head pops up from behind a screen and Iris almost screams.

'Oh my God,' she says, 'Norman.'

'Yeah, hi.' He raises a hand. His face doesn't betray any emotion. No surprise, no anger, no particular interest. It simply says: there you are.

'Sorry, you surprised me.' Iris doesn't know why she's apologizing.

Norman moves his cracked glasses from his nose to the top of his head. He's lost a lot of weight. His skull juts through his greasy skin; his grey hair is long and limp. He doesn't brush it away from his face.

'How's it going?' he says, in his weird, undefined accent. He forces a smile, showing dark tombstone teeth.

'Fine,' says Iris, before correcting herself. 'Well, not really. No one's fine.' She has barely ever spoken to him before. 'Where have you been all this time?'

'Here and there. Mostly here.'

Iris's heart throbs in her chest and her throat feels numb. She's so nervous, the way she was whenever she spoke to Roger at Freedom & Co – a feeling of insignificance, near-invisibility. It seems stupid and pointless to feel this way now, so near the end. He's just a person, she tells herself.

'You're the last one,' he says, walking over bits of broken equipment, till he's standing inches away from her. He glances at her belly. 'The last *two*.' He smells unwashed, bitter, like he hasn't bathed in months.

'Do we win a prize?'

'A one-way ticket back to Earth. Ha!' He smiles wide, as if this is the funniest thing he has ever said.

'But actually, you're the last one, Norman. I'm leaving.'

'You won't be able to come back.'

'I know that.'

'No, you don't know.' He crosses his arms across his body. 'You people don't know a fucking thing.'

Iris's heart is thumping so hard it hurts. It really does feel, uncannily, like she is about to give a big presentation at Freedom & Co, the kind that will reassure her superiors that she deserves to keep her job. One last dazzling performance, a self-sacrifice.

'How do you know I'm the last one?' she says.

'I saw you on camera. I haven't seen anyone else in days.'

'But they're all broken.'

'One of them still works. Look.' He gestures at a screen on the wall, filming an empty corridor. 'Do you have an imaginary friend?'

'Huh?'

'I keep seeing you talking to someone.'

Iris shakes her head, ignoring the question. 'What have you been doing all this time – hiding in this room?'

'I was taking a break.'

'You abandoned us. You didn't have the decency to announce the end of the show, to make some kind of plan –'

Norman scoffs. 'There was no plan. You knew the risks.' He rubs his face with his fingers, moving dirt across his skin. 'No one forced any of you to come here.'

'Well, everyone's gone now.' Iris realizes she knows nothing about Norman – whether he was married, whether he had children, who he left behind on Earth. Nobody spoke of him in those terms, as if he were a real person. 'What are you going to do now?'

'I'm staying till the end.'

Like the Dido song, Iris thinks. 'When is the end?'

'The end is the end.' He pauses. 'Do you regret coming here?'

'What a question.'

Iris moves away from the room back to the chamber, facing the window. She doesn't feel ready, but will she ever? When she swallowed those pills, twenty years ago, she had felt ready. If they had worked more quickly, if she hadn't puked, she would have been wiped clean, gone, at the age of sixteen, and none of this would have happened.

'Go ahead,' says Norman. 'Open the window. What, you don't want me to watch?'

'You're a real arsehole, you know that?'

Norman points a finger at her and says, 'You don't get where I am without –'

'Without being an arsehole? You're just a man in a room.'

He sighs, avoiding her gaze, and then moves back towards his seat, clambering over the equipment, almost tripping over.

'Good riddance to you all,' he mutters.

He hits a button and the doors close.

Finally, Iris is alone, more or less. It feels like nothing special, being close to the end. Like any other moment in life. Iris tries to remember the Kaddish, to sweep away these dull feelings – not even the words, just the feel of it, its cadence – but of course she can't. She can only remember 'Amen'. She's never believed in God, but it quietly slips from her mouth as she contemplates opening the door.

'Amen,' she says, 'amen, amen, amen, amen.'

It wasn't supposed to be like this. It was supposed to be . . . I don't know, poetic? That's what religion does, right? It lends poetry to these empty moments. She does remember one prayer off by heart: the Lord's Prayer. She learned it through repetition, not belief, but now that she thinks of it, it seems suitably grand and meaningful. It conjures up the smell of the polished wooden floors and dusty drapes in her school's assembly hall. Early-autumn chill on her bare legs. An itchy green skirt. Youth.

First, she kicks off her trainers. They're falling apart, black with sweat on the inside. She wants to die barefoot, with the sand between her toes.

'Our Father,' she whispers, 'who art in heaven . . .'

The baby turns, appreciatively. *Yes*, it says. *Continue.* Iris's eyes begin to burn with tears. She wipes them away and carries on reciting the prayer:

> *hallowed be thy name;*
> *thy kingdom come;*
> *thy will be done;*
> *on earth as it is in heaven.*
> *Give us this day our daily bread.*
> *And forgive us our trespasses,*
> *as we forgive those who trespass against us.*

Does Mona forgive my trespasses? Probably not. Do I forgive Earth? Maybe. It's not such a bad planet, not entirely. Iris reaches for the metal handle. It's cold to the touch. She lets go. Not yet.

> *And lead us not into temptation;*
> *but deliver us from evil.*
> *For thine is the kingdom,*
> *the power and the glory,*
> *for ever and ever.*

She pauses and breathes twice, before saying, 'Amen.' In her head, a thousand girls say it together, wearing their leprechaun-green uniforms. The sound echoes around the old hall. Goodbye, she thinks. All these memories will soon be gone, all these thoughts.

She reaches for the handle, inhales deeply, holds her breath and opens the window. Before she can think twice, she bends down and steps outside. The sand is soft and lovely against her feet. She kicks the door shut and sits on the ground. It's much hotter out here, perhaps forty degrees, like summer in Seville. Once I breathe, she thinks, it'll be over. Holding it in, she looks around at the pale pink expanse and the ruins of Hub 2. To her right is the farm; to her left, the control quarters – both of them abandoned now. She feels the sun on her face, warm and nourishing. The breeze brushes her forehead, cooling her sweat. What bliss. The lake glimmers in the distance, on lower ground. Without a window in front of her, it feels closer – it looks real. She's still holding her breath. The baby kicks. *Breathe, Mother, breathe.* She can't restrain herself any longer. The processes that keep her alive can kill her, too.

Iris exhales and pauses, then inhales the Nyxian air for the first time. Hmm. It doesn't burn her lungs. It tastes fine, normal. She exhales and inhales again. She isn't dying. She leans her back against the Hub. Her body feels heavy against the hot metal. She's breathing oxygen, she's sure of that. *Or perhaps I'm dead and this is this heaven? I've said the Lord's Prayer, after all. St Peter decided I was OK and let me in, despite my sins.*

She grabs at the window, putting her fingers around the edges, but it's sealed shut. It can't be opened from the outside.

She slowly stands up, leaning against the Hub for support, and strips down to her dirty underwear, leaving her clothes on the ground. Who cares, there's no one here to see her. The sand is hot under her feet and the lake is so far away. In old movies, when people are trapped in the desert, they walk towards the oasis. That's what she'll do. Iris trudges forward several metres before turning to look at the Hub one last time – but it's gone, it's no longer there. Just pink sand and blue sky, pink sand and blue sky, as far as she can see. Even her clothes have disappeared.

'You won't be able to come back.' That's what Norman told her. 'You people don't know a fucking thing.'

I must be dead already.

Never mind. Nothing surprises her any more. She turns and walks on.

Half an hour passes, and then an hour. The lake becomes fatter and clearer, more violet than indigo.

Two hours later, Iris is covered in sweat. She is so very thirsty. She didn't bring water.

Other colours and shapes start to form more clearly around the lake – pink, blue, purple, orange and yellow; wild, alien plants, flowers and trees. A mirage! she thinks. She hums the tune from *Lawrence of Arabia*. Sweat trickles into her mouth, down her back and her legs. She licks the salt from her lips. She wants to rest, but if she does, she won't be able to carry on.

The trees around the lake have pink trunks and blue leaves, their branches heaving with orange fruit. Iris has read about this before – how when you're close to death, you have one last, dazzling dream. It happens so that you go peacefully, willingly, like a stunned animal to the slaughter. Iris doesn't care. She's happy. Adrenaline fills her body. She starts running. She isn't dead yet. After death there's nothing and this doesn't feel like nothing.

    The sand ebbs away. Her feet begin to bleed as she treads on twigs and rocks. Under the canopy of trees, the air is cool and moist. Some of the fruit has fallen to the ground. She picks one up – it's soft yet firm, like a ripe mango – and digs in her nails till it comes apart, revealing its pink flesh. It tastes sweet and sour, like a pineapple crossed with a strawberry, with the texture of an avocado, but unlike any of these things. It is the most delicious thing she has tasted since she left Earth. Her hands become sticky with juice. She licks her fingers. Birds are singing above her. No, not birds – some Nyxian creature with wings. She bats away a fire-bug and it stings her on the shoulder. Her skin burns and swells, but it's OK – no worse than a bee sting. It's a novelty to be stung for the first time in years.

At last, she reaches the lake – iridescent, flat and clear. Iris dips a toe into the water. It's slightly cold, just right. When she walks in, the sores on her feet begin to sting, gratefully. The water covers her belly, soaking through her underwear.

'This is a lake,' she says to her baby. 'We had them on Earth.' Iris lets the water pour through her cupped hands, and then she drinks it – delicious, cool and sweet. A breeze blows on her face, making her shiver. She smiles deliriously. 'This is the wind,' she says.

She closes her eyes and enjoys the feeling of her skin rising in goosebumps. Small creatures swim around her, tickling her legs. They don't have names yet. A light patter of rain falls on her face. She drops down, under the water, holds her breath and swims a few metres without coming up for air. She could be anywhere. She could be on Earth. She could be in the pond on Hampstead Heath. When she comes up and opens her eyes, she notices that the sky is darker than it was over the Hub, and the sun is peachy and low. She can even see a star in the sky, or another planet, twinkling. She has reached the edge of the Twilight.

Bodies of water.

A breeze.

The sun on her skin.

Rain.

Stars.

The night.

All of these things, she has them now.

The lake is still shallow enough for her to stand. It comes up to her neck. She is about to dive down again when she hears something – a shout, two syllables, a female voice.

'What?' says Iris.

The person shouts again. On the third go, Iris hears her name. It's a familiar voice.

'Iris! Iris!'

There's a woman on the shore, in front of the trees, on the darker side of the lake – too far away for Iris to recognize. She looks either naked or half-naked. The figure waves her hands in the air. Iris squeezes her eyes, trying to focus. The woman has long, curly hair down to her waist, like Mona did. Of course. It's my sister. She's waiting for me to get out. We'll put our clothes on over our wet underwear and walk home across the park, shivering in the dusk as the sun comes down.

'Iris!'

Shush, she thinks, closing her eyes. I'm not here. I'm on Earth. I'm in the pond, feeling the weeds touch my toes. The cold water feels so good, like it could cure anything. A large white swan floats past, followed by three fluffy grey cygnets. It's my favourite place on Earth. There's no sign of London. It's like the city has disappeared – gone!

'Just a minute, Mona,' she whispers. 'I'm coming.'

Acknowledgements

Emma Paterson, the best literary agent on this planet (or any other). My brilliant editor at Viking, Mary Mount, who pushed me further than I thought I could go. Rosanna Forte, for her hard work and insightful suggestions. My sister and first reader, Julia Sauma. My old pal Poonam Vidyarthi, who helped to name Ravinder and Kiran. The rest of my family and friends, for all their love and support. As ever, Tim Goalen – for everything.

The premise of this book was partly inspired by 'Hostile Planet', an episode of the podcast *Love + Radio*. I highly recommend it.